Trichome Star

Fractals of Time

Teodoro Castro III

DEDICATION

Boo Boo Bear

Kuma Bear

Fudgee Bear

Boring Bear

Lady Frank & Farmer Hank

This Dimension and all the Multi Dimensions in the Universes, Stars, Earth, and my Home.

To Music, the doorway to the infinite.

To Dreams in Reality.

ACKNOWLEDGMENT

My family for supporting me!

Kuma Bear, Aura Sky, Tara Sage, Mikiko.

Desirée, my sister, for believing in me 100%.

My Rock, The Wise Tree, Mother Dearest.

Lastly, to Me, Myself & I, for not giving up on a Dream of the other DREAM!

ABOUT THE AUTHOR

Teodoro Castro III channels the power of creativity through the innocent lens of a child. He is an explorer, multi-dimensional thinker, writer, creator, artist, producer, musician, and inventor. He has toured extensively across America, Europe, and Asia as an electric shamanic lead guitarist, prophetic lyricist, and vocalist. T. Castro has produced, written, and created over 100 original multimedia immersive theatrical performance art shows that blend story, music, dance, circus arts, and theatre. He is a key figure in the art, music, live performance, theatre, and circus arts scenes in Los Angeles and beyond.

T. Castro's original roots stem from the Mojave Desert full moon music gatherings to the Los Angeles music and art warehouse scenes. He then moved into national and international touring, participating in gatherings in Asia, India, Europe, and Latin America. These experiences sculpt his creative process.

T. Castro is fascinated by astronomy, history, philosophy, science, metaphysics, and higher consciousness, integrating these interests into his work. He believes in natural healing, ancient shamanic practices, and harmonic frequency balance, and champions free thinking and individuality.

T. Castro is a technology enthusiast who envisions combining the ancient, present, and future in harmonic resonation. He is continuously curious, eager to learn with an open mind, and dedicated to manifesting innovative concepts and thought-provoking ideas. To be alive with excitement and enthusiasm!

Teodoro is a Lover of Life...

TABLE OF CONTENTS

PRELUDE

A gentle breeze coasted through the small gap in the windows of the moving car. Zaya sat in the backseat, listening as her parents talked about the day ahead with smiles on their faces. She was not much older than seven, and her eyes were drifting in and out of sleep. The car seats were large and comfortable, and she felt at peace with the sounds of the tires crunching on the gravel road, which wound through the large forests, interspersed with the familiar and comforting voices of her mom and dad. Her head lolled to the side, and she smiled as she sleepily noticed her dog Kuma on the seat beside her. She reached a small hand to stroke at his soft fur, and he stirred slightly, his eyes also sleepily fighting the rock-a-by lull of the drive. His floppy ears twitched ever so slightly, and the wetness of his nostrils expanded as he took a deep breath in.

At Zaya's stroke Kuma, the dog readjusted and lay his head to rest on Zaya's lap. That was the last warmth she needed, the soft weight of his head finally tipping her over the edge into the world of dreams. Kuma, too was in a state of utmost serenity. There was nothing like the feeling of being included and altogether with his family. The soft tuft of his eyelids fell heavy, and before he knew it, Kuma had also passed over into the world of dreaming, entering a landscape unlike no other.

THE FIRST CHRONICLE

The Trichome Star — Part One

Deep in the far reaches of space, the winds of the etherium carry celestial tones, resonating with crystalline memories. Within endless folds of realms and possibilities, fractal galaxies spiral like helix serpents, flowing ever further into states of quantum indeterminacy. Across all realms, across all possible timelines, a story is unfolding. A story stretching the length of time since the very first primordial chanted the frequency that set everything we know into motion. And all of it rests in the heart of a dream, in the mind of a dreamer that exists within all beings at all moments. A dream that surpasses the limitless boundaries of space and time.

On the smallest scale, particles dance and interact in

ways beyond human comprehension, creating a rich tapestry of subatomic activity that fuels the universe. Meanwhile, on the largest scale, galaxies spin and collide in a cosmic dance that has been ongoing for billions of years.

Despite their differences, the microverse and macroverse are intrinsically linked, each influencing the other in mysterious ways. Even the tiniest particle can impact the larger universe, just as the movements of galaxies can affect the smallest building blocks of matter.

This cosmic balance, both beautiful and terrifying, reminds many of their small place in the vastness of the universe. Yet, it also underscores the interconnectedness of all things and the infinite potential for growth and change that exists in both the microverse and macroverse. In this way, the universe is a never-ending symphony, with each note playing its part to create a masterpiece beyond imagination.

In a conceptual realm, untouched by mortal eyes and before the universe's creation, a cosmic pendulum swings above a round table where the three Infinite Ones dictate the forces permeating into the material plane. Zeno, Alo, and Xmo, cosmic architects of the timelines of infinity, exist in a paradoxical state—they have always existed and were never born.

Before matter even existed, before time was ever conceived, before space was even thought, the three Infinite Ones existed in a place where nothing is all there is, nothing but themselves, bound to one another like immaterial forces in the inconceivable reaches of infinite perpetuity.

In this realm beyond all that is known, what can only be described in wordlessness, the three Infinite Ones are in constant flux with one another, each representing a different force that has yet to be born.

They exist as aspects of one another, bound by the balance that each One holds. Together, they communicate in a language that surpasses verbal dictation. They speak in a language of forces, with each representing the sides of Harmony, Chaos, and Preservation as tongues in their mouths and the whisper of Fate in their voices.

Infinite moments passed by, moments so long they would encompass the entire creation and destruction of universes in a single flash. It was timeless their debate of forces, seeking, trying to understand one another in balance. Until, at last, the singularity found convergence, and their forces aligned in a perfection that had never been before.

This convergence formed the first spark of life. In the fraction of an infinite splice, balance was found, and the universe took its first breath inwards. The three Infinite Ones formed a perfect opposition and attraction, and this spark of energy was their birthing, in which they created, for the first time, something in the realm of nothing.

Interlude One

All dreams transition from one state to another in the relative world of duality and matter. As the car jostled and city horns mingled with the buzz of life, Kuma, the dog, was suddenly awakened. To the dog who dreamt so easily, one reality was hardly distinguishable from the other. There was no segmentation of mind alluding to the illusion that a dream was any less real than the world of waking. As his eyes adjusted, he sat up. Zaya was still asleep on the seat beside him, head tipped slightly over, limbs limp, and eyes flickering beneath closed eyelids.

The car moved slowly through a thick line of traffic, and as Kuma stuck his head out the window, he was awarded a vast amount of stimuli — people, objects, and scents. Two-legged beings walked quickly passed one another, not paying anyone any mind. Others lay slumped on the ground, holding out hands for change or food, amongst the plethora of vendors who kept their grub for paying customers. There were loud noises and complicated smells weaving this way and that through the air.

Kuma felt all of it inside of him, and together, it blended into a cocktail of anxiety and excitement. His tail began to wag, and he propped himself up higher, sticking his head further out the window, tongue lolling out to cool him down in the smoggy heat. Then, something amidst the chaos tugged at his attention, causing him to hone his focus on a single thing. There, in the mouth of an alley, was a large tabby cat. Instinct kicked in. Kuma barked once, then with one kick of his hind legs, he propelled himself out of the window, dashing through the honking cars directly towards the alley.

Kuma appeared at the entrance to the alleyway, ears perked, tongue panting in the summer heat, and tail wagging. He barked playfully at the tabby cat which sat atop the garbage bin. But the tabby cat began to recoil, arching its back, and raising the hairs on its body, letting out a low hiss. Kuma quirked his head, tongue lolling out to the side. He ran up to the garbage bin and stood up on two legs, reaching for the tabby cat who sat atop it. Again, he barked playfully, little strands of fur falling from his coat, drifting in the light breeze that trickled through the alley tunnel like a small river current. The light that crept through the gaps in the buildings illuminated the drifting strands of fur as they spun.

The tabby cat wanted no part in this dog's game and retreated in a quick flash of movement, leaping from the top of the bin to land on another. Kuma quirked his head, watching for a moment, and just as the tabby cat landed on the ground, he wagged his tail, and the chase began.

The wind brushed through Kuma's fur as he ran, ears flopping loosely on the side of his head, ducking and weaving between the alley obstacles. As he ran, the light seemed to follow him, as if some sort of spotlight was set on his life, like watchers observed from some hidden seats, watching the play like an audience in the theatre. The tabby cat ran for its life, or what it seemed to think, taking a sharp turn into an alley where two sets of people, beings of another kind, were standing and talking, holding a strange and pungent-smelling plant between them. The tabby cat, swift and nimble, dashed between them seamlessly, but Kuma, on the other hand, rammed right through the beings.

Stars cascaded from open hands. A sparkle of golden plant dust reflected in the spotlight that shone between the cracks of the wall. But Kuma did not care. He was caught in his play, chasing the tabby cat, thoughtless, bound by his open heart, unbeknownst to the flickers of crystallized light that began to coat his fur and the single large trichome landing on his paw.

A single act.

A single moment in a single day.

A single moment that would spark life in the most unexpected of ways.

As Kuma continued to play, chasing the tabby cat through the alley, the golden trichome dust began to glow and swirl around his paw, illuminated and activated by the stray slants of light. Kuma didn't notice the transformation, but the dust continued to expand, forming a complex and intricate microverse upon his paw.

Within this single act Kuma's paw became host to something else entirely. Kuma ran, completely oblivious to the tiny world sparking to life. As Kuma moved, the micro-universe shifted and changed, affecting the lives of its inhabitants in ways they couldn't comprehend.

In all things relative, entire universes can exist within a single speck of dust, and wonderous miracles can arise, hidden away from the eyes of the world. Meanwhile, Kuma chased, completely unaware of the incredible power that lay at his feet.

A vortex formed instantly, a spark of energy imploding upon itself, reversing and exhaling, thus creating the first warp of physical space beyond the conceptual realm. Time unwound alongside space, becoming inseparable from one another, bound in a great cosmic union.

Growing from nothing more than a seed of light, the multiverse suddenly was shimmering into existence with the forces of ether converging. It was bursting outwards, expanding, and creating all physical, astral, and gravitational elements to form the first spark of life in the material plane.

Alo, the Creator summoned the energies of the ether, and in its wake, a white hole formed, opening the boundaries of the infinite so that matter could be born into the universe of finite things, bridging the worlds for the first time. As Zeno and Xmo's forces coalesced, the convergence burst through the inversion of concept into matter and ushered the great story into motion.

Their energy set free into the first void and brought forth the essence for the spark of life. Forged in the etherium fire of the Infinite Ones, the void began to expand. It radiated its cosmic code, coalescing the untapped ether of primal material into the first atom. Thus, everything in the universe was birthed at once from this single inversed implosion, forming a toroidal loop of infinity. The single focused point of awareness to which nothing became all we know.

Matter was created in a single bursting exhale from the inversion of the first spark. The vision of the three Infinite ones birthed the multiverse into existence, an infinite dream held in the balance of their forces in convergence with one another.

Everything happened at once from the perspective of heightened awareness, but within the realms of relative time-space, a cosmic procession was underway, to which an origin point occurred. The center of the material universe expunged the infinite energies from the imploding white hole, and scatters of cosmic radiant energy burst forth at the speed of light. The first quantum building blocks were born, operating as a divine code that had been created as a result of the three Infinite Ones' harmonic convergence. Sub-atomic particles mingled and joined forces in this divine code to form the first electrons and quarks. From there the first atom was born, which grew into molecules that bonded into the elements which created all matter thus forth. This is fragmented and divided into an infinite permutation of vast multiverses, all bound within the single continuum of the single toroidal timeline. The timeline to which everything we know rests in a delicate balance.

Eons turned a score for the great cosmic symphony, and from nothing grew all matter that we call our universe. Galaxies birthed, stars lived and died, black holes swirled, and asteroids carried information across systems. And so, it began.

The Great Alignment of the three Infinite Ones occurred simultaneously in a chance agreement, dictated at odds spanning trillions by trillions of impossibilities. For three separate forces to converge in balance is a feat the universe had yet to see. This alignment birthed an imploding neutron star, surging with primordial fire and inverting upon itself to create a reversed dimensional plane, tearing a rift in the fabric of the void itself.

An unfathomable force, trillions upon trillions greater than anything the multiverse had ever seen, created temperatures so hot it became cold, all forces inversing upon themselves to a state of absolute zero, producing a fusion star made of sentient liquid diamonds. The primal pulse of this star took its first breath and beat its tempo into the field of existence, opening its eyes and shining its high-frequency rays like ribbons of diffracting light.

These ribbons of infinitely colored aurora beams came together, encapsulating everything. Every soul, spirit, and thought came to be reflected in these planes of light. Every universal event, every word, every emotion felt, and every intent to be manifest throughout the past, future, and present were all encoded in the non-physical plane of Akasha.

The Trichome Star breathes its song in the universe, holding all of infinity in its frequency. The rise and fall of immortal Beings are found in the folds of its light. Celestials so grand their very gestures swirl galaxies into motion. Within all life, throughout the entirety of all multi-dimensional planes of space and time, the life of the Trichome Star shines fourth unseen.

And so, the balance of the pendulum swings. The realms of infinity and the World of Zero are born in tandem measure with one another, bound by the subsonic Ohm, which contains all life within its vibratory womb. If one listens deep enough into the fabric of our universe, one can hear the eternal breath, chanting the seed syllable, which holds all frequencies of possibility within its echo. Its waves of energy lap against the ocean of existence, sound against the shore of time and space and expand forever into the deep sea of creation.

A part of the Trichome's liquid diamond existence fragmented and flew into the far reaches of creation space. Billions upon billions of years, it travels at a speed faster than light as we know it, passing innumerable star systems, each galaxy a being in their own right, and passing the continuum of newly forming worlds, past the vision of the great Cosmics who sailed the void, until at long last, it found its way to the Planet Lumaria. A liquid diamond meteor shower cascaded through the atmosphere, raining into the land that lay waiting. The liquid burrowed, extending its ventricles and rooting itself, dendrites sprawling like a web into the very core of the planet. Reacting with the energy emanating at the center of the planet, the liquid starlight hardened and crystallized. Giant crystalline structures burst forth from the surface of the planet, shimmering in rainbow hues and humming the song of the Trichome Star from whence their genetic code originated.

It would come to be known as the Singing Forest, whispering the records of infinity in the diamond facets of its solidified light. And from the primal force emanating from the crystals, Souls were called from the Infinite one, birthing sentient life into physical form, imbuing these beings with the power of Gods, eternally incarnating with the knowledge of source running through their very veins.

The first beings to be born on this planet were known as the Lumarians. They were born in harmony with the rhythms of the three Infinite Ones, setting up the architecture and embarking the first chapter of the great story into motion. The Lumarians were beings of the closest firmament to the frequency of the source, and in their nature was the very essence of the Trichome frequency, a pure emanation of balance, dilated from the very essence of the origin point.

This frequency goes by many names. That name has changed throughout time and throughout civilizations. It is the force that grows all things. It is the force all beings yearn to become, whether conscious or unconscious. The Lumarians, within their singing forest of crystal light, set the foundation for the blueprints for the evolution of the soul.

Their word spoke the true timeline, a truth beyond illusion. All beings strive to evolve towards this truth. All souls yearn to remember the lost knowledge. This is not a knowledge of mind and thought but a knowledge of frequency, a remembrance of being. All who seek the mystic path past the sun will eventually return to the ancient singing forest of our Lumarian ancestors. Remember well, remember true, and know oneself to be what the Trichome Star reveals within its light folds.

Yet, in time, all such stories are solely relative. For in this great multiverse, universes start and birth all the time. Sometimes, in the most unlikely places.

THE SECOND CHRONICLE

Crystals of Lumaria

Upon the crystalline planet of Lumaria, a wondrous civilization emerged over many eons. They were beings of subtle matter that existed in the highest frequencies of light. The Lumarians were some of the first of the soul archetypes to manifest within the physical realms of existence. But they were not entirely physical. They existed as bridges between the subtle spiritual planes of ether, coexisting within the higher densities of reality closer to the source whilst also incarnating in forms within the three-dimensional plane.

The Lumarians had what could be described as a light body. A body made of pure photons that vibrated in such a way that it could take form into a fixed state of potential.

It is unlike the physical bodies that many beings are used to having. The light body is more etheric substrate material than it is physical. It vibrates at a very high frequency and is impervious to aging or entropy. It is practically insubstantial and has very few limitations.

The Lumarians didn't have forms like most beings can conceive. They were not limited by things like hair color, height, shape, or skin tone. Yet they were expressed in a pentagonal ratio within the sacred geometry of the universe. That is to say, they resembled a humanoid shape, with a head, two arms, and hands, as well as legs and feet. This humanoid shape would continue to appear throughout the universe, and not in any connection to a particular race of beings, but because it was of a specific geometric frequency. The body is in ratio with the pentagrammic symbol and holds the blueprints for many other soul incarnations and sentient beings. This being said, the Lumarians were very malleable in their form, having no fixed facial features or sizes etc. Instead, they reflected one another's souls, adapting and morphing and communicating in ways that were very different from typical speech.

The Lumarians spoke in light language. It had no fixed verbal or grammatical structures but was more a language of emotion, feeling, and psychic impressions. Their words and tonalities were manifestations and expressions of their own internal state, transposing and transmitting emotional frequencies that could be understood in complex ways. They also existed within a collective mind, having their own unique individuality within the three-dimensional plane, but at the same time, they were not separate from one another. All thoughts – which were pictographic in nature, consisting of images, empathic emotion, symbols, and color – cohabitated within a collective mind as if they all swam within one mixing pot of experience.

One might see these beings as having no privacy, but for the Lumarians, there was no need for secrets amongst themselves. Their state of being and manifestations of thought were so pure that there was no need to hide or obfuscate anything. There was no shame, no guilt, nor any dark desires. Their existence was one of pure tranquility and harmony.

The Lumarians are extreme empaths, able to feel one another on profound levels down to the core of their individual souls. This collectivism is partly what made them such a thriving civilization. The Lumarians dedicated themselves to the one true timeline, offering their energy to protect and serve, becoming the gatekeepers of the sacred knowledge embedded within the realms of the singing crystal forest.

Over time, organic and intuitive technology grew from the very substrata of their mind technology that lived with its own consciousness, operating as an extension of the Lumarian soul. This technology can be referred to as bio-organic technology. To some beings that exist within the higher planes of reality, there is a mode of extending their self outwardly. The Lumarians, existing as a collective mind of aware individuals, were able to utilize the etheric planes to manifest and create new living objects equal in density to the expression of their own form. However, this would not be as solid and dense as the objects known within the typical third dimension.

Think of this technology as an extension of their selves, of their collective mind. Their inventions thought, breathed, and lived just as they did. Their buildings of light were alive as they were, and their celestial towers and technology were as organic and alive as anything else. They can be related to trees – though not in the sense of matter, more so in the sense of metaphor. Trees are alive and offer a function. Not only that, but they release chemical, electrical, and even sub-atomic impulses to their surrounding environment through an aura of biochemistry and through their root systems. Trees are able to communicate and make sense of the impulses that other living organisms receive.

This is what technology was like in Lumaria. The Lumarians were able to create spacecraft as extensions of their minds that were just as conscious as themselves, for it *was* them. As stated previously, the Lumarians were not limited by their form, nor were they limited by the typical three-dimensional mentality of creation. If it was in alignment with their path, they could manifest anything they so pleased. Their organic technology grew to help them evolve and better understand the universe, and from this, a deep knowledge was formed. A science of all things grew from their knowledge, a science so advanced many sentient beings would call it *magic.*

The Lumarian civilization flourished in harmony, guided by those who rose to become revered wisdom keepers. These leaders were esteemed not for their power, but for their unwavering dedication to pursuing the true timeline and their role in transmitting sacred knowledge. Even among these enlightened beings, this knowledge remained a riddle—a song to be decoded and revealed to all incarnating souls.

Amongst the immortal Lumarians' they were less bound to form. They were the original blueprints for the first primordial form. Born into the golden ratio, they had heads and bodies, with arms, hands, legs and feet, just like many of the beings that came after them. Their souls were free, and they could express themselves through the shifting of features, able to shift from one gender to another as they so pleased.

Upon Lumaria was a soul who for all modes and purposes came to be known as Zaya, though names were not a thing of the ancient Lumarians. She was as pure as light could be and embodied the heart of a child, known for her playful manner, and often caught playing with the stars.

She sang with the cosmos and had a love for all things, and it was through her dreams that many beings came into existence. She dreamt of dolphins who splashed in large oceans of water, playing and twirling through the stars, dancing with one another amongst their pods.

She also dreamt of giant whales, who sang deep tones, carrying the memories of sacred knowledge, swimming on the currents of the galaxy, and travelling from world to world as record keepers of Times already passed and yet to come.

There were few like her, even on the beautiful crystalline planet of Lumaria. She was a soul seemingly shaped from the tears of the Creator itself. A sparkling gem in the vast void of the cosmos.

Zaya was an attendant of the Oracle of Twelve. This Oracle inhabited a floating island of crystals and stood in a temple woven from the fabric woven from their own essence where the Oracle resided. They again were not known by a name but by the collective cluster, they represented. Being many in one, a single mind joined through the union of twelve souls spent most of their time within the inner sanctum of the temple.

Zaya took care of the dreaming garden surrounding the temple, overflowing fountains of light cascading over the edge of the floating island, dripping vision and prophecy down to the people of Lumaria below. She cared for the crystal buds that blossomed with the passing of the cosmic cycles.

It was upon the floating island where the moon sat, and Zaya spoke with the moon constantly, helping her to ease from the bright of her full shine and into the eclipse of her darker side. Zaya took on the form of a young humanoid with translucent starlight skin and long teal-colored hair. Many myths to this day draw upon the archetype of her ancient form and weave fairy tales into stories around the imprint she left on the mind of the cosmos.

It was not often that she got to step within the deeper folds of the temple. She attended to the main altar, which was a growing splay of crystal records that sang the tones of the cosmic score. From the main altar, the Oracle of Twelve had carved Zaya a crystal flute, which she used to guide the melody of her waking dreams and cast her spells into the still-growing ether.

The universe as we know it was once a very different place. It was so close to the source of creation that the concept of physicality had not yet become a notion for minds to comprehend. While Zaya resembled an archetype, it is not accurate to limit her as such. She had many things and many faces. The freer the soul, the more one was to *be.*

Many of the Lumarians who lived in the cities beneath the temple of Oracles were like children in heart and mind. Still young in spirit and innocent, despite having lived for countless eons. Time did not have the relationship with space as it does now in the three-dimensional modality.

When one thinks of dimensions, it is typical to conceive from the bottom up, starting with the zero point and growing upwards to one, two and three, etcetera. But the truth is that within the linear framework of perception, the dimensions formed from above. Opening from the source, an infinite place, and refracting downwards, creating the lower dimensions as creation grew, just as a sunbeam stretches from the source of light and diffuses based on the atmospheres or mediums it passes through.

Zaya and her people lived in the upper etheric realms before all had become what we know today. It was a starting ground. The closer a being is to the source of creation, the less delusion they divulged and the more their consciousness was aware of. That being said, there were others who existed. For the universe, its balance was created with duality. The Lumarians were not the only ones to inhabit the early notions of the cosmos. Amongst the odd and strange manifestations of life, one was the extreme opposite of the Lumarians. They were dark and malicious in every way and would come to be known as the Dystopians, though their influence would not be seen for quite some time.

Many of the laws and mechanics of the lower universal planes were dreamt into life through the first drops of source into individuality. That was to say, the Lumarian race. Whilst Zaya did not know her dreams would become the groundwork for different aspects of reality, she dreamt in all moments, not needing to sleep or wake.

The Lumarians lived in a state of liminality. There were no power structures within the society, and they all shared a mind as much as fish share an ocean. Their minds swam within the same currents and tasted of the same salt despite perceiving the whole from different perspectives.

They were unblocked from the channels of creativity. Their imagination was limitless and on the level of godly. Entire star systems could birth with the wink of an eye, yet all dreams were dictated through the laws of the source code. As beings of the source, they could not stray from their natural law. And so, the great Oracle of twelve warned. This fact is important to note, for it was the deviation of the first Lumarian that would eventually lead to their own downfall. But that story will be revealed a little later on.

The cities of Lumaria were constantly shifting and as malleable as the tides of the ocean. Made of light shining through one source, the Lumarians and their cities lived within the spaces of the singing crystals. Their cities were fractals of multidimensionality, living in so many angles and dimensions that it would be impossible to conceive of.

Their architecture was in alignment with sacred geometry and the law of numbers. Some semblances of this notion can be seen in some of the more ornate temples within the third dimension today. Patterns and sacred geometric patterns are depicted in two dimensions or even three, but try to imagine what these patterns would look like if they were infinite in dimensionality. The mind will almost break with just trying to imagine a fourth dimension, but that is a showcase of how much consciousness has fallen since its time. Do not mistake this fall for a negative, however. All things are relative within the great cosmic mind, and its dreams are unfolding.

Zaya knew more than many of her kin, but still, she was naïve in comparison to the great Oracle of Twelve. The Oracle took on the greater teachings, the ones of polarity, shadow and form, in order to allow the rest of Lumaria to continue existing in the play of their dream. Knowing the true course of time is a real burden, and the Oracle carried it for their people.

For eons, the Lumarians lived in the tranquil peace of their existence. But one among them started to change. For countless times, the idea of *question* was not something to be known. One did not *question* the law; it was merely accepted. With its beauty, its love, its attraction, there was no reason to question anything. To imagine this life was to imagine nothing wrong, pure peace and serenity.

However, as the dream developed and the Lumarians grew in consciousness, they developed modalities such as thinking. Before, it was not this way. The Lumarians simply dreamt, swimming in a state of aware unconsciousness, like how dreams manifest, and one can remember them, yet the dreams have a course of their own.

It was through dreaming that they developed their language of light, a system of thinking with the infusion of emotions and images. But there was one among them who, amidst deep, playful thoughts, suddenly asked the first question. The question was simple, and at first, it did not trouble them. This Lumarian's name was Lekiam, but would later be known as something else entirely.

How *did I get here?*

It was the question he asked himself. A question that changed the course of his life. It was not instantaneous but rather happened over several eons, just as how a seed planted will one day grow into a large tree. One may ask how such an innocent question could lead to such revolution within his own mind. But to do so, one has to not think with the waking mind. One has to think with the mind of a dreamer.

To become aware of a dream is not a simple feat. Though many beings have claimed to have done so at least once. Imagine the question rising within the unconsciousness of a dream. *How did I get here?* Dreams often start from nowhere and begin in the middle of things. There is no true linearity to how a dream begins. At least not in the beginning, not until the dreamer investigates deeper.

Not only that, but one question always leads to another. Lekiam could not shake this question from his mind. It repeated over and over again, and Lekiam became obsessed with answering it. He even asked others around him. *How did I get here? How did you get here?* Little did he know that the question would act like a drop of poison, slowly infecting the delicate balance of the harmony. The word poison is used, but that does not imply negativity. It simply was what it was.

For in the grand unfolding of the universe, there was not just one created but an infinite multitude. Within the framework of infinity, each universe had varying degrees of mirror dimensions to itself. It was a multi-dimensional spectrum, and through this spectrum and the laws of duality, the universe in which the Lumarians resided had its exact opposite. The Dystopians. The Oracle of Twelve knew of this inverted universe. At this point in time, the veils and boundaries that separated one universe from another were very thin, and in the deep recesses of the Oracle's temple, in the deepest shadows of the crystal's songs, the Oracle of Twelve could perceive this alternate universe and the beings who were most opposite to that of the Lumarian ways.

. Not much could be said on Dystopians now, but with the veil as thin as it was, whispers and traces of their ways managed to slip past the Oracle of Twelve's guard. It was these whispers that began to wriggle their way into Lekiam's mind. Lekiam dreamt deeply, and in the far recesses of his dreams, the Dystopic spirits of the inverted realm began to infiltrate his dreamscape, penetrating his mind and making him question his reality in such a way that he thought these thoughts were his own.

Since the minds of the Lumarians were so connected, soon, many of the Lumarians were questioning their origins. But Lekiam was eons ahead of their thinking and, with the influence of the Dystopians, had come up with many more questions. Like, *what came before me?* And *how is it that I am?* These are questions that many a being might recognize. They are the foundation of many philosophies and sciences.

Inherently, they may have no danger and may even

bring us closer to the truth. The Oracle of Twelve had answered many of these questions long before Lekiam, but as their role within the temple and in the law of the source, they were unable to influence or steal the free will of any soul or being. The Oracle knew Lekiam questioned, and yet they could not do anything to guide or stop the course of action once it had begun. It was written in the stars, fate for the course of the soul's journey.

As Lekiam continued to question, he began to grow frustrated with the obfuscation of certain knowledge. This frustration grew from the Dystopians seed of contradiction. He looked up to the temple in the sky where the Oracle resided and resented that the knowledge was kept from him. Lekiam did not understand the truth that the Oracle was protecting him. Some knowledge and awareness can fracture and break the soul if not introduced at the right time or in the correct way.

The truth was that the knowledge held within the Oracle's temple was the external manifestation of all the Oracle of Twelve had found for themselves. They were not bestowed with any greater gift; they had simply dug deeper into the nature of reality for themselves. True knowledge and understanding, like many things, must come to be found internally. The error in Lekiam's thinking was that he perceived the knowledge to be *outside* of himself. It was exactly how the Dystopians had designed it, corrupting Lekiam from their obscured realm, invisible and unknowable to Lekiam himself.

As his frustrations grew, he began to question the

very law of the universe itself. *Why was there a law at all? Why did he have to follow these rules to create?* And perhaps the greatest question of all arose. *What happens if I break the law?* If the universe and its rules flowed one way, Lekiam questioned if it was possible to flow in the other direction.

In his frustrations, he had grown tired of following rules, and he asked what would happen if he made his own. Gathering a great horde of followers within Lumaria that he had accumulated by spreading the seed of the Dystopians corruption, Lekiam did the unthinkable. Whilst the rest of life breathed, he held it. He pushed against the current with his dreams. He broke the sacred geometry and, in his act of creation, inverted the sacred law on its head.

A great fracture took place, and almost instantly, Lekiam and his followers were cast out of the high etheric realms of Lumaria. This was not by the hand of some God but by the choices Lekiam made of his own free will. Upon inverting the matrix of the sacred law, Lekiam had created the Lumarians' first opposition. The first is internal polarity. While the Lumarians lived in peace and tranquility, in love and creation, Lekiam did the opposite.

Thus, Lekiam and his followers fell from grace, and nightmares grew from the dreams of those who had chosen the path that directly opposed the natural law. They fell like comets, descending from the high etheric plains of Lumaria and dropping into the lower densities. Lekiam became his own and began to create his own systemic matrix, deviating from the natural law. He shed his former name and would soon be known across the many universes as Lekiam *Dominus.* The latter title was given because he was now the creator of the matrix in which he and his fallen followers existed. He had dominated the sacred law and inverted it, making him a god within his own lower-density dreamtime.

Though, with this godlike privilege also came a curse. As he descended into the lower densities, his higher spirit became inverted, and the frequencies within these low-density realms were slower. As his body shifted from photonic light to gross matter, wavelengths slowing, Lekiam lost connection to the high-frequency knowledge of Lumaria. Lekiam lost his connection to the vibratory field of the crystal-singing forest.

As he deviated from the law, his form became twisted and so did those of his followers. From forms of light, they grew dense bodies of thick matter whilst still retaining many of the powers they had before. They held on to the ability to change their form, except it was no longer through angles of light but by manipulating the cells within their own body, by stealing and snatching the forms of other beings.

Whilst Lemuria was in harmony, Lekiam and his followers entered disharmony. They were now bound by the laws of entropy within the lower densities. Lekiam ruled his people for many eons, though eventually, his physical body perished and faded. The original Lekiam soon far exceeded any of his followers and became an archetype, a notion within the universe no longer limited by his form. But he gave rise to many followers and many children races, which extended from his new law and source, spreading throughout the universe as it grew and inhabiting planets as they developed. Amongst these races, one prevailed over them all. They came to be known as the feared and infamous *Draconians*. These beings carried the genetic strands of the first offenders. They were themselves the children race of Lekiam.

Over the eons of time, through endless folds in the continuum, many beings began to develop. All who sought the great mystery eventually found themselves at the shores of the singing forest, and all who sought were welcome. But to every soul born of Law, a balance had to be struck, and so was the direct transmission from the three Infinite Ones. The universe was a constant push and pull of opposing forces, set into motion by the questions Lekiam asked before he underwent his transformation. One without the other would mean collapse. Stars could not be born without the destruction of another. In the passage of eternity, a great firework display of bursting star systems and galaxies imploding to scatter their dust and be reborn from the ashes.

This was to say that with harmony came chaos. Chaos eventually reached the shores of Lumaria in the form of the Draconians the aggressive, ego-driven, shapeshifting race, the descendants of Lekiam. At the core of their being was the drive instilled in them through the inverted law of chaos and destruction. Also seeded were the first questions and frustrations that Lekiam had thought countless eons ago.

Over time, Lekiam became more than a form; he became an archetype and a force. However, his children lived on with him in the core of their fragmented souls. Whilst the source of the Lumarians influenced and guided them through the natural law, Lekiam became such for his people in his own inversion. He drove them through war and conquest and, through his force, led them in the way of destruction and disharmony.

In their ego-driven minds, the Draconians felt inferior and thus threatened by the prosperity of the Lumarian beings. The Lumarians only shared and offered small measures of their sacred knowledge in tiny bursts to the physical beings who sought the mystic road. You see, the return journey of the soul, back to the singing crystal forest, was a long and arduous path, one that spanned over countless lifetimes.

The Draconian race disapproved of the withholding of this knowledge, craving it not from a place of true yearning but from a place of desire for the power that was embedded within the secret codes. This was, of course, a misunderstanding. The knowledge was never purposefully kept or hidden by the Lumarian race. The Draconians were viewing it from a narrow perspective that did not consider the truth of this knowledge contained within the singing crystal forest.

The crystal forest was not a physical place, nor did it exist within the folds of time. One could only acquire the knowledge that lay there under certain conditions. Once a being rose to a state of significant spiritual development, they would organically be led there. Lumaria has and always will be a place within us all. Once a being has reached the right stage of evolution, then, and only then, can they access the library of knowledge within their own inner being. The Draconians only saw the physical manifestation and representation of the Lumarians and their forest. They did not see them from a multi-dimensional perspective.

Amongst the Draconians, a chaotic and corrupted leader rose in the reptilian ranks. Whilst love and harmony were revered in Lumaria, so the balance sought its opposition, and thus Domitor Subjectus was born into a fate outside of his control. He was acknowledged as a leader because he most embodied what their original creator, Lekiam, stood for, and Domitor Subjectus ruled over his race with hate and fear, evoking the primordial forces of chaos, seeking to conquer and subjugate the planets he took over.

One might place blame and feel anger or injustice towards the forces of *evil*, the forces of chaos. But one must understand he, too, had a role to play in the cosmic story. In the dense physical incarnation of the Draco constellation, the shapeshifting Draconian were subject to a chaotic three-star system, which propagated near-impossible survival conditions. The weather patterns as a result of the three-body problem, were unpredictable and intense. The Draconians had to fight in order to survive, and thus, their souls grew in such a way that there was simply no time or privilege to seek love or harmony. Survival was their only agenda.

From this struggle, they developed crude and brutal forms of technology that were very much opposite to the harmonic frequency and organic technology of Lumaria. Eventually, despite the unforgiving conditions of their home system, they managed to evolve far enough to leave. And they left with a vengeance, conquering all the nearby sentient planets and growing an Empire to be feared and hated.

It is said that even the darkest of demons may unlock the secrets to the universe, and the Draconian aspired to do just that. Instead of harnessing the natural and harmonious technology that could be developed as an extension of the soul, they developed external machines of stone and metal. They mined planets till their death, and they sapped the systems they conquered of their resources, seeing the universe and the planets as insentient materials to repurpose for their own selfish gains. They enhanced their bodies' abilities with external materials and defiled the very nature of the soul's evolution, as was the course set out by Lekiam all those lifetimes ago., as was the course seeded by the dark Dystopic beings and their invisible influence within the cosmos.

Dreaming is the conduit between all dimensions, multi-universes and timelines. A golden string ties living entities in this dream state to this universal order of The Zero Ohm Frequency, harmonically resonating from the World of Zero to various spirit souls throughout the physical timeline from future, past and present.

The realtime zero harmonic dream frequencies are secret mathematical equations to open these dream portals to navigate, look and experience in these dimensions.

Various entities emanate different magnetic vibrations which attract each other through The Zero Ohm Frequencies. This shapes the dream state and physical reality of each being in existence.

The Draconian race emanate lower vibration frequencies that attract the dark soul spirits from the dreams of the Dystopian race that reside in the anti-verse, a dream in a dream, communicating in the inverted dimensional plane. The dark Dystopian spirits whisper thoughts from their dreams into the dreams of the Draconians which shift reality in their waking universe.

War and destruction followed their path, all under the lead of Domitor Subjectus, who employed the vicious and tyrannical High Commander Decepti Mortor to carry out his dark wishes. Many, many cycles after the fall of Lekiam. Millions upon billions of years later, the Draconians, through their cycle of incarnations, had forgotten where they came from. They were caught in the webbed mind matrix Lekiam had cast over the lower density of their consciousness. Eventually, word reached the cruel Draconian forces of the crystalline planet of Lumaria and the knowledge that lay embedded in their singing forest. Domitor became obsessed and set all his sights on reaching this planet.

Giant void-ripping machines were used to open artificial wormholes, violating the natural order, which began to upset the balance of the lower-density systems. The Draconian force became a deviant race, collapsing timelines and branching forks in the organic order. Domitor gathered all his forces and prepared them to invade the physical aspect of Lumaria .

This Arc took place billions of years after the fall of Lekiam, within the relative framework of time. The Lumarians, having existed in the higher etheric realms of creation, were not subject to the tides of Time as those in the lower densities were. Billions of years passed in no relativity to the Lumarians. To them, it could have been a matter of days, hours, or minutes.

Right beneath their noses, an entire universe was growing in the dense realms of physicality. Planets were forming, civilizations were emerging and still, the Lumarians dreamt. But, amongst the Lumarians was a grand oracle. While many on Lumaria took on individual genders, upholding a balance of the duality, this oracle was neither and all genders, a divine hermaphrodite, which in spiritual law is the highest attainment of gender.

The oracle did not consist of one single soul but had an oversoul system of twelve light beings. An oversoul is a being who holds more than one soul within their conscious self-incarnation and karmic destiny. Most beings live in succession, in division, in parts, in particles. In the meantime, within all beings is the soul of the whole, perceptible only through intuition and not to be communicated through words. This divine spirit is the source of all moral and intellectual growth, for the heart, which abandons itself to the Supreme Mind, finds itself related to all its works and will travel a royal road to particular knowledge and powers. It is said that all beings walk the road towards the supreme oversoul, which one could call the Source. The Oracle of Lumaria was the highest incarnation of their race and, thus, the closest to Source. They had no name and were simply known on an intuitive and empathetic level.

They communicated through twelve souls, each offering a unique perspective and understanding, each a different facet of one another, like a mirror of light reflecting in twelve different ways.

The Oracles saw the upset in the timeline's continuum, were well versed in reading the rays of crystal forest, and were forewarned of Domitor Subjectus's plans. They had been watching and knew that when the time came, there would be nothing they could do. Just as the turning of time wiped out the dinosaurs in a single cataclysm, all is subject to fate, and all is subject to the cycles of balance. The Oracles of the Lumarian council gathered to peer into the folds of possibility and pursue a course of action.

They were not beings of war. That was not their nature. They would not fight and kill. It was against the very ideals they upheld. If they resorted to violence, they knew it would go against the very reason they existed. The coming of the Draconian Age was written in the very stars themselves. It was written in the astral currents and in the wind of the etherium. Instead of fighting their nature, the Twelve Oracles banded, channeled directly from the records within the singing forest.

Each of the twelve aspects of the Oracle created a single chapter, a memento of which they folded and compressed the knowledge they held within a manuscript, later known in time as the Lumarian Book of Prophecies. They created from the very folds of their mind, as an extension of themselves, a living manuscript, imprinted with the direct transmission of light codes through the act of psychokinesis, a psychic transmission within written symbols of light language, symbols that morphed and changed, only readable to those who have reached an attainment that allows them to receive the transmission.

The Lumarian Oracles of Twelve peered deep into the One Timeline and saw that the fall of their civilization was always an event that was meant to come to fruition. It was in the very order of cosmic balance. If they fought, they would be solely responsible for altering the course of the great story. The single timeline demanded that the Lumarian planet be sacrificed and eliminated for the cycles to progress.

Even though the Oracles knew this and conveyed the

fate to their people, it was not easy to accept. The Lumarians, being half spirit and half physical over the millennia, were subject to physicality, and grief came along with the knowledge that their way of life was coming to an end. The Lumarians knew they were no longer safe, and neither was the singing forest. The Oracle of Twelve declared that it had to be relocated.

Kuma, the dog, chased the tabby cat, but she eventually sprung up a garbage can and onto a high window sill that Kuma could not reach. He barked playfully, and she watched with narrow eyes, smartly satisfied that she had gotten away without a scratch. Kuma didn't want to give up the chase, but even as he tried to stretch his paws up, the cat's new perch was much too high for him to reach. His tail drooped, and he turned away, and the cat began to resume her grooming. Kuma padded out through a different exit to the alley, slightly defeated, when suddenly something caught a scent on the current of his senses.

THE THIRD CHRONICLE

Rise of the Draconian Age

Metal, fire, ash, and dust. Churning furnaces, the size of asteroids, cover the surface of the dead Draconian Planet. The pound of factories beat to the rhythm of war, producing toxic, radioactive materials, harnessing void black energy, and crushing the very life of everything around it. Thick fumes obscure the planet in a dark haze as the weave of spacecraft flies in and out of the industrial port.

The three suns of the Draco constellation circled in a chaotic dance, threatening to tear gravity itself out of order. They were like titans fighting in the sky, with Draconia at their centers. It was no wonder the Draconians evolved the way they did. In their early history, a mass extinction could occur at any moment, setting evolution back by millions of years at a time. The gravitational orbit of the three suns was nearly unpredictable. There could be stable weather for sixty days, followed by heat so hot it would send everything up in flames for a single day, then become so cold that not a single thing would survive the sub-zero temperatures.

Yet, life found a way to adapt. The Draconians evolved in this crucible of harsh unpredictability, surviving mass extinction after mass extinction. For eons, their existence seemed doomed to randomness.

Until science developed upon Draconia, and their forms became adapted to these changes. Eventually, they were able to understand the movement of their three stars.

The Draconians developed giant technological titans to counteract the sun's destructive forces. This break-through spurred rapid technological advancement previously unavailable to them. But the harshness they had grown in was now permanently engrained in their being.

The Draconians were vicious, cold-blooded and brutal in their traditions. The trauma and cruelty that runs in the history of their genetics left little to no room for anything else. This not as a criticism but a testament to their will to survive. Imagine any being in such conditions. It is unlikely many would be able to withstand such pressures.

So, take into reason the privilege of kindness. The privilege of empathy, love, and compassion. Such qualities may only arise in the climates and conditions where they may. And yet, even in the beautifully balanced and lush climate of some planets, it is still possible for a being to fall subject to cruelty, not realizing the blessing they have been bestowed with.

One can see how fear is spread within a world that has lost its connection to the harmonious order. As the eons of time passed in Draconia, the population began to skyrocket, as they no longer endured the brutality of the three suns fighting amongst one another. But their mentality remained stunted and stuck in this violence. They lost touch with the natural relationship of the universe and became slaves to materiality, pouring all their resources into furthering their technology. Draconia has become overcrowded and uninhabitable. This was the beginning of their expansion and conquest into other star systems. They left their dying planet behind, using it only for industrial purposes to produce the nuclear and toxic energy that fueled their atrocious weapons and machines.

Their race soon became infamous amongst the sentient species of life spread throughout many realms and galaxies. The Draconians dominated and enslaved other species with no regard for the lives slain or the civilizations they ruined. The Draconians were masters of war, having adapted near unkillable bodies through the years of brutal evolution. They developed bipedal lizarian bodies with the ability to regenerate limbs and shapeshift, amongst many other traits. This made them not only great fighters but incredible infiltrators. Most species never even knew the Draconian had arrived until their governments began to crumble from the inside out, and when the planets were at their weakest, the hordes of the Draconian army would sweep in and destroy everything in sight.

They not only sought physical domination, but they collected the scientific findings and knowledge of other planets, adding them to their arsenal, taking only the most valuable and leaving the rest behind. In the religion of their science, they looked only to one thing. The blissful chaos of the inverted realm. An existence-less existence they held in regard above all others. A realm that many beings feared. But to the Draconian, the chaos that it offered was revered above all else. Their religion was directed towards this realm, though they could not see it. They could not touch it nor knew how to travel to it. This was, of course, the realm that the Dystopians inhabited. If Lekiam was the father of the Draconian race, then the Dystopians were the spirit that had imbued Lekiam in his fall. The myth of the Dystopians was the bedrock for their religion, which intermingled with the advanced sciences they had developed.

Their quest and hunt for knowledge became their sole drive. They desired eternal life, a desire based on the fragment of what they once were. They were descendants of the fallen Lumarian Lekiam, but they had fallen so far that the amnesia of their race left them distant and entirely separate from what they once were.

They wanted, more than anything else, unlimited power so that they could sit upon the throne of the cosmos and claim it as their own. They invaded ethereal planets of light, where beings existed for millennia, tearing the peaceful realms apart and sending them back to the void. Slowly, they worked their way through these planets until the knowledge of the singing forest appeared before them.

Domitor Subjectus knew that the knowledge he sought would be buried in the tomes and records kept there throughout eternity. He began his infiltration as a master shapeshifter. And when the time came, he commanded his Empire to board their nuclear-powered, void-energy warships and set course for the planet Lumaria , ripping holes in the fabric of space-time to do so.

The warships were giant metal contraptions built from the mined minerals they stole from other planets and their own. They were giant behemoth crafts, made in some way to resemble a locust, one of the only insects to exist on their planet, able to survive the drastic conditions, surfacing every dozen or so years to feast on whatever food they could find. The Draconians were inspired by this creature's adaptability and resilience and was thus the inspiration and became the symbol of their warships.

The ships produced a terrible buzzing sound, with powerfully propelled wings used in atmospheric conditions and giant ionic thrusters in the back of the craft that allowed them to travel at great speeds within the void of space. These ionic thrusters were atomic fusion-fueled rockets that produced a thick dark smoke and were in terrible counter frequency to organic life. Their ships produced such harsh frequencies that when they landed on planets, all plants and organic material would wither and die around them.

Domitor Subjectus always led his swarm in the largest warship of them all. The locust father ship was the size of a city and required obscene amounts of resources to power. Their violation didn't go unnoticed, and their craft created giant ripples in the fabric of space-time, which was how the Lumarian Oracle of Twelve was able to foresee the Domitor's encroaching procession toward their planet.

Domitor himself was the darkest and most powerful of the entire Draconian race. His domination and leadership were earned through vicious murders, conquests in war, and the brutal subjugation of foreign planets and civilizations. Domitor had seen traces of the Lumarian planet hidden in the myth of the civilizations he destroyed and soon gathered enough intel, finding the star map to the planet upon which they were anchored into the physical dimension.

He devised a plan to infiltrate their ranks and destroy the Lumarian race. But the Oracle of Twelve had known that the Draconian was coming long before Domitor had even made the decision and planned to do so. The Oracle knew that battle was not an option, even though their spiritual technology was far more advanced than the primitive machines of the Draconian. If the Lumarians so wished, they could have destroyed the entire Draconian fleet in a single thought. This would have eradicated the entire Draconian race and would have saved the universe from many unnecessary horrors and grief. But this was not in alignment with the Lumarian cause. The Oracle saw what many didn't. They saw how the Draconian race would play a role in the greater timeline's purpose.

The other members of the Lumarian race did not understand, as the Oracle of Twelve did, what role allowing the Draconian to live would have. Many of them sought other options. One female especially, the priestess Zaya, devised a plan of her own, one she thought to be of her own free will, a plan that would take millennia to oversee. But the Oracle knew her soul and had foreseen her action as well. They knew that she would have a large role to play in the eons that would ensue after the fall of the Lumarian civilization.

Even though there was talk of rebellion, the Oracle's plan eventually took root in all the minds of Lumarians, and they had to come to terms with the fact that it was in the universe's best interest not to fight. So, the preparations to save the knowledge they cherished were set into motion.

Using a form of conscious and organic mind technology, the Lumarians were able to transport the singing forest in a cloaked bubble of light. The Lumarians managed to escape secretly at the last second, and when the Draconian fleet arrived, the crystalline planet was empty.

This came as a great surprise and embarrassment to Domitor Subjectus. He had spent a great deal of resources and money and had ceased all conquering to focus all his troops on the Lumarian Project. When the fleet appeared on the empty planet, there were those with strong political influence and power that declared their leader had failed. Domitor Subjectus was thus dishonored in the eyes of his ranks. He was labelled a fool and a heretic for pursuing such a phantom goal. It was in these moments that the High Commander Decepti Mortor seized this opportunity and cut off his Emperor's head, claiming the position of Emperor for himself.

At this point in time, the Draconian were still considered a mortal race. They could live on average for three thousand years, a lifespan that, at this point in the universe's timeline, was relatively short. Through countless hours of dark meditation, Decepti Mortor had discovered a way to prolong his life, feasting on the energy of souls by concocting methods of blood sacrifice, harvesting the latent energy in warm-blooded beings to fuel their reincarnation when Draconian bodies became too old to function.

Like vampires, they thrived and prolonged their life by draining the life force of other living beings. This was a dramatic revelation and he shared some of his knowledge when he rose to power. This made him widely venerated in the eyes of the Draconian, and he used this rise in popularity to distract his inferiors whilst he pursued in secret the work of the former Emperor.

Decepti had also unlocked other powers through his long periods of dark meditation. When the first fleet had arrived in Lumaria he had been able to sense an energy signature that no one else had been able to. He had felt the presence of the Lumarians disappearing in their cloaked technology.

Even though they were invisible to the naked eye, their energy could not be cloaked. He felt them warp and tracked their technology across the universe. He knew where they had gone, and he would follow them to all corners of the multiverse if it meant laying his hands upon the knowledge they so selfishly guarded. Or at least that was how he saw it. From his narrow perspective Decepti did not understand the nature of the Lumarian knowledge. He thought that they withheld its powers purposefully to keep power. It was no surprise that he felt that, considering the mentality of his race. He did not understand that the knowledge was open to all who sought harmony and peace. It was open to all who should seek the path of the eternal source, the path of the soul's highest calling.

As soon as he had taken control of the war fleet, he gave his people what they wanted. Decepti turned his attention toward the beautiful crystalline planet of Lumaria and smiled. With a single gesture, he unleashed the totality of his arsenal on the planet and watched as it exploded before his eyes. Lumaria was a crystalline planet; even with the singing forest gone, most of the planet thrived with the glow of rainbow quartz crystals. Shards of crystals were sent hurtling through space, reflecting the mass of his fleet in their facets.

And so it was that the Lumarian race was sent running, forced to hide like insects. Decepti thrilled in their weakness, thrilled in the predatory chase that would ensue, and let them get their distance on him. For he knew that no matter where they ran, he would find them, and he would bring them to their end. But he had to ensure that they could not get the better of him again. If he appeared before another empty planet, he was sure to share the same fate as the former Emperor Domitor.

Decepti was patient. However, he was cold and calculating. He would not make the same mistake as his predecessor. So, he focused the attention of his fleet on other matters. He allowed them to do what they did best, allowed them to continue ravaging the sentient life forms and souls on other planets, allowed them to feed and grow strong, allowed them to lay waste to planets and grow the wealth of their resources. All the while Decepti held the sights of Lumaria's knowledge in the back of his mind. He wanted more than anything that they had. When a being reaches a certain level of wealth and power, they see that resources are fickle and finite, but knowledge is infinite. And thus, knowledge becomes the true power and wealth to seek.

THE FOURTH CHRONICLE

The Kingdom of Trichomia

All stories begin somewhere. Or so that is what many beings were taught. However, within the grand scheme of the multiverse, there is no beginning or end. Or rather, there are many, and none. Ancient history can equally be modern knowledge, long ago, right now, and the past can stem from events in the so-called future. All of time and space is one grand cosmic machine that has no linearity in its endless folds. Such shapes of the universe cannot be conceived from the limited perspective of the three-dimensional mind. To see how all events, connect, one's mind must extend beyond time. For now, let us say that the tale of Trichomia is an ancient one and still yet to happen. Let us say that it took place long ago. Long ago and far in the future all at once.

The light and ethereal beings of Lumaria grieved as they felt the heart of their planet destroyed. They sought a course with no direction, following the internal guidance of their intuitive compass, following the map of fate and the shores to which it would take them. Guided by the supreme vision of their Oracle, the Lumarians travelled far through the cosmos.

The journey was long, not because they travelled slowly, but because the grief the Lumarians carried was heavy. Their planet was as much a part of them as the souls in their eyes. The loss of their home world was like losing a part of their heart. But their Oracle remained true to their promise, carrying the infinity of the living knowledge stored within the singing forest and taking their people to a lush and paradise planet they named Trichomia, which had been foretold in the Oracle's prophecy.

Trichomia was located in a small solar system within the spiral arms of the Milky Way Galaxy that would one day come to be known in a different dimensional frequency of space time reality as Mars. Of course, it was not known by that name at this point in time. Trichomia was mostly covered with a calm and crystalline azure ocean that sparkled with the reflected light of the star to which it orbited. Lush jungles and forest biomes grew abundantly on the parts of the land, and wild animals of all kinds roamed amongst them.

The Lumarians were in awe at the spectacle of this paradise planet. They had lived eons within the crystalline frequencies of Lumaria , which was magical in itself, but it did not express such a diversity and abundance of plant and animal life. To them, it was altogether foreign. They knew of planets such as these, had seen them in their visions, and had interacted on the metaphysical plane with beings who existed in similar environments. But never had they stepped foot with the physicality of their forms and beheld it with their own eyes, never had they smelt the pollen of flowers, or heard the chirp of birds in their ears, or the feeling of sand beneath their feet.

Upon their arrival, many animals wandered out of the forest to behold them. You see, the animals had never seen anything like the Lumarians either. Of course, the animals held no fear, for the Lumarians radiated a frequency of calming tranquility and love. Instead, the animals nuzzled up against their legs or stared deeply into the Lumarians' souls. They were able to communicate with one another because the Lumarians spoke the language of the world. It was a language that forwent any verbal dialectics, a language that spoke from one soul to another through an unfiltered and direct transmission of communication.

The Lumarians found laughter and joy with their new-found friends and, for the first time, found hope after the loss of their planet. The Oracle stepped forward as they sensed another being about to emerge from the thick of the jungle. All Lumarian and animal heads turned to behold the great energy that stepped forth. A beautiful, proud, and strong male lion stepped onto the sandy shore. The wind blew gently through the hair of his mane, and his eyes held great and silent wisdom in their ochre depths.

At this point in time and on this planet, the Lion did not need to feed on meat. In fact, all animals on Trichomia lived in harmony with one another. There was no food chain, no prey, and no predators. The Lion was the guardian amongst them, the leader to which all the animals of the jungle looked for wisdom.

Recognizing this, the Oracle of Twelve stepped towards the Lion and knelt so that their eyes and foreheads were levels with one another. They both acknowledged one another as equals and acknowledged one another as leaders in their own right. The Oracle saw the archetype of this being's soul and realized, at that moment, that the Lion would be the guardian and protector of the knowledge contained within the crystalline diamonds they had travelled so far with.

The Oracle bowed and touched his forehead to the Lions, and in a single moment, the infinite realms of knowledge were transferred to him. It was a test as well, for if the Lions heart was not pure, he would not have survived the transmission. The Lion came to be known as Ashka and was raised to be King of Planet Trichomia.

With the knowledge Ashka gained, he received eternal life as a blessing and was known as the first Enlightened One. Ashka vowed to protect and uphold the sanctity of knowledge and nurture the crystalline diamonds through all eons of time. One must understand that this did not simply happen in a single instant. Ashka had to go through his own spiritual journey within himself and find enlightenment on his own. Enlightenment was not something the Lumarians or any being could ever bestow. Ashka was already in a place where he was ready to embark on the process of becoming the guardian of the eternal crystalline knowledge. It was written in fate, and his soul had incarnated through many lifetimes, arriving at that point in time and on that planet for the sole reason of stepping into his enlightened destiny. No being can grant enlightenment. It is not the way the universe works; one can only guide and try to point the way.

The Lumarians planted the seed of their singing forest upon the soil of Trichomia at the north pole. Over the next eleven years, the crystalline seed took root and grew once more into physicality, whispering the knowledge of the universe and producing a light like the aurora borealis that stretched across all Trichomia.

Trichomia was known for its beauty, and amongst the vast biodiversity of life lived the small yet brilliant electric grasshopper. It resonated with the new frequency planted in its world, and like an ocean wave passing through the sky, the shimmering critters took to the sky. Ashka and the Lumarian's watched as the first procession of the electric grasshoppers took place above them. With all of them together, the soundwaves of their chittering syncopated in such a way that it produced a harmonic overtone, like the resonant afterglow of crystal singing bowls. The sun reflected in their shimmering wings, and the gong-like echo in the air filled every cell in the Lumarian's body, watching the beautiful insects with pride.

It was the first procession of thousands to come, and each year, the electric grasshoppers would travel to the crystal singing forest to mate and procreate and lay little golden cocoon eggs within the bath of the trichome resonance. When they arrived, millions of facets and reflections of their insect form could be seen in the mirror of the crystals. The crystals hummed, and the electric grasshoppers then mirrored the resonance back, attuning to the resonance of the Trichome frequency that was channeled through the singing crystals.

It was the marking of many new changes.

The Lumarians, with the help of Ashka, set to create a sacred geometric grid across the planet, utilizing the telluric and etheric energies of the planet's ley lines in alignment with the cosmic order. This was a multi-dimensional grid, one that did not only exist in the three-dimensional plane but extended upwards through many densities, all the way back to the source.

Etheric pyramidal structures were installed from the conscious projective technology within the Lumarian soul. They were placed on the intersecting ley lines and aligned with the stars, and in this way, a great cosmic and ethereally energetic circuit was created, not only on Trichomia but with the rest of the solar system. Within this grid was a grand and cosmic plan, which the Oracle of Lumaria had set into motion. One that would be revealed at a later time.

Eventually, after many years and none at all, the Lumarians left planet Trichomia behind, entrusting its safety and protection to its new King Ashka. The Lumarians were once again saddened at having to leave the paradise of Trichomia, but they now understood that their lives would never settle on a single planet again.

The Lumarians, now homeless, left Trichomia behind, traveling in translucent bubble ships made from the extension of their own consciousness, and spread themselves throughout different lands and universes, knowing that they would lose their connection to the great ethereal forest of knowledge. Just leaving their forest behind, they found their knowledge and connection to the timeline diminishing. But each held the trust and hope in their hearts that someday they would be reunited with their source once more.

It was a sacrifice of epic proportions. They gave up everything they knew for the greater good of the universe and turned away from the beloved light of their knowledge and the crystalline song of their hearts, all so that we souls who came after might have a chance to one day return to that which we came from.

During the years that passed, King Ashka, married Queen Xamira and his people lived in absolute peace and harmony. In many ways, this was his downfall. Without the polarity of suffering and under the cloak of protection that the Lumarians set up, there was no threat that befell the planet or King Ashka's people. He passed his days in tranquil meditations, but he soon grew bored of that, and desire slowly started to seep into his psyche.

He was no longer content with simply being as he had been for countless years. Ashka began to learn how to develop supernatural powers, moving past the awakening and growing into a truly powerful being. By mastering the different faculties of his body, he soon learned how to levitate, untethering his body from the ground. He learned many other things, like how to materialize matter from the etheric substrate of the universe, primarily creating anything he so desired at will. But the truth was that the King did not know hardship after eons in peace. As his focus moved away from simplicity, he grew complacent.

King Ashka had been tasked with protecting the sacred crystalline forest, but there was nothing and no one to protect it from. Years went by, and the lion King began to doubt that there was any danger at all. The stories and warnings the Lumarians had told him soon became a distant memory.

As the King's powers grew, he manifested a magnificent palace, becoming decadent and arrogant in his ways.

He sat upon his giant throne every day, mighty and powerful, and his pride grew too large to contain. There was nothing for him to do, for there was no war, no famine, nothing for him to solve or fix. The planet he was meant to be guarding soon began to feel like a prison. He grew restless and desired more from his life, more from his people. Why should he sit back and safeguard his civilization from a threat that never came?

The King realized that if the Lumarians had visited the planet Trichomia, then there must be other beings existing within the cosmos. Perhaps he could open his planet for others to visit. Perhaps he could be a shining example for the universe, a brilliant ray of hope. Not only that but he had knowledge, vast amounts to share. He had developed incredibly advanced technologies, ones that he could share with the universe and help guide other beings to a harmonious existence.

Sometimes, the problem with eons of peace is that those within the bubble of safety grow complacent about their freedoms and become naïve to the dangers that truly lurk beyond the bubble. King Ashka had never seen a day of war in his entire life. The field that the Lumarian's had set up completely cloaked the planet of Trichomia from any outside life, but that did not stop him from seeing.

The King was limited by the resources within his planet, but not only that, Ashka had become bored and lethargic ruling over a perfect Kingdom. His ego grew large with no struggle and no one to challenge him, and like many a leader, he set his sights away from his own planet. For long amounts of time, he observed other civilizations and found the natural dynamics within their planets fascinating.

He saw the rise and fall of Kingdoms and the many exotic, strange technologies each of these planets possessed.

For a while, simply observing them was enough. For a time, he found pleasure in living vicariously through the lives of these other civilizations. But that did not last long in the grand scheme of things. The King was bored of his immortality and yearned to interact with the other beings within the universe.

So, he started by reaching out to a small but spiritually advanced civilization known as the Ganeshian race. They were elephant-headed beings with humanoid bodies, possessing immense telekinetic capabilities. The Ganeshian race were almost monastic in their traditions, but they had developed extremely advanced technologies.

Technologies that cleared and opened up channels in the very tunnels of space-time. They acted like cosmic plumbers, helping the natural order along. Much like if a river began to dam, creating all sorts of migratory problems, the Ganeshian race would clear the debris away and let the river flow once more. They were largely a migratory race, creating spacecraft from their own telekinetic powers and traveling together throughout the cosmos in large herds.

The King thought that these benevolent beings would be a great place to start. Ashka reached out to one of their leaders, who went by the name Elephantus. The leader replied with great reciprocity and honor, and so King Ashka invited his herd to the first reveal of the planet Trichomia.

The coordinates were psychically transmitted, and

only a small section of the veil surrounding planet Trichomia was opened to let them through. King Ashka welcomed them with a giant celebration, inviting all of his Kingdom to greet the newcomers from another world. King Ashka was overjoyed to meet a new race and spent days discussing the ways of Ganeshian life.

Elephantus was a great person and a true leader of his people. He was brave and kind and had a purpose. King Ashka was overjoyed to have met him, and over the weeks that Elephantus's herd stayed, they shared much wisdom and technology and soon became very close friends.

But, like all good things, it had to come to an end eventually. The Ganeshians were migratory, and it was not in their nature to stay in one place for too long. King Ashka sent them off with another grand celebration, offering to welcome them back anytime they wished. He was overjoyed with how the first experience went and soon sought out other races within the cosmos.

They had not only gained a great amount of knowledge and technology from their interaction with the Ganeshian beings, but they had opened and established their first interplanetary trade root. It had been so long since the Lumarians had been on Planet Trichomia that to Ashka, their presence was almost like a distant dream.

King Ashka welcomed another race soon after the departure of the Ganeshians. This time it was a race of gaseous telepathic beings that resembled small clouds of various shapes, colors, and textures. Within the cloud was a small orb of electrical impulses, like lightning charges, forming an advanced brain and nervous system.

These beings were known as the Ephemera. They did not have a power structure like on Trichomia and even the Ganeshians. They were homogenous beings with no race or gender and no concept of names either. Yet they had a complex system of language that involved tones and the shifting of their gaseous colors to imply emotion or expression.

Being telepathic, they could transmit and convey great amounts purely through the mind. They did not trade in resources or currency and survived on the vast amounts of available radiation within space. Instead, they traded in knowledge, and they had a lot of knowledge to pass on. They had never needed to develop technology, but with their knowledge traded other beings for space-craft with which they could control by inhabiting the very circuitry itself.

Ashka was again in awe of these strange beings and made a great show of welcoming them. Beings came and went and soon Trichomia had become well known for its hospitality and wealth. So, it was done. King Ashka opened a gateway in the cloaking device, a small hexago-nal opening in the light grid from which he sent a signal to the various star systems throughout the galaxy. Beings from every corner of the universe began to flock to the planet Trichomia, and with the trade resources he gath-ered, Ashka built a great space-port just outside the

boundary of the cloaking field. Every time a new being arrived on their doorstep, a huge celebration was thrown in
honor of their arrival, one that would begin with a procession, always leading the beings to the giant thrown upon
which Ashka sat.

It was there that he would greet his planetary guests
and treat them to the spoils he had acquired. Trichomia
became a booming and bustling trade planet, and for a
long time, it operated perfectly. Ashka kept the border of
Trichomia under tight control, only allowing certain beings through. The crystalline forest remained hidden, for
it lay on a forbidden quadrant of the planet that was not
open to foreign visitors, and Ashka once again felt like a
King.

Many beings came through to visit him, but perhaps
one of the most notable of all was a race of beings known
as the Owlinian Archons. They were a nocturnal race of
highly advanced sorcerer scientists. They had evolved
from birds many millions of years ago into what they are
today.

They still had feathers, but they walked bipedally, and
from a joint in their wings, arms had grown with four
feathery fingers. They could still fly, though, within their
society, it was not socially acceptable to fly in the company of others. Flight to them was the guilty pleasure of
past time, as they had become highly devoted to their
magical sciences.

They came in all shades and colors and had large void

black eyes. They were highly intelligent and were psychically connected to the 'hall of records' or *akasha* as they called it. A vast library of cosmic information, to which many of their kinds were attendants and scribes within. While the hall of records was not a physical place, many of the trained initiates could soar there on wings, not of the physical world.

Imagine an endless row of shelves that extended forever in every direction, like a complex labyrinth within the very substrate of the astral ether itself. The Owlinians could exit their physical bodies using a method of soul traveling called astral projection. It was through this method that they were able to access the Akashic records. It was in this astral realm where they were always permitted to fly amongst the shelves, gaining eternal knowledge and bringing it back to the physical world to convey with their cohort of scientists.

At first, when the Owlinian race arrived at the spaceport of Trichomia and was granted access, the King was not sure what to make of them. They were a quiet bunch and spoke in a trilling bird song of a language that was hard to decode. They showed no emotions on their faces and were very still beings who came off as rather stiff and dry.

It wasn't until King Ashka became proficient in their language that he truly began to understand them. Whilst they did not express emotions with their physical features as Ashka was used to, their emotions were hidden within the intonations of their bird-song language. The nuance and subtlety of each tone was so hard to pick up that, at first, Ashka could not tell the difference between one trill and another.

But the more time he spent with them, the more he began to see how deaf he had truly been to their language. A halftone down followed by tone trills three steps up conveyed curiosity. These were heard as overtones that acted almost like a second voice, resonating above the frequency of their whistle-like language structure.

A race that Ashka had once thought emotionless was in fact, expressing great magnitudes of feeling in every moment. It was these differences and nuances that inspired the King to keep his gates open. The diversity within the cosmos was truly breathtaking. The Owlinians always spoke with melody and with the fuse of feeling within their words.

It was very different from the typical phonetic language he was used to and, of course, less transparent than the direct psychic transmission of feeling and intention that he had grown accustomed to from other beings. Within their societal structure, the most venerated and honored were not those with high material wealth but those who had attained the highest state of knowledge. Two of them had been granted titles of High Priest and Priestess.

The High Priest, whose name could be loosely translated as Barradow Gray, was what Ashka expected when he thought of a leader. He was young in relative years, though he came across as a composed elder, slightly reserved with constant scribes and attendants by his side. But the High Priestess of the Owlinians, Neve, was very different. She was quick-witted, fun, and even feisty with her remarks. She appeared to have a fiery childishness about her, but it was backed by serious strength and power.

Ashka had observed her once going through what appeared to be a kata of some kind, a warrior's dance, wielding fan knives and utilizing her claws and beak with deadly precision. She could often be found training in the art of battle and had even tried to coax Ashka himself into a bout, which he evidently refused.

The Owlinian's Sorcerer's had a home planet, though they said that they were very different from those who lived as citizens. The citizens had normal tasks and duties, occupations and families. It was the task of the High Priest and Priestess to navigate and explore the uncharted darkness of space, and to be frank, the task suited them well.

They even asked Ashka in a formal request to make Trichomia their *perch* indefinitely. A term that was used to describe a planet upon which they were residing temporarily. Ashka accepted because he felt that there could be a great benefit from the knowledge they had obtained.

They stayed for many years, and upon the return of the Ganeshians on their herd's migration, a brilliant idea struck the mind of the great Trichomian King. He proposed that a galactic coalition be formed. A coalition that would come together and congregate and share the learnings of space. He invited both the Owlinians and the Ganeshians to be the first amongst a new order that would come to be known as the Trichomian Alliance.

It was the first of its kind. Most races within the galaxy may never learn that there were others out amongst the stars. Only those with sufficient advancement could truly hope to navigate the vast and infinite reaches of space. If it were not for the advanced astral technology and knowledge left behind by the Lumarians once upon a time, then Ashka doubted he would have ever known life outside the planet of Trichomia.

This was a great celebration, for it was a start in the new chapter of the cosmic order. As the Alliance grew, so would its members, and perhaps a unification of peace and shared knowledge would spread across the galaxy. Both the Ganeshian and Owlinian races eagerly accepted. It was to be a collective, with none of them above the other, an alliance of true equality.

Ashka called a feast to commemorate the Trichomian Alliance and invited all and many. It was a celebration said to have lasted days, with exotic liquors and substances, massive feasts, and performances alike. On the third day of the celebration, The Owlinian High Priestess Neve stood atop the highest tower of the ancient temple of Trichomia that rose high above King Ashka's palace, her eyes scanning the horizon for any signs of danger. Trichomia was a safe place, it was heavily guarded, and Neve approved of the security measures in place. Despite that, she could not help herself from being on the lookout for any potential threats. She had seen the dangers within the cosmos for herself and fought in many battles. Neve had been trained since birth to serve as the guardian and protector of her people, and she took her duty very seriously.

Within the Owlinian society the High Priestess and Priest were chosen from birth, based on the basis of certain signs that indicated that they were reincarnations of the past lineage of High Priest and Priestess. Neve's role was very different from Barradow's, though there were several similarities, including being the spiritual leaders for their race. While Barradow focused more on alchemy and the formulation of medicinal and spiritual plants, the High Priestess was born to protect her people and trained in the martial combat of Owlinia, known as *Owlinian Arts*. The martial combat was an ancient style that was channeled from one of Neve's previous incarnations, though she could rarely ever access the memories that belonged to her past lives. This was not from a lack of trying as she often attempted to sit in meditation to access higher forms of consciousness with the aid of the plant medicines that Barradow formulated.

As she looked out over the sprawling city of Trichomia she could see her people mingling with the Trichomians and felt a great sense of pride and responsibility wash over her. The people of Owlinia looked to her for guidance and protection and she would do everything in her power to keep them safe. Neve was not just a warrior, though. She was also a powerful sorceress, capable of wielding magic that few others, even amongst her own race, could even comprehend. She had spent her entire life studying the ancient tomes of magic and mastering the complex spells that would aid her in battle, and the battle was where her true passion lay. It was not the killing or bloodshed but the practice of her art form and the honor of being on the front to protect her people.

She was also tasked with also leading her people spiritually and spent hours each day in meditation and prayer. This part of her role was harder for her to connect with. She could recite the texts perfectly, but their true meanings and metaphors were hard to truly integrate. Barradow, on the other hand, was much more accomplished in this field, though he lacked the warrior spirit. However, Neve continued to be disciplined and meditated even if the hours would go by in frustration and the desire to return to her martial practices.

Despite the weight of her responsibilities, Neve took great joy in her duties. She loved nothing more than seeing her people thrive and prosper under her care, and when danger threatened, she was always ready to stand at the forefront of the battle, wielding her razor-sharp fans and her magic with deadly precision.

Never felt the breeze rustle against her feathers, and it inspired her to move. She fell into one of her kata forms, flowing with the wind and shifting from stance to stance, channeling energy through her body. There were many forms depending on different scenarios. The swift form was inspired by the movement of the wind itself and was best used for evasion. It was a form that did as little damage to her opponent as possible were she was in combat and focused more on a flowing style of redirection that would put an enemy off balance. She spun on her feet, twisting like a leaf in the breeze, even flapping and rising up into the air for short bursts, twirling before landing as light as a feather. She was coming to the end of her kata when she felt her senses tingle and noticed a heartbeat that had not been there before. It was the Kings. Neve did not stop instantly but instead went through the rest of her kata, not wishing to break the flow of energy that she had already started.

When she did eventually finish, Neve closed the practice with an honoring bow towards her lineage before turning to face the King. She looked at him with a sharp gaze, feeling relaxed and peaceful after moving through her form. He had an awe-inspired look on his face and greeted her with a smile. Ashka approached Neve and invited her to go on a walk with him. She had been on Trichomia for a while, but he still very little about her in comparison with the High Priest Barradow.

"Your fighting style is beautiful," Ashka spoke with praise. "It was almost like you became the wind itself." Neve gestured with a melodic trill that implied a smile and the emotions of humbleness.

"Thank you, King Ashka. I can't help myself. It is where I find peace." She spoke in her language, hands and wings clasped behind her back. "Many find it in meditation or in the arts, but I feel most at ease when I move through one of my past incarnations of katas. It helps me attune with the natural laws that permeate our universe."

"It is an incredible thing to witness, and it makes me all the happier that we are allies. I would not like to face you on the battlefield." He replied jokingly.

Neve trilled, gratitude, with a tone for peace as well, but she sensed that there was something more. Neve turned to him. "Was there a reason you came to see me, King Ashka?"

The King was about to answer, but in that instant, one of Neve's attendants approached her with haste, trilling a couple words which alerted Neve right away. Neve excused herself from the King's presence with apologies, leaving him behind. The King watched her go only for a moment before someone stepped beside him. It was the High Priest Barradow who greeted Ashka with a quiet trill.

"Neve rarely has any time. She spends most of it worrying about our people, and it is because of her worrying that we are safe." He paused, then looked up to King Ashka. "I would like to show you something very important to my people."

Barradow Gray then pulled King Ashka aside. The two had spoken frequently, Ashka speaking in his language and Barradow in his own. They had the technology to translate, but something about that felt like it didn't honor the other. So instead, both sides had committed to learning each other's languages, though it was physically impossible for Ashka to reply in the Owlinian language with the set of vocal cords he had, and the same went for Barradow. They understood each other, however, and that was important.

The Owlinian priest reached into his wings and, from a hidden area beneath his feathers, withdrew what looked to be some sort of liquid substance. It was contained in a spherical glass flask and glowed slightly. The liquid was thick and only slightly translucent, constantly in motion like the currents of a slowly flowing river.

The King questioned Barradow of its contents and the Owlinian High Priest revealed that it was a secret substance very few of their kind ever tried. It was a drink meant to be shared, and apparently, only the Owlinian priests partook in the ancient ritual. They had scientifically designed it using some of the local plant life on their home planet. With their knowledge they had combined the roots, stems, and leaves of several plants to make a powerful alchemical elixir. Barradow revealed much to Ashka, not only about this particular elixir, but of the great importance of plants and their role as spirits within the evolution of beings.

The plants were alive as much as the sentient beings that existed amongst the universes. In fact, in Barradow's eyes, plants were divine representations of the sacred code of the universe. They had spirits, and some plants that existed had incarnated into physical form to aid in the expansion and growth of consciousness for sentient life forms.

These plant beings were known as the sacred teachers of the soul. Barradow went on to reveal that the first Owlinian sorcerer had arisen when he followed the words of nature to consume the leaves of a rare plant. This plant had granted the first sorcerer the ability to soar beyond the physical world. It was he who taught many of his people how to travel in the astral dimensions and retrieve knowledge from the Akashic records.

King Ashka was enthralled and amazed by the knowledge Barradow shared, and soon, the conversation wound back to the elixir before them. It was made by combining several natural plants and tinctures, and it allowed those who shared it to merge their minds. It could be shared with one or as many as so desired, but the more minds, the more complex the experience became.

Ashka was honored and bewildered that the High Priest was bestowing him such an honor. Somewhat tentatively and perhaps driven in part by the rich wines and exotic foods, Ashka agreed. In fact, how could he pass up an opportunity such as this? Was it ever possible to know another's mind? Truly? One was severely limited by the perceptions they had. Even through psychic communication from other beings, Ashka had never been granted privilege into the depths and wonders of their innermost minds. They conveyed simple things like intention, emotions and will, but that was surface level in comparison.

Ashka led the Owlinian High Priest to his own chambers, which were grand and lavish in the center of the great palace that looked out over all of Trichomia. King Ashka and Barradow told stories and drank from the liquid whilst they waited for the effects to take place.

It started slowly at first. Whispers of bird whistle thoughts in the back of the King's head. He felt light impressions, like the soft fluff of feathers on skin that was not his own. Their voices began to blend together, and Ashka could no longer tell who it was that was talking. Was it trills coming out of his own mouth?

Then, he began to see through Barradow's eyes. Oh, how incredible that felt. His vision was keener than anything he had ever known. He could focus on miniscule details and spot the scuttling of an insect from hundreds of meters away. And then he saw himself through the Owlinian's eyes. He saw himself seeing himself, an infinite mirror of perception that almost sent Ashka tumbling into the vastness of it all.

But Barradow was experienced in this meta perceptual nature. He eased the King's nerves, and as he did, Ashka was no longer himself. It was no longer him and Barradow put them together as one unit. Two bodies, one mind, swimming in the absolute uniqueness of one other.

What arose was a sparkling compassion that quickly blossomed into... Love. Not just the love between two bodies but an indefinable and unquantifiable love. It was profound and all-consuming, something Ashka had never truly experienced before. Ashka was Barradow, and both their memories merged together as one, streaming and sharing the most intimate parts of one another like a root lay bare. Their physical bodies met, and what once was a merging of minds became a merging of form, soft feathers ruffling against his tender mane.

The King having a Queen had never known an intimacy such as this. It was profound and terrifying, and *magnificent*. Magnificent to not only feel the stroke of one's own pleasure but that of the other, a feedback loop of perpetuity. They rode and wove on waves of pleasure that peaked to heights neither of them had ever known.

It was on this night that Barradow and the King found love in one another. Love from two beings born and raised galaxies away. They shared in one another for the entire night, exploring the depths of pleasure and the depths of one another, the effects of the elixir only wearing off as the morning sun began to rise. And even as their minds began to separate once more, their sense of selves returning, they continued to lie in one another's presence upon the King's bed.

It felt almost like a great loss to disconnect from one another in mind, but they had dived deep into one another, and the King felt a great satisfaction of being able to love this being as himself. He watched as Barradow slept, for the day was when all the Owlinians slumbered.

When eventually nightfall came again, Barradow arose, and they shared their side of the experience for many hours. But just when Ashka thought to order some food from the servants, Barradow stood and informed the King that he would not be able to stay any longer.

It was not because of the intimacy they shared, though they both thought it best that it be kept silent. But the High Council of the Owlinian sorcerers had been planning to depart after the festivities ended. Neve had caught wind of a potential danger to their home roost from foreign invaders, and she was anxious to set off. Barradow had ensured her that he would accompany her until the situation was quelled. Barradow promised Ashka that he would return soon, and from his wing, he plucked free a feather and handed it to the King as a reminder of the night that they shared together.

It was a great pain for Ashka to bid farewell not only to Barradow but to the rest of the Owlinians, amongst whom great friends he had made. And it was not only them who took the need to set off but also the Ganeshians. They needed to set sail once again on their migration, for without their aid, the rivers of the cosmic etherium that they carved would overflow or grow stagnant. Ashka watched as their spacecraft departed, and as he did, he could still hear the sound of bird trills whispering in the back of his head, emotions fluttering in the beat of his heart.

With the absence of the Ganeshians and the Owlinians. King Ashka sought out the company of other races. The great Trichomia Alliance had been formed and he would look for other beings to enter into the council, although no official decision could be fully made without the presence of all three monarchs from the various races.

Decades went by in a blur, and a part of Ashka began to grow lonely. Not only that, but his mind began to be pulled outwards. He was enamored and astounded by so many of the visiting races and their strange ways. He forwent his austerities and spiritual practices and began to fully dive into the role of a galactic ambassador and tradesman King.

He became caught up in material technologies, fascinated with the strange and exotic wares that merchants would bring. He grew much too used to being praised and became decadent in his tastes, draping himself in gold and fine weavings from other star systems, indulging in rich wines and foods. He even began to partake in many of the various psychotropic drugs and substances that the foreign dignitaries and their council brought with them to the lavish parties. They were incredible and new, and Ashka partook in them without restraint, losing himself in their temptation.

King Ashka sat on the great throne within the grand halls of his newly built palace. The Kingdom of Trichomia was prospering. Soon, beings from every corner of the universe were coming to visit him. He sat with a large goblet of wine that had been laced with a foreign stimulant, cast in gold with shimmering sapphires encrusted on the exterior, his mind swimming with the bright colors of the drugs in his system.

The rich violet substance tasted fine on his tongue, and he sat watching as ambassadors from other Kingdoms brought gifts of finery to his feet, his mind in the sloshy exuberance of the liquor. With a simple wave of his fingers, Ashka's attendants picked up the offerings and placed them in a pile by his throne.

He waved again, and the next beings in line approached him. His eyes twinkled as they revealed strange formations of crystalline gems, odd technologies, and intricate tapestries. He tasted spices that made the mind elate and smelt fragrances that granted hallucinatory visions.

With all the new and exciting discoveries, with the meeting of beings completely different from himself, King Ashka soon forgot his original purpose. It had been eons, countless millennia, since the Lumarians had arrived on the soil of Trichomia after all. And with all this new excitement, the King's mind was drawn outwards. Fascinated and enthralled by the riches of materiality.

He could not believe that he had kept his planet hidden for so long. He feasted and reveled with ambassadors and foreign Princes and Queens. With his new riches, he expanded his palace, turning a once humble monastic temple into one of grandeur and extravagant luxury. Ashka, having been born of the Leo constellation, bearing the anthropomorphic form of a lion and bearing the genetics of pride, this great wealth and prestige exonerated his ego to new heights.

He once had deep powers of introspection, powers that allowed him to reach even the farthest reaches of the internal world. He had once spent most of the day in quiet meditation, diving deeper into the nature of reality. However, slowly, over time, those hours became less and less. And as his practice diminished, he fell from grace within himself, slowly and unknowingly falling into the whims of unconsciousness, a state he had never known before.

The grasp of illusion and materiality had seduced him, and his attention was pulled outwards, emotions no longer in control, wild and lusting for more. He consorted and took to bed many different beings, only choosing the prettiest and most exotic of them all. His lust became ravenous, and what once satiated him was no longer enough.

He decided to divorce his Queen because he no longer sought comfort in simply being but *needed*, required pleasures to make him feel good. Indulging in all subsatnces, combined with a gala of orgies, feasting, and fornicating to his heart's content. One of the exotic new technologies that had been brought to Ashka was from a race of amphibian beings named the Silteki. They did not wear any clothes, their tender areas on full display adorned with elegant jewelry. Their society was founded on a relatively new revolution that empowered the exploration of pleasure and freedom of passion. They brought Ashka, a machine that was soft and supple to the touch, made almost of an organic bio-material that was as smooth as a dolphin's skin. The machine was large enough for him to sit in, and when activated, it stimulated regions and nerves in Ashka's body that he didn't even know existed. It sent surges of pleasure through every cell in his body, creating full-body orgasms that could last for hours.

Ashka indulged greatly in the stimulating Orgasmic XTC Machine, and it only fueled his desires for pleasure more and more. The King never felt satiated. His pride and confidence grew, but with it, so did his entitlement. He turned away those who could not offer him material goods, even if they made up for it greatly in wisdom and knowledge.

He had spent millennia seeking wisdom, and that had driven him to boredom. Why did he need the insubstantial riches of knowledge when he could so easily lay with the finest of consorts and drink any problems of mind away? King Ashka had lived his life in a bubble. He had never known hardship or war or famine. His people had always prospered. And whilst that was a blessing in itself, it also made him naïve.

The King drank belligerently with no fear of consequence. He had no concept of addiction or dependence, and at first, he did not feel the effects of the comedown. He did not feel the headaches or nausea. But as he continued to fall from grace, the effects of his actions soon followed. The problem was that King Ashka was already too far gone into his unconsciousness to return. He yelled at his attendants, grew bitter with rage, and demanded more and more each day.

The only things that would bring him comfort were

the gluttonous indulgence in rich meats, the smooth tannin of foreign wines mixed with other psychoactive substances and, of course, the sweet taste of flesh beneath the bed sheets.

But with the spread of Trichomia throughout the cosmos, and its rise in popularity also came unwanted attention. Through the wide web of the cosmos, word had reached the Emperor Decepti Mortar's ears who been waiting patiently throughout eons of time. The emperor has been living his immortal life through dark sorcery and vampiric blood magic.

Through his network of spies, informing him of Trichomia and the great riches it was accumulating. But more so, he had heard rumors that the great planet was hiding something extremely valuable. Something that was rumored to be more valuable than any gold or material wealth.

Devising a plan and knowing that the planet was heavily guarded, he ordered his most deceptive spy, Illuminatus X, to find a way to infiltrate the planet unseen and investigate what lay hidden there. Illuminatus X had unrivalled shapeshifting powers, able to shift seamlessly into any race he beheld. Whilst many Draconians could shapeshift well, Illuminatus came from a hybrid Draconian race. The Draconian raped and pillaged many of the worlds they conquered, and through that violation, they had created several Draconian sub-species. One of them had been with a serpentine race of sentient beings. The hybridization of their two genetics had created an unexpected result. The sub-species that were born, known as the Dracoslivians, had been born with extremely enhanced shapeshifting abilities. They could not just change their outer appearance like the Draconian, but they could alter their molecular make-up cell for cell. Illuminatus X was the offspring of that violation and would be these powers that he used to his advantage. He had been recruited by the Draconian Empire to take a position as one of the Illuminatus, a secret organization within the Draconian agenda that infiltrated and controlled entire worlds from the shadows.

He had forgotten his true name long ago, that was if he ever had one. Amongst the brothers of the Illuminatus, he was known simply as X, for the title of *Illuminatus,* was given to those who had passed the initiatory rites within the secret cult. All who joined were given new names, each as nondescript and anonymous as X himself.

Through their network of spies, Illuminatus X had heard of the Trichomian alliance and knew that if he could shapeshift into one of their ambassadors, he would most likely be granted unrivalled privileges and would be able to infiltrate Trichomia with ease. He had heard of the Owlinian Archon's but despite their extensive spy network, the Owlinian race could not be tracked. So Illuminatus X turned his attention towards the Ganeshians. They were well-known throughout the galaxy. They had a home planet, but it had never been worth invading. The Ganeshians were migrators, using tunnels in space-time to travel large distances, altruistically cleaning up the cosmic currents.

On one of the many cosmic cycles, Elephantus and his herd were en route to cycling back towards Trichomia as they had been invited by King Ashka to witness the procession of the electric grasshoppers. Elephantus and King Ashka had formed a great bond over many years and were not only partners in trade but also great friends.

Using this knowledge, Illuminatus X cloaked himself in the advanced Draconian technology and followed Elephantus and his herd. He infiltrated the signals coming to and fro from their mother ship and learned of their plan to visit Trichomia. It was perfect. All he had to do was infiltrate the ship and disguise himself as one of them. They had no alarm systems, as they were extremely telepathic. For many a Draconian infiltrator, that would be a huge problem, but Illuminatus X had invaded psychic races before. He knew that telepathy worked as an extension of the mind's senses, able to pick up on minute electromagnetic signals, like thoughts, emotions, and bodily impulses. Illuminatus X, being part of the Dracoslivian subrace, had a vast amount of control over his body. He could still his mind to perfect silence and reduce the electromagnetic output of his cells so that they were unreadable and could even become invisible to the naked eye. To the Ganeshians, all they would sense was silence. If given time, they may realize that the silence they sensed was not natural, but by that time, it would be too late.

Quietly, when most of the Ganeshian beings were in a

cycle of sleep, save for the guards, Illuminatus X snuck aboard the large mothership in absolute silence. As he passed by one of the guards unnoticed, he flicked out his forked tongue. Illuminatus X's senses were so acute that just one taste and he had the data he needed to become one of them. As soon as he was out of sight, he shapeshifted into the guard he had passed, molding his mind to theirs so that they would not sense him with their telekinetic powers, before making his way towards Elephantus's quarters. He would become a mirror of their leader. An exact replica.

Illuminatus snuck into the sleeping Elephantus's chambers. He knew that he would not be able to kill the ambassador in any conventional way. If Elephantus's mind awoke for even a single moment and acknowledged that he was being killed, the entire herd would be alerted. So instead of slipping a knife into his chest, Illuminatus X pulled a small vial from his belt and removed the stopper, which released an odorless gas. It was a neurotoxin of Illuminatus X's own invention. It slowly pulled any who inhaled it into a deeper and deeper sleep, until they entered a comatose. This would disconnect Elephantus from the psychic connection for enough time to let Illuminatus X insert the a specialize metaphysical weapon, a dark-necro ceremonial sacrifice knife. This would stop his heart instantly and shock him to be awake and paralyzed in a frozen conscious horror, simultaneously realizing a foreign perpetrator is absorbing his essence.

He carried it out, and there was only one second between the death of the Ambassador and the time it took for Illuminatus X to become him, mimicking his mind and tuning himself into the psychic mind field of the Ganeshians. No alerts went off. He had succeeded.

Illuminatus X then shed his previous skin and took that of Elephantus, assuming the identity of the herds' ambassador. With this skin, he would be granted the highest levels of authority and, knowing the connection that King Ashka and Elephantus shared, would also be privy to a seat by the King of Trichomia himself.

Instead of taking the long migratory route that had initially been planned, Illuminatus X, disguised as Elephantus, rerouted them directly to Trichomia. Some amongst his ranks upon the ship questioned this decision, but Illuminatus X wove lies of his own, and with the face and voice of their leader, none of them questioned him any further.

The spacecraft that the Ganeshian beings had did *not* contain 5`advanced, but as migratory space farers, they did not use that form of technology. They knew that creating artificial wormholes in the fabric of space left behind a tear, which could disrupt and clog the natural flow of the cosmic currents. Much of the work that the Ganeshians did was stitching these holes back together. They were like the caretakers of the cosmic river. However, they did utilize the natural formation of tunnels that formed within the fabric of time and space. They would journey from tunnel to tunnel, bridging vast amounts of space each time until they arrived at their destination.

The estimated journey would take several months, but this gave Illuminatus X time to master his disguise. He mimicked the mannerisms and eccentricities of the Ganeshian race, and after those months had passed, he had become so immersed in his new identity that he could barely remember his own name. In all manner of speaking, he had become Elephantus, and he referred to himself as such, even in his own head.

Everything was identical, save for his purpose. Illuminatus X, now known to himself as Elephantus X, held onto a single purpose. To infiltrate the Trichomian ranks and find out what powers and secrets they held within the forbidden quadrant.

The Ganeshians were a peaceful and spiritual race known for their giant temples and wisdom. After a long, arduous journey, they eventually reached the Trichomian spaceport for inspection. Even under the close and scrutinous eyes of the Trichomian Elite Guard, Elephantus's shapeshifting was flawless. They let him and his ship through the hexagonal gate and into Trichomia's atmosphere.

As expected, Elephantus X and his people were welcomed with the highest of praise. King Ashka even left his throne to greet them personally, as they were the first beings he had ever made contact with outside of his own planet. For the first days, Elephantus played his role well. He took part in hours of conversation, exchanging stories of his travels that he had gathered from the memories of the former Elephantus.

Ashka was overjoyed to be in the company of Elephantus and hastily ordered one of his squires to send a message to Barradow and the Owlinians. They responded, taking up the rare opportunity to reconvene at Trichomia during the procession of the electric grasshopper. However, Barradow informed Ashka that it would only be him joining as the High Priestess had to remain behind to oversee a potential system uprising from a pirate group of beings.

Illuminatus X had not anticipated this, but he held his disguise well.

He had heard of the Owlinians and knew that they were keen of sense. Had he not spent the many months imitating the former herd leader, he most likely would have been spotted. But Illuminatus played his role as Elephantus well, and despite the Owlinian's sharp wits and intelligence, they did not catch him.

Together, the High Priest and Priestess, along with Illuminatus X and Ashka, talked about new trade deals and negotiated prices. They celebrated, indulged in wines and rich foods, and shared what they had learnt on their travels and watched as the great ocean of shimmering grasshoppers flew overhead. Illuminatus X stared at them and wondered where it was they were heading. They spent many long nights alone with King Ashka, catching up and reveling in their shared prosperity. After such discussions, Elephantus X asked if he and his people could stay for a couple more months. He wove lies that his people loved Trichomia, and it had become like a second home to them. A pilgrimage away from the motherland. So, few planets, after all, were habitable to the Elphantus race, Trichomia being one of the only ones within this galaxy.

Of course, King Ashka agreed and was honored to host them. So far everything was going according to Illuminatus X's plan. After these long-winded days and nights, Ashka and the High Priest would spend time alone. Of what they were doing, Illuminatus X soon found out. He was shocked to see the King and High Priest in such intimate activities. But this was also the perfect opportunity. The secrecy between Barradow and the King meant that he dismissed many of his guards and servants. Illuminatus X waited for these times, and when the King was occupied, Illuminatus X began his covert mission of trying to find the secrets that the King held.

He started by following his hunch and tracking down where the grasshoppers were flying to, which happened to be in the forbidden quadrant of the planet and found that it was heavily guarded from all angles. This only confirmed Illuminatus X's suspicions that whatever was guarded here was extremely valuable. One night, when the moon of Trichomia was hidden in a near eclipse, Elephantus X infiltrated the forbidden quadrant.

For a long while, he saw nothing, for most of the area was cloaked in the Lumarian technology. It was only when he reached the core and center of the forbidden quadrant, did he find what he was looking for.

Illuminatus X stared in absolute awe, beholding the singing forest of crystalline knowledge. This was more than he could have ever anticipated. It was a singing magnificent structure to behold. Giant crystals grew up from the earth, the infinite mirror of reflections within the shimmering rainbow facets fractalized time in repeating geometric patterns that swirled so deep that even Illuminatus X could not make them out. He could walk amongst the towering crystals, and all of his body was filled with the high resonance. It made his body shudder, and he could not stay next to them for long, for their amplitude was too great for his soul. He scurried out and knew at once that this was what his leader, Decepti Mortar, had been looking for.

It had been right here this entire time, right under their noses. Illuminatus X spared no moment of delay. Eager to move up amongst the ranks, Illuminatus X sent confirmation to his Emperor using a technological beacon device, transmitting that he had found the lost crystalline forest of Lumaria He was so wrapped up in his discovery that he did not think of what defenses were in place against foreign signals coming from within the planet.

King Ashka woke in the night to alarms blaring within his chambers. These were the defensive alarms that the Lumarians had installed eons ago. Ashka shot up in his bed and rushed to his command post, beholding the foreign frequency of the signal beacon. After millennia, the singing forest was under attack. With all the distraction of opening his border, King Ashka had almost completely forgotten about the original task he had been entrusted to carry out.

The Lumarians had tasked him as the protector of knowledge. The knowledge that, if held in the wrong hands, would truly spell the end of life as they knew it. King Ashka put the planet on high alert and sealed the borders before sending his elite guard to the singing forest, joining their ranks himself.

He was absolutely dumbfounded and shocked to find Elephantus hiding out in one of the icy caves. For the first time in his thousands of years of life, King Ashka felt the bitter stab of betrayal. How could his greatest friend and closest ally betray him like this? Of course, he did not yet know that this was not Elephantus at all, but the notorious Draconian spy Illuminatus X in disguise. Illuminatus X ran from Ashka and tried to escape the planet but found that his ship had been forced into lockdown and all the flight quadrants were shut. There was no escaping Trichomia. Being a master in stealth, he managed to elude them for many days, but the Ancient Lumarian defenses were too advanced for Illuminatus X to truly navigate by, and he was eventually caught.

However, the entire time he had dodged King Ashka and his soldiers, he had been pinging the location of Trichomia through an entangled quantum lock, and his efforts had given the beacon more than enough time to make an entangled signal lock with Decepti's main warship. With the confirmation of the singing forest's location, Decepti set a course for the Milky Way.

Ashka, the Beast King, and many of the animal citizens upon Trichomia had evolved much in the millennia since the Lumarians had inhabited the planet, and with his knowledge, many had developed into bipedal sentient beings. Ashka was furious and perplexed at finding Ambassador Elephantus hiding in the most sacred and forbidden corners of his planet. It was Ashka himself that managed to corner the elusive ambassador and capture him. While Illuminatus X could cloak himself, Ashka had the capability to sense his frequency without the need for eyes through the heightened sense of his whiskers. The quantum device pinging the location was what ultimately gave the master of stealth away.

Once captured, Ashka ordered the Trichomian Elite guards to take Elephantus prisoner. It was only once he was imprisoned, Ashka had dowsed all veils of deception away with the remnants of the Lumarian technology that he saw who it was running around in the body of the ambassador. Ashka stared in shock at the reptilian being before him. It was the first time in all his life that he had encountered a Draconian in the scales and blood.

Ashka questioned Illuminatus X for days, employing all methods at his disposal, but Illuminatus X never said a word except to spit insults. Having been disguised as Elephantus for so long, he could barely remember his own name. It was one of the side effects of taking on the body of another.

Dracoslivians knew that to shapeshift was not only to look like someone else but to become them, thoughts, memories, and all. It sometimes took weeks or months for a Draconian to remember who they really were. Ashka had no other choice but to violate the boundaries of the Draconian's mind, and with invasive technologies, peered into the folds of Illuminatus's consciousness, psychically interrogating him until he found the information that he dreaded to uncover. He saw to whom the beacon was transmitting its signal, and there was very little time to prepare. For now, he knew that the Draconian Empire was on its way to his doorstep.

Ashka was panicked. The legends the Lumarians had told him were true. He had been a fool to question them, and now there was an entire Draconian army headed his way. He knew how precious the knowledge that lay within the singing forest was and, when in the wrong hands, could bring about the end of the universe as they knew it.

Acting out of pure necessity, King Ashka divulged the Lumarian secrets he had been bestowed to protect, telling them to the High Priest of the Owlinians. Ashka begged Barradow to aid and find a way to transfer the knowledge within the crystal forest. Barradow of course, knew of these secrets already, as they together had partaken in the elixir that merged their minds to one. In fact, he had been thinking for many years about a way synthesize it so the Trichome crystals could be transferred into a biological container.

Ashka knew that if he didn't act quick, the Draconian army would steal the knowledge and lay waste to Trichomia. So, under the lead of Barradow and his scientists of sorcery, Ashka ordered them to make the transfer. Thousands of them gathered around the singing forest and began the ritual. To a lesser being, the ritual could be called magic, but amongst such highly realized spiritual beings, the working of their spell was purely scientific.

They used sonic frequencies, which they emitted from instruments and their voices, to begin the transfer process. The Owlinian sorcerers liquified the diamond crystals with cosmic frequencies, infusing the knowledge and energy through bio-sonic waves into the first two strains of a biologically cloned living organism.

The Owlinian sorcerers had created a plant vessel, an organic crucible. It was cloned, grey and bleak in appearance, with no active genetics for it to carry out any proper living functions. But as they transferred the liquefied sonic energy of the Trichome crystals into the neutral plant vessels, the plant began to transform.

On a genetic level, the Trichome crystals began to reprogram the plant vessels, imbuing them with life, and a bright burst of golden light sent a shimmering shockwave of energy across the planet. The *cannabinoid* plants were living crucibles, vessels into which to transmit the Trichomian crystal knowledge. Barradow and his sorcerers had long been testing the effect of using plants as living vessels to transmit knowledge. It was said that the Owlinians first began to evolve due to eating a powerful seed. This seed was said to have contained active components that began to expand their minds and open them to other realms of possibility. The Owlinians used that seed to catalyse their growth and map the etheric dimensions. Eventually, they no longer needed the seed, but it was the primal source of their alchemical sorcery, so they knew the potential and power that could be bound within plants. The sorcerers performed their ritual, and as soon as the transfer was complete, the plants began to glow a rich and vibrant gold. They came to be known as The Golden Trichome.

Whilst Barradow and his Sorcerers carried out their work, Ashka could feel the fabric of time-space rippling as the Draconian warships encroached on their location. Ashka knew that they would be upon Trichomia very soon, and he assigned his Trichomian Elite to guard the task of protecting the secret of the Trichomian crystal knowledge.

Ashka couldn't believe that it was coming to this. The Draconian Empire was coming, and that only meant one thing. War. Ashka was a peaceful being. Even the elite guards he had trained had never seen a day of battle.

They had been trained in the sacred martial arts passed on by the Owlinian High Priestess, but Ashka knew they would stand no chance against the power of the Draconian forces. The Draconian had been bred and forged in the fiery chaos of their home world. They were natural-born killers, masters of destruction.

Ashka knew that there was only one option. They would have to run. It was not an easy decision to make. But Ashka ordered his Elite Trichomian guard to seal the newly synthesized vessel of the golden plants in ancient Lumarian diamond cylinders and evacuate the planet immediately. He tasked them with the near-impossible mission to scatter and plant them throughout the multi-verse and through all timelines. A plantation that not only anchored in a single reality but in all, created a consciousness grid that would operate in the substrate of the multi-dimensional ether that permeated through all things. He also knew that once the Draconian arrived, there was little to no chance that they would spare any semblance of life. With great grief in his heart, he asked his priests and priestesses to gather as many of the animal citizens on Trichomia and spread them across many worlds, dimensions, and timelines so they would not go extinct.

The transfer had worked. Barradow and his sorcerers had successfully synthesized the trichome crystals into a living plant that could be transported. Electric Grasshopper insects swarmed around the sacred plants as they put them onto the spacecraft, they instinctively clung on the crystal cylindrical containers that protected the golden plants because they wanted to be with the trichome energy. Unbeknownst to them they were about to migrate on a epic journey to other planets and dimensional planes. It was here that the King made his final decree. He begged Barradow and his people to flee. Barradow refused at first, demanding that they stay to help him fight off the invasion.

But Ashka knew that even though the Owlinians had power, they would be no match for the sheer quantity and force of the Draconian might. With a final touch of their heads to one another, Barradow left, knowing that he would likely never see the King again. They used their ships to JUMP away and left Ashka alone with a handful of warriors and a small group of citizens that disobeyed the King. They refused to leave and prepared to fight for their planet.

Ashka sat at the north pole, upon the throne of the King and watched as the first swarm of beautiful emerald-green grasshopper ships carrying the knowledge he failed to protect took off into the sky. They were extremely advanced ships working in the physical dimension using advanced electromagnetic pulses and transmuting the natural gravitational force to create anti-gravitational propulsion. He watched with tears in his eyes, knowing that their journey would be long and perilous. In the opposite direction, another swarm of grasshopper ships carrying the citizens and animal beings of Trichomia took off. All the fleets jumped into hyperspace through a maze of wormhole coordinates that would span millineum if not eons of time. It was the only way to throw the Draconian off their trail. You couldn't find something that didn't exist within relativity.

Ashka now sat and waited. He had failed his mission. He had failed to protect not only the crystal-singing forest but also his citizens and his beloved planet. It was only now that Ashka saw how he had become caught up in the materiality of his ego. He had become complacent and arrogant and ignored the warnings that the Lumarians had handed down to him. He could only sit and hope that it was not too late for his people or the sacred knowledge stored within the crystalline forest. As for him… He would meet the retribution of his errors. He was a King foremost, and he would go down with his planet.

He had issued a planetary wide evacuation, which extended to the spaceport that was inhabited by many other beings from across the universe. A visual symphonic cacophony of Electric Grasshopper spaceships with some of the ships on a secret mission to bring the sacred golden bio-sonic living organism that has been infused with trichomian crystalline magic and knowledge. The Electric Grasshopper spaceships escaping the atmosphere of Planet Trichomia, is a beautiful orchestrial sight yet, it is a frantic exodus into the unknown, a journey beyond, travelling into multidimensional planes of infinite realities. A ASTRAL ODYSSEY of time and space. But some were slow to take heed. In a giant tear through the fabric of space, King Ashka watched in horror as the dreaded swarm of Draconian ships emerged before the spaceport. Thousands of ships jumped through the artificial rip in spacetime. King Ashka was appalled. Their practices were unnatural and defiled life itself. The damage they did to the natural order, using such primitive nuclear technologies, was catastrophic.

Ships belonging to different races began to flee, but

the Draconians were not going to just sit by and let that happen. Orders were sent out to eliminate everything in sight. Swarms of Draconian ships broke off from the father fleet and began firing on anything that moved. Soon, the space around the trade port was littered with giant chunks of ravished spacecraft and lifeless floating bodies.

Decepti Mortar stared calmly at the destruction before commanding the nuclear missiles to be released. They were deployed in an instant, and Ashka watched in horror as the spaceport went up in a giant explosion that lit up the entire sky. He couldn't grasp the reality of the situation nor the arrogance within him that had allowed this to happen. Ashka had believed himself invincible and, in that belief, had given up everything that was dear to him.

The chunks of metal from the spaceport began to rain down before the Draconians even entered the atmosphere. A rain of metallic meteors pummeled towards the surface of Trichomia in the light of day. Flaming, asteroid-sized chunks. The first one to fall hit the ocean around the city, where Ashka watched the demise of his planet. A giant tidal wave rose from the catastrophic impact.

Rage boiled in Ashka's blood, and he found he could no longer sit idly by. Old powers that he had once possessed came frothing to the surface. He used the remnants of his powers and wrestled with the towering waves, controlling them using the elemental principles of the universe. But it was not only one tidal wave he had to contend with. The chunks of the spaceport were falling all around him, and as he fought earthquakes and waves, the Draconian fleet invaded.

They all poured in through the hexagonal gateway like a swarm of insects before fanning out, eclipsing the sun with the sheer number of ships that flew into the atmosphere. The Draconian fleet dove straight down towards the surface of the planet, and just like locusts, the primitive ionic thrusters that burned on overdrive trailed black smoke, choking the plants that still lived and singeing everything they pummeled past.

The peace that lived within Ashka was crushed and splintered into nothing. Only rage fueled him now, and he lashed out against the ships with his power, redirecting waves to engulf ships and manipulating gravitational forces to send ships hurtling toward the ground. Decepti Mortar saw this powerful being fighting his ships off single-handed, and his snake-like pupils narrowed, reptilian brows furrowing, with a bright glow of greed blazing deep within.

There was only one way a being could possess such power. Whoever this was had unlocked certain secrets of the universe. He had peered into the knowledge stored within the crystalline forest. Decepti ordered his fleet to fan out and search the entire planet. Ashka, on the planet's surface, breathed heavily as he watched the ships disengage and fly out of his reach, his mane billowing in the devastating wind all around him.

He shouted out to them to come fight him. The King's

voice roared in the air, and Decepti laughed. But he didn't laugh for long. His army had scanned the entire planet and there was no sign of the crystalline forest. Eventually, he got a report with a set of coordinates. Decepti guided the giant locust father ship and saw an empty crater. The energy readings of the ground held the traces he had picked up on eons ago when the Lumarians fled their planet. But there was no crystalline forest in sight. Ashka's evacuation plan had worked.

Fueled with rage, Decepti Mortar let out a roar of his own and slammed his fists down on the control panel. The knowledge had slipped from his grasp once again. The heart-pumping cold blood around his body surged with anger, and he called his fleet back. Ashka watched as the locusts retreated. For a moment Ashka thought he had done it, thought he had saved his planet. That was until the fleet turned around again in space, and a rain of subatomic antimatter missiles fell from the sky.

The enraged Draconian Commander has no regard for life because he will use whatever means to gain ultimate power in the universe. He fired these ungodly weapons not concerned that one mistake can eliminate all of reality. These new antinmatter weapons were stolen technological from another universe.

"No..." Ashka, still a thousand years young in his immortality, dropped to his knees.

The world around him went silent as he watched the

bombs and missiles rocket toward the surface of the planet. The Draconians were brutal and unforgiving. This planet was just another of the thousands they had decimated.

Then, the first of them hit planet Trichomia, and everything went white, bleaching out all life in a single moment.

*

In a distant time, relative to now, roughly sixty-six million   years ago, the grasshopper spaceships belonging to the remaining citizens of planet Trichomia set a series of JUMP sequences travelling at vast speeds through the geometric spirals of interdimensional portals. Their advanced spiritual technology allowed them to tunnel through the fabric of spacetime, utilizing the natural gateways that existed there already. Unlike the Draconian, their machines did not rip or tear. Their machines were both made of matter and not, utilizing the astral dimension to navigate the corridors of time-space at will, able to phase between the frequencies of the multiverse. A knowledge and form of travel they had learned from the Ganeshians.

As part of their mission, the Trichomian Elite Guards had split into many groups, each one travelling to a different universe with a vast multitude of infinity. Ashka had decreed it as one of his last orders as king, assuring that the knowledge he had been tasked to protect would exist across multiple universes.

Raha, High Commander of the Trichomian Guard, was the first to exit the astral plane and phase through the dimensions into third dimensional reality once more. It could be said that through the corridors of space-time, he travelled into the future, phasing into a timeline that brought him away from the invasion of Trichomia. Though, that linear framework of thinking was not quite correct. His ship and a small fleet materialized in front of a planet mostly covered in a deep blue ocean. There was one central land mass and an arctic pole on either end.

Raha had been one of Ashka's first disciples. He was an ape, raised to sentience through the knowledge contained within the crystalline forest. Upon arriving in range of the planet the first thing he did was check the readings of their home planet. Quantum sonar imaging, entangled with the atoms of Trichomia, revealed to him what had happened.

The fur of his brows creased into heavy lines of grief, and he allowed himself to shed a single tear. Trichomia had been destroyed. It was now nothing more than a hulking dead planet of red rock. But there was no time for grieving now. He had a mission to carry out.

First and foremost, he had to get his people to safety. Once they were settled on solid ground, they could begin the seeding process. Raha reached towards the control panel with long ape fingers and ordered his fleet to approach the blue planet. Though little did they know that something devastating had been caught in the tides of their portal through space-time.

In the chaos of the invasion, King Ashka did not have the time to deal with Illuminatus X properly. The Draconian shifter had been confined in a prison cell, with walls made of a strong plasma field. He had could feel that his Draconian brothers had arrived, and also felt that the Trichomian secrets he had been tasked with finding, were getting away.

When the explosion came, the first wave rolled over his plasma prison walls in great plumes of roaring flames. Explosions shook the planet, and Illuminatus X could feel his end drawing near. He took in a twisted breath and shapeshifted back into the figure of Elephantus. The older and more experienced shapeshifters within the Draconian race often lost themselves in their work. Not knowing who they were without the guise and personality they had shifted into and impersonated.

To shift, one had to become the other. Illuminatus X had to become Elephantus, and he took a dark pleasure in mirroring and impersonating Elephantus's personality and attributes without flaw. He liked thinking how the ambassador thought, acting in the strange ways these beings did. It gave him a rush like it did every time he went on a mission undercover, living through the mind and body of another.

When the second wave of explosions hit, they created an incredibly large atomic and nuclear reaction. The very threads of atoms were torn apart as the Draconian weapons acted like particle accelerators, hurtling atoms at near-light speed. In the wake of this destruction a small black hole within the core of the planet Trichomia.

The flames and explosions burnt at his skin, whilst at the same time, the black hole sucked him in. The black hole was only open for a fraction of a femtosecond, but it pulled Iluminatus X in before sealing it shut in another giant explosion.

Illuminatus X felt his body being crushed and elongated, stretched through the passage of the black hole like an elastic band. Were it not for his Draconian regenerative abilities, he would have died at that moment. But even as his body was crushed and decimated, it healed itself simultaneously. The only true way to kill a Draconian Elite was to lop off their head. Even then, the results were questionable.

The black hole stretched for an eternity and Illuminatus X saw the true darkness of space, beyond where all light reached. He thought he knew darkness, thought he knew what true void felt like. He had, after all, travelled for countless years through the dark of space. But it was nothing compared to this all-consuming crush of light into a density so thick that not even a single photon could shine.

All at once, he was hurtled out through a white hole that opened up into another dimension and was sent crashing toward a dark and empty planet. He collided with it, and it was lucky that he had remained in the body of the Ganeshian prime, as the beings did not need to breathe as most did.

His body regenerated itself, although the process was not painless. In fact, it was quite the opposite. For agonizing hours, Illuminatus X teetered on the brink of death, healing at an excruciating slowness. But at last, his body had recovered enough that he could stare out at the strange realm he had entered.

At once, Illuminatus X knew that he was no longer in his own universe. The vibrations in the fabric of space-time were altogether foreign. No. Not foreign. Rather, they were directly the opposite wavelength of the universe he had come from. He stood on the desolate planet and, using the enhanced senses of his copied Ganeshian body, realized that it was also resonating at the exact *opposite* wavelength of Planet Trichomia.

The black hole had acted as a gateway and transported him to a dimension that was a direct mirror of the one he originated from. A mirror dimension, or a polar dimension. He knew of their theoretical existence, but even though the science of the Draconians was advanced, they had not yet managed to explore one for themselves, though they had managed to utilize some of its energy within the Draconian temples to extend their life. This anti-matter universe had been spoken about by the Draconian Elite sorcerers in their scriptures, which also included the fall of Lekiam and the origin of the Draconian race.

Illuminatus X, however, was the first of any kind to have stepped into this anti-world. When he looked down at his body, he realized that his form was different as well. He had not known it when enduring the painful regeneration, but his atoms had inversed themselves, naturally adapting to the different universe. The polarity of his atomic makeup had reversed itself. Negatively charged electrons had become positively charged, and the charge of protons had gone from positive to negative. This was not just an inverse world of matter. It was a mirror dimension of anti-matter.

Illuminatus X reveled in this altogether new experience. If it were not for his extreme adaptability as a Draconian shifter, the second his atoms collided with this world, he would have triggered an explosion so great that it would have taken out an entire galaxy. Matter and anti-matter were not meant to come into contact with one another. The result was an explosion that eradicated both polarities at once.

Had his body intuitively known to shift its atomic arrangement as he passed through the black hole?

Regardless, He was now alone in an undiscovered realm. What sort of beings existed in this dystopic environment? He was definitely the first of his kind to travel to such a place, but was he this universe's first visitor from the outside?

The questions began to thrum a vicious need to find answers. Using his abilities, he morphed his back into dark wings, from a race of beings that the Draconian had enslaved long ago. He had liked infiltrating their ranks. He had enjoyed destroying their way of life from the inside out, and he had enjoyed becoming one of them.

The blueprints of their atomic makeup were engrained in his memory bank, like all the other beings he had impersonated, and the bat-like wings grew from his back, forming bone and muscle and tissue in the reverse atomic makeup of this antimatter universe. He swooped upwards and hurtled towards the sky, set on exploring all he could and uncovering the secrets of this vast and undiscovered universe.

THE FIFTH CHRONICLE

Underground Knowledge

The full fleet, two dozen of Raha's ships, entered the planet's atmosphere. It was a young planet named Tiamat at the time, but it would later come to be known as Earth. It had completed its terra forming eons ago and had its own eco-system and air to breathe, but as of yet, no warm-blooded beings had not yet evolved on its surface. The oceans covered most of the surface of the planet and were greatly inhabited by a plethora of sea creatures. The land was fresh, and while plants and insects were abundant, there were also amphibians and reptiles roaming the surface.

Raha shared the coordinates of a landing spot, a humid, open plain where they would not have to destroy any of the marshlands or jungles to make space for their fleet.

The grasshoppers landed, and the remaining citizens of Trichomia stepped out onto their new home for the first time. Families, guards, and merchants all become one under this new atmosphere. They were survivors.

Even though the air was rich and clean, untouched and pure, there was a heavyweight in the ether. It was the weight of grief that the Trichomians carried with them.

King Ashka was sure he was dead. He opened his eyes to nothing. A single crystal the size of a spacecraft hung suspended in the darkness, glowing a moonlight aura in a zero-shaped spotlight around him. But beyond that spotlight was only nothingness. Not even darkness lay beyond the light because even darkness was something. The only something came from the glowing crystal and the aura it radiated.

Ashka remained seated, knowing that this was his eternal exile. It was what he deserved for his failures.

Every ounce of the guilt he bared hung in the air, thick with self-loathing and devastation. There was nothing to be done now but sit eternally in this nothing place, sit forever in the knowing that he had caused the destruction of his planet and sent his people running like ants into the cosmos with no knowledge of the true knowledge they were tasked to guard.

Ashka sat for unknown amounts of time, reliving his last moments repeatedly in his mind. He saw the terror in his people's faces. He saw the way the non-sentient animals had fled and screamed. He saw how he had abused the knowledge he had been granted, saw how he had used it to fuel his own rage. Rage that had ensued only because of the mistakes he made. This purgatory went on for lifetimes. Eternities.

Ashka's guilt blinded him, and in his blindness, he could not sense the presence that encapsulated him from all angles. The presence held Ashka together and kept the King from dispersing into the nothingness that he was. The presence was nothing. It was naught. It was zero. And yet, from its seat in zero-point awareness, it was also the base of everything. The architect of the container Ashka found himself in was known too few as Master Zero. An immaterial being that had no true form. It was one of the primal forces that held the multiverse together. Everything that was sat in the womb of Zero. And through this truth, Zero was.

The Master of Nothingness bound the sonic frequencies and elements of the universe together in the primordial silence that permeated all things. The silence with sound as it was known to the great cosmic architects. And it was through frequencies that Zero reached out to the fallen King. It was here that he revealed to Ashka where he had ended up.

The World of Zero was born from the implosion at the center of the Trichome Star, a direct polarity to the Trichome Star, the first force to coalesce, the first power imbued with the ability to create life. Their relationship with one another was dual in nature. The Trichome star upheld the binary code of one, encompassing the emergence of creation in its very principle. And like an anchor in balance, the World of Zero was its polar neutrality.

Bound by gravitational laws, the World of Zero orbited the Trichome Star. The World of Zero was created in the very forge of the Trichome's ethereal fire, with pressures so high that it created extremely precious crystalline metals at its core, full of large, cavernous chambers, with a powerful secret hidden deep within a catacomb. The sonic Ohm resonates, containing all matter within, fueled by the crystal diamond frequency of the Trichome star. Together, the two celestial bodies syncopated in a harmonious relationship with one another. Together, they acted as the seed code for the vast multiverse existing at all of the creations centers. Within the matrix of an inverted white hole, their nature exists in the gravitational rift of the vortex portal.

No mortal being had ever seen or set foot in the realm beyond space and time where these celestial bodies exist. This hidden place marked the final journey in the architectural blueprint of the soul, a place witnessed only by masters who are mere moments away from returning to the source beyond materiality.

Within this realm in spacetime, three moons orbited the liquid purple sky of Zero. Moons were not mere moons but the physical manifestations of beings beyond the universe of known things. Alo, Xmo and Zeno. The three Infinite Entities occupied a place within their own space and time continuum, expressing through the moons that rotated around the planet Zero. The three moons rotated around Zero in an atomical orbit, much like the electrons around an atom, passing one another in great cycles that turned the tides of time themselves.

They did not influence the realms and worlds of matter but held the balance in their rotations, ever consistent, bound by the law of vibration set in the frequency of the Sonic Ohm. Master Zero, the being and guardian of balance who inhabited the World of Zero, held all atoms and molecules in their place, bound them with the sacred geometric code of the pattern of life that ran in the ether substrate of his Ohm frequency, binding all matter as one.

Master Zero existed from the beginning of creation. He was born from the sound of his own Ohm and existed as a product of himself, fluid and infinite in the eternal dream state of his consciousness. His dream is the unconscious stream that runs unseen beneath the creation of the Trichome Star.

All that we know results from the two celestial bodies relationship, manifesting the physical places of matter, as well as the ethereal planes of spirit, and soul consciousness. Should the Master of Zero, the dreamer of worlds, wake, then he, as well as all of creation, cease to exist in the flicker of a blink.

All beings rest upon this fragile balance. Like a feather atop the tip of a needle, our world rocks gently back and forth in the breath of his slumber. The zero aspect to the one of the Trichome Frequency. Zero and One. They are the algorithm and code of life within the physical plane. All beings who dive into the nature of reality find these two numbers at their core.

In the cocoon of zero, the origin of Ohm echoes eternal within the physical manifestation of his planetary form. His body is made of metal alloys and precious gems that have never existed anywhere else, and the sound they make is like a deep gong echoing forever into the fabric of space. At the heart of the planet is a cave known as the temple of sound, inextricably linked to the glittering wind chimes of the Trichomian light fractals that manifest as liquid crystals of amethyst rain cascading to create glistening moments of time.

It was by Master Zero's awareness that Ashka found himself in the tomb of his eternal self-exile. Ashka was shocked when the crystal above him began to hum, filling the nothingness with light. Time had no relevance until the first sound emanated from its shimmering facets. Ashka, in his own mind, had lived eternities in his guilt, which was only a flicker of nothing to Zero. The being reached out to Ashka in the language of the universe, the code of sonic frequency and vibration. It revealed a tapestry of information in one single utterance. It was so much information that even as he realized what being Ashka was, he could barely contain the eons of data that flowed through his mind in a single moment.

But the King could not bear it. His frequency was stunted by the shame and guilt to which he felt. He turned away from the knowledge that the Master of Zero offered him. He was not worthy to see. He was not worthy of anything besides his non-existence. And as the frequencies passed. Ashka bowed his head to that guilt, allowing the infinite purgatory to consume him once more.

✸

Raha, the Captain of the Trichomian Elite Guard, returned to his ship and stared with glazed-over eyes at the motherload he carried. An entire chamber of the spacecraft had been dedicated to a single-diamond-coated cylindrical vessel. Giant sonic machines held it in place, and the capsule floated in the air. Within it was a shimmering bio-sonic plant, beautiful and golden, shimmering with the trichome crystals in its flower.

Raha powered down the machine that suspended it in the air, and slowly, the capsule began to descend. Raha walked over to it and caught it in his long ape arms. It was large, roughly half the size of his body. As he held it, a warm glow emanated from the cylindrical chamber. Within, he heard whispers, silent angelic whispers, singing crystalline tones. The codes and secret knowledge that had led to his sentience whispered inside, and Raha was overcome with reverence.

He emerged from the ship carrying it, and all the citizens of Trichomia bowed as he came into view, prostrating themselves on the ground, knowing the true divinity that Raha carried in his arms. They surrounded him in a circle, and Raha, one step at a time, made his way to the center. He placed the diamond-coated cylinder containing the alchemized crystalline-trichome plant on the earth and kneeled before it in prayer.

As he did, Raha could feel it reaching out to him with an altogether superconscious sentience, reading his intentions, reading the fabric of his very soul. It hummed and glowed a joyous tune, and right before his eyes, the diamond-coated cylinder began to melt away into the earth, leaving the bio-sonic plant hovering in the air.

Raha stared at it with reverence, but the light it emitted was too bright, and he had to cast his eyes away lest they be burnt from his skull. He began to dig into the earth with his bare hands, feeling the rich foreign soil of earth in between his nails. Once the bed was dug, he reached out cupped hands, and the plant gently lowered itself into them, whispering beautiful songs of light as it did.

Raha gently placed the golden trichome plant into its bed, and filled in the loose soil, giving it loving pats, like how a mother would tuck her child into bed. As soon as he was done, Raha stood up and backed away slowly. He joined the circle and all the citizens of Trichomia stood. One by one, they held one another's hand. The bio- sonic plant began to pulse and glow even brighter. Muscle by muscle, bone by bone, cell by cell, the Trichomian's felt the golden light permeating their being.

Then it began.

The golden bio-sonic plant began to assimilate with its new planet, growing its roots at the speed of light.

Branches and veins sprawled and extended downwards and in every direction, twining with the roots of everything already there, touching every living plant and tree. As it did mycelium sprouted for the first time in great abundance, creating a living dendrite nervous system, a network between all living things on land, a planetary mind. It stretched towards the ocean, merging with the mangrove trees that bore their roots in the water. A golden pulsar wave stretched the entire circumference of the planet. As the golden energy of the plant dispersed amongst Tiamat, the color faded from the plant itself. It assimilated with the nature and biome of the living planet, and as the last of the golden light seeped into the soil, the plant turned into a bright and beautiful green.

There were tears in every Trichomian's eyes. Raha squeezed the hands of those next to him, and the gesture was passed all the way around the circle. They had done it. But at that exact moment of relief, a reptilian cry echoed through the air. Heads turned frantically towards the sky, anticipating the worst, but there were no Draconians in sight. There came a stomp, a loud cracking tree trunk, and another stomp. Heads turned and saw a giant reptilian monster appear in the clearing.

It was giant, standing on two powerful legs, with a giant tail swinging behind it for balance. Its head was massive, and it had two small arms. It was the Trichomian's first ever witness of what would come to be known as a Dinosaur. Raha held up a hand to subdue the panic. Calmly, he extended his consciousness to the ships and emitted a cloaking field around them. The dinosaur growled and let out a frustrated roar once more before turning and lumbering back into the jungle.

But the danger was not over yet. The ancient Earth lay within the same star system as Trichomia; the only difference now was that the Trichomians had shifted density from the higher seventh planes of reality they once inhabited and, through multiple universes, emerged into a lower third-density reality.

The Trichomians eventually set up a base on Tiamat, surrounding the sacred plant in a protective field, cloaking them from eye view, and emitting a frequency such that any dangerous creature that walked towards it was unconsciously navigated elsewhere. But with the threads of their portal through space and time still open, they unfortunately did not have much time to get settled.

In the cataclysm of Trichomia, giant chunks of the planet had been sent hurtling in all directions of the star system. One managed to follow the Trichomians through the portal they had escaped in. Mere moments later, just when the Trichomians thought they had escaped and landed safely on Tiamat, a massive meteor approached at a deadly speed. It was so large it practically filled up the entire skyscape. The entire jungle was in pandemonium, for even though the beings that inhabited the planet were not sentient, they still had the instinct to know their destruction was coming.

The Trichomians were in shock. It seemed disaster

followed them wherever they went. Raha stood atop his ship, watching as the meteor approached. They had only just managed to seed the planet with the sacred plant. It had not even been a full hour. The meteor eclipsed the sun but filled the planet with a red and terrible flame, drowning the world in long, dark shadows. There were those amongst the Trichomian's who's instant instinct was to flee yet again, but Raha knew better. He had stared into the trichomes, heard the whispering melodies of the crystalline forest, and felt their will.

Raha raised a protective gravitational forcefield in a large dome over the clearing. It would be their fate to live out the rest of their lives in the aftermath of catastrophe. With fear in their hearts, the Trichomians all gathered to watch the apocalypse unfold. As Raha stared at the giant, burning ball of fire hurtling towards them, he felt contradicting emotions. He knew little to no life would survive such an event. He felt the despair and horror, and yet he couldn't help but see beauty in it.

As he watched, he was filled with a great and profound realization. The universe operated in cyclical eras. Like clockwork entire species and civilizations could be eradicated. The physical world was bound by these laws, bound to the shifting of epochs, just as the earth was bound to quake in tectonic shifts.

Raha couldn't help but feel awe as he witnessed one of these cycles coming to an end. How many could ever look up into the eye of a cataclysm? These sorts of things only happened once or so every hundred thousand planetary years. In this realization of the great cosmic cycles, Raha understood that Destiny was as much a force in the universe as gravity or time. But then again Destiny was just another concept to explain something far beyond explanation.

What was the force that destined these events? Deep in his heart Raha knew that the fall of Trichomia and now the extinction of all current life on earth would only make room for new life to grow. What would come after? What new story would rise from the ashes of their fallen worlds?

The last thought barely had time to pass through his mind before the meteor hit, and once again, everything was filled with a blinding, burning light. For years, the planet burned. Raha and the people of Trichomia had, of course, survived. They watched as the planet was sent into turmoil. Tsunamis crashed upon desolate land; the land broke into pieces and shifted, and yet through all of it, the sacred plant stood tall beneath the force field.

Raha spent hours every day meditating in front of it, and through the plant, he felt the spirit of the planet. The Trichome plant had embedded its roots deep in the planet, safe form the tumultuous chaos incurring on the surface. The planet was alive, a sentient metaphysical being and the sacred plant acted as a medium translating not only the planet's mind but deeper secrets of the universe. The more Raha meditated, the more knowledge he realized was contained within the trichomes. The crystals are sung and whispered like beams of the aurora borealis. It would take an eternity to learn everything. Raha saw the greater plan of Ashka. This planet, in this particular time-line, at this particular point in time, was a convergence.

Raha was not only entranced in his meditations but bound to the fate of the trichomes. Thousands of years existed, and Tiamat struggled in turmoil after a large chunk of the planet had been broken off. Within the protective field, the Trichomians were protected from the toxic atmosphere of the planet. And in such close proximity to the sacred plant, their lives were suspended in time.

Raha travelled deep into the astral consciousness of the planet, traveling through the vast network that the sacred plant had woven. Raha witnessed a new age rising on the planet and saw that Tiamat would soon come to be known as Earth. He could not quite grasp the importance of Earth's role in the grand cosmic play but knew that it would be a central point of contention and evolution for a new kind of being.

Eons continued to roll on, and Raha was immersed in meditation for the entire time. The Trichomians went into a meditative slumber until the time was ripe for them to awaken once more. Eventually, Tiamat stabilized and no longer was it ruled by molten earth and tidal waves. The elements settled, and once again, the planet was ready to harbor life upon its surface and within the depths of its oceans. During that time, in a profound state of meditation, Raha had learned to extend his astral body from his physical one and travelled to many planets throughout the cosmos. Through dreams, he communicated to beings of his choosing, beginning to seed the start of a cosmic revolution.

Raha's eyes shot open to the physical world once more. To him, it seemed as if an eternity had passed in a single breath. Except he was no longer the same being who had left Trichomia all those years ago. As he awoke, so did the people of Trichomia. They rose as if a great spell had been lifted, yawning and stretching to a new age.

Raha knew he had to keep the secret of the trichome from centralizing into a singular concentrated energy frequency. He would have to act as the keeper of the garden on Earth, managing the distribution of the trichome's energy so that no traces of it could be tracked by forces who wished to steal its knowledge and corrupt the power that it contained.

Now that it was time, Raha and his people deconstructed the force field that had protected them for so long. Tiamat would now come to be their home for the great variety of sentient animal beings of Trichomia. But in so doing they subjugated themselves to the natural cosmic cycles taking place on the planet.

You see, all planets in their relative spheres go through their own process of multidimensional evolution.

Earth was still young in relative terms and had countless generations of growing to do. As the cosmic scales tip and turn, the tides and unseen forces of the universe take their influence on spheres of consciousness.

What was being set up now on Earth was a blueprint for the consciousness of souls. Even Raha, in his newfound revelations, could not truly grasp the entirety of what was playing out. In the scheme of the universe there are waves of energy, rises and falls of consciousness. It is why civilizations could rule in absolute peace and harmony for thousands of years, then suddenly crumble. It was these natural waves of energy that led to the fall of Lumaria and Trichomia alike.

Being extremely highly evolved souls, the Lumarians understood this, and in the wisdom of their oracle, they had foreseen all these events coming to pass. Raha was just at the beginning of his journey and while his former king Ashka had grasped these concepts once, Raha was still learning.

He relinquished his role as leader of the Trichomians and let them partake in the experience of Earth as they so pleased. While he had once been one of them, he was no longer. The trichomes had changed him, and he was now their guardian and caretaker. In his new role, being so closely interlinked with the trichome knowledge, he could see these cycles as they came every couple thousand decades or so.

He watched as the once sentient Trichomians fell with the dip of cosmic energy, their consciousness reverting to more primal ways, their consciousness subjugated to an obfuscation of sorts. He watched those who were once his people devolve into mammalian animals, void of the sapience that they once had.

He, however, continued to evolve with the knowledge of the crystalline trichomes now alive in his very DNA. The trichomes changed him and altered the very core of his being. Slowly and over many years, Raha began to stand taller, losing much of the ape hair that had covered him before. Raha evolved over millions of years, being reborn over and over in a cycle granted by the trichome. The planet Earth, including all the beings upon it, also integrated into his central consciousness.

Raha was to be the new blueprint for the next generation of souls to partake in the cosmic symphony. Raha evolved into what many would soon call a human. The genetic code of Raha was perfect, a sacred mathematical masterpiece of organic development. At this point in time Raha had developed extremely advanced spiritual technology within his own body, and it would set the precedent for all humans that came after. The apes existing on earth at the time followed in his footsteps, and soon, there were souls incarnating into the new vessel of sapient consciousness.

Raha's perfection came at a time when the earth was in a Golden age of its cycle. All sorts of animals and creatures existed on the planet, and all of them lived in harmony with one another. Humans now had no need for physical reproduction. The female polarities of this new race knew how to communicate with the realms of souls and, through immaculate conception, call in a soul to begin gestation within their wombs.

This act was an initiation into the human experience.

And with the foundation that Raha had created, guided all the while by the trichome knowledge, Tiamat, which came to be known as Earth, had created a frequency to which only those born by the power of an earthly womb could survive in its realm. One had to incarnate through the womb of a mother integrated with the Earth's frequency. If other beings tried to conquer or take over, they would not be able to properly align with the Earth's frequency and would fail to survive.

The first matronly civilizations of the earth began to form. At this point in time, however, the individuality and sense of ego had yet to form. The minds of humans were all one, like a great ocean of consciousness, open and shared in a collective mind. Humans did not need to feed on physical matter. Through spiritual technology inherent in their bodies, they could simply survive off the ether that was abundant everywhere.

Fruits were plentiful, however, and were only consumed as a means of pleasure and enjoyment, for the trees that produced them handed them out willingly, growing in perfect hand-sized forms for humans to experience.

Each fruit carried a frequency of experience, a knowledge grown by the trichome's influence. And so, humans began to experience sour, and sweet, astringent, and bitter. This would set the precedent of duality and polarity. A concept that humanity would have to integrate further down the line.

No human harmed one another for they did not understand the concept of separation. They did not see themselves as separate from one another. It was a paradise, a beautiful garden that Raha named Edan. This all took place many millineum before the common era.

Raha of the sacred trichome crystals, the immortal master, lived, died, and rebirthed as his body evolved from each life he lived for eternity.

Raha's essence fractured by the loss of his world, various humanoid species branched off from his energy, some became more advance, and others reversed their spiritual evolution over time.

Different dimensional beings moved to the light that were harmonically attune to the universe, other humanoids connected to physical energies, some evolving and others devolving into interdimensional beings, some sought out to develop advanced technologies disregarding their connection to the universe.

A group of interdimensional humanoid beings were seen as demigods by subhumanoids they genetically cloned, a created race that was programmed to be a subservient species, to work collecting minerals, precious metals, and gems for their interplanetary time travel machines so they can travel back and forth to different dimensions of time and space. The demigods became ego driven forgetting the origins of their ancestors, as all cycles rise, they too must fall.

Raha the immortal master watched with a great feeling of loss as the fall of consciousness occurred. Even though he understood that this was what was meant to unfold, as obfuscation was a natural process of soul evolution. Still, it hurt him to see that humans, dimensional beings and spirit began to view themselves as separate from one another, focusing primarily on the surface physicality to which they existed and forgetting the deeper truths of reality within them. They lost much of their knowledge and began to need food for sustenance to keep them alive. The women forgot their divine ability to call in souls, and physical reproduction began to take place between the various sexes. There was division and separation. There were sects and religions of all varying beliefs. The oneness that humanity once knew became fragmented.

Not all humans, however, lost their connection to the deeper aspects of their nature. Raha decided to form a secret society. One that would live through the countless cycles of earth's history, one that would carry and protect the wisdom of the sacred plants, harboring its knowledge and passing on the magic it possessed.

It was so referred to as The Third Eye, and all who came to be a part of it would be marked with its symbol. It was not a mark that could be seen with the naked eye. It was a mark engrained in their very energy body. Something only one with sight beyond the material plane would be able to see. The Third Eye would be the keepers of knowledge and remain hidden, influencing in subtle ways until humanity was once again ready to understand. But it was not only on Earth that this secret society began to grow. Through Raha's deep astral journeys, he had begun teaching beings from other planets, star systems and times through their dreams, guiding and awakening souls, and initiating them into the Third Eye Order and into the knowledge of the singing forest.

Millions of years went by in a relative universe. But Raha had escaped the Draconians by shifting in density. The linear timework of this density would be entirely different from the rest of the universe. The Draconians whilst they had descended far, could manipulate the cosmos with such precision that they could shift between densities in order to conquer or take over specific planets. Earth, however, was still unknown to them. Whilst millions of years of evolution occurred, it would be a long time before the Draconians ever caught a glimpse of the planet, for they existed in another polarity of matter. Time is dependent on the throttle and movement of frequency and the density it inhabits. Once the universe unfolds past perception it can become a tricky and complex shifting of times to navigate. Though the Draconians used an almost primitive technology to shift through time, much more is possible. With advanced spiritual technology, an advanced being can manipulate the throttle of time, using gravitational forces and controlling the movement of space to slow or speed up time as they please. Many use advanced alchemical sciences with the aid of conscious altering plant medicine. It is possible to navigate these realms as one controls the speed of a car. Unfortunately for the Draconians, they did not have a quantum location within the space-time fabric to try and manipulate these laws. Raha and the seed of Trichomia were lost to time and the infinite realms of density, though their knowledge lived on through the Third Eye Order.

Kuma, the dog, went on his way, taken in by the grand sights of the city. For a moment, he felt something calling from inside of him. A thought, perhaps, or the semblance of a memory. A young girl and a family. He looked around, searching for them, suddenly feeling a little lost. But before the emotions could truly set in, a rush of people began to move his way. One pair of legs stumbled over him and cursed, and another accidentally kicked him on the side.

Kuma dodged the next set and wove his way against the current of people, trying to find somewhere safe to be. He began to run, and whilst people shot glancing looks towards him, none of them tried to stop him.

He ran across an open street, where large machines blared loud noises and screeched to a stop before they could crash. The noise and chaos were all too much, and Kuma ran as fast has he could, ran and ran, letting instinct guide him, until at last, the sounds began to dwindle, and instead of horns and angry people, Kuma heard laughter.

Children playing by a park. There were kites strung high, wide open fields, and as the wind gently blew, it rustled the silver leaves in the trees. Kuma began to feel his heart grow warm once more, and he approached with a jaunty gait towards a child who sat by himself on a park bench. There was light in the child's eyes as he enjoyed, one lick at a time, the frosty coolness of a bright blue ice cream.

THE SIXTH CHRONICLE

The Trichome Wars

Thousands of years had passed since the Draconians had destroyed the Kingdom of Trichomia, and still, the search for the elusive Trichome crystals had yet to fall into legend. The Draconians were not one united front but a divided group of many. And each of their leaders desired the power of the Trichome for themselves. There were traces of it laced throughout the entire universe, and yet, somehow, it's presence still eluded the Draconians. The Trichome was a power to which entire worlds crumble and new ones born from their ashes. So, despite its elusiveness, the hunt could not be forsaken.

Amongst the powers of Draconia, Decepti still reigned supreme in his score of the universe. But that was not to say he was the most powerful. Decepti had survived for countless years harvesting the life force of warm- blooded beings. It was an immortality that took a tole, and he was not the Draconian he used to be. Hundreds of thousands of years he had waited, conquering and destroying civilizations, and harvesting the planets of all their resources.

Over the years, he had grown even more bitter and cruel, not feeling the fire of war any longer. Ever since the Trichomians slipped from his fingers, his eyes had been ever set on the power they hoarded. He needed it, craved it like an obsession.

But the multiverse was a vast and infinite place, primarily consisting of void and darkness. There had been talk that Decepti had lost his way, but all whispers that returned to him were quickly snuffed out in death. Whilst Decepti clung to the old ways vengeful and destructive towards even his own kind.

Meanwhile, a new commander had risen elsewhere. Commander Arelix was young and still full of power and ambition. He had begun by seizing control of his quadrant of the Draconian Militia, and then he began to unite the other Draconian separatist forces. Arelix was different than the majority of his kin. Firstly, he stood out. He had been almost discarded at birth, born with a rare oculocutaneous mutation that made all his scales devoid of their usual colors. Instead, they were a silver grey, bleached with a moonlight white. He was not born with the muddy emerald and dark shades that his species had adopted in order to survive on the forsaken home planet. Being a shapeshifter, as all Draconians were, he could have changed his appearance, but instead, he wore it with pride.

He was ridiculed from the day he emerged from his birthing pod, but the ridicule only served to bolster his power. After all, Draconians thrived in harsh conditions. With all the odds against him, Arelix grew to be fearsome and brutal in battle training, decimating any who challenged him. He was granted status as a low frontline soldier and quickly rose among the ranks.

But what truly made him different was his ambition. Other Commanders got caught up in the game of pride and power amongst the other Draconian elite. There were many clans, all with separate flags and often times these clans warred against one another, fighting over planetary resources like unruly space pirates.

Arelix, however, saw how great the numbers of the Draconian race had become and had much larger goals. He heard whispers and rumors circulating on one of the conquered planets in the Draconian's grasp. An extremely plentiful planet abundant with gold and precious gems. It was a treasure horde for the Draconian, as their space drives needed gold to function.

Upon this planet was a foreign slave race known as the Iki. They were brought to the planet but were not the original inhabitants. The Iki was small in stature with short and stubby arms and legs and very broad top skulls that tapered to a thin face. Their planet had been destroyed hundreds of years ago, and the Draconians had enslaved them and used them to mine gold and precious resources all over the universe. They had once been a race of metallurgists and jewel crafters and were perfect in build and stamina, capable of working long hours that most races would not be able to persevere through.

The original inhabitants of Fareen, however, were almost the opposite. They were tall and elegantly skinny, boasting a once radiant golden skin, though, through generations of enslavement, their glow had dwindled and became almost pale in comparison. They had sharp and striking features and had once ruled a peaceful matriarchy, known for their attention to detail. Ever since the Draconians took over their planet thought, the Fareen had been growing paler with a sickly purplish tint, the vibrancy of their golden glow dimming under the tyrannical subjugation. They were once keepers of records, not only cataloguing everything imaginable on their planet, such as the shapes of the clouds on particular days or the feel and texture of the wind, but they took great pleasure in collecting ancient knowledge and manuscripts from across the universe. They had never developed an army nor had ever had the intention to. So, when the Draconian invaded, they were forced to surrender and submit to the Draconian will.

In succession to the royal line was the highly revered Princess Cherena. To her people, she was seen as a goddess, beautiful beyond measure and equally fair. She was the child of King Bahran and Queen Samin. Whilst Princess Cherena's mother and father had submitted to the

Draconian rule, Cherena secretly conspired against them.

She herself had been initiated into the knowledge of the Trichome, granted the privilege to witness the Ancient Manuscript by a member of the Third Eye Order through an Iki spy slave known as Griek. A keeper of the Trichomian secrets and bearer of the ancient manuscript detailing the prophecy of the great Lumarian Oracle, which was granted to him by the work of Raha in his time of astral meditation. The Iki did as they were told and worked long, hard days in the mines, harvesting the gold of their planet. But in secret, Griek revealed to them the knowledge of Trichomia, and with the help of Princess Cherena, they began to rouse a rebellion.

Fareen was a colony of Decepti, and he was not a fool. He had many spies riddled amongst the ranks of the Iki, working alongside them undercover. The spies heard wind of this rebellion, but no matter how hard they tried, they could not find the leader.

Princess Cherena knew well the pressure her parents were under. They had been allowed to keep their titles merely because the Draconian had control of planet Fareen's economy and could profit greatly with the illusion of civility upheld. Cherena had to keep her involvement with the rebel Iki a secret even from her parents.

Griek remained well hidden and knew who amongst his people were spies, granted the vision to see through the Draconian veil. He purposefully spread false information, and the time soon came for the rebellion to arise.

Griek knew that planet Fareen was too valuable to destroy, and in the rebellion, the Iki succeeded.

With the head of the rebellion, Princess Cherena took charge, forgoing her royal attire and escaping the palace in the old and weathered cloak of a beggar. She wound through the streets of her home city, knowing that she may never see it again. The planet had been under the Draconian rule for hundreds of years now, and as a divine empath, she could feel the spirits of her people breaking.

She followed a trail in the ether, a trail left behind by the member of the Third Eye Order, Griek, in a realm just beyond the physical, a realm only those initiated and allowed were able to see. She knocked thrice on an old wooden door and was ushered in by an old Fareen woman. Cherena was led into a cellar and shown a secret tunnel that led down into the gold mines where the Iki worked.

A secret chamber had been dug, one infused with magical veils and protective enchantments, one that could only be found if the intentions of those seeking were pure. Cherena was led through the tunnels and met by Griek, who brought her to the front of a podium carved in the rock. Before her were thousands of Iki slaves. They all raised their hands, consisting of four large, amphibian-like fingers, holding three up in the symbol of the Third Eye Order.

It was on this day that Princess Cherena revealed her plan. But it was not only the Iki who would take part in the rebellion. She had secretly been forming another rebel group of her own people who were willing and able to fight across the great shimmering desert of Tenar. Her plans were already underway, and even as she spoke, fighting began to ensue in the streets above. Cherena knew very well the status of the Draconians. Their resources were spread thin across many galaxies and solar systems, and currently, the rebels she had raised outnumbered the Draconian soldiers.

That wasn't to say that the fight would be easy. The Iki and Fareen were not fighters by nature. They were archivists and tinkers, whilst the Draconian had been bred to be ruthless vampiric killers. It was a fight that would either make or break the two races. But what other choice did they have? Cherena knew that if they did not stand up and fight for their freedom, their spirits would break long before their bodies did, and once that happened, there would be no hope for either.

She rallied the emotions of her people and the Iki with the powerful waves of empathic energy that radiated from within her. She not only fought for the freedom of her planet but for the freedom of the universe. If Fareen took a stand and succeeded, it would plant a seed of hope that would spread like wildfire to all the Draconian colonies. It was time for the light to rise once more and for balance to resume its rightful place.

The fighting began, and there was blood and slaughter in the streets of the capital city of Fareen. The city of Ural was constructed of a pure, cloud-white stone that shimmered with the sparkle of quartz. The white walls were quickly stained red and blue, with the blood of Fareen, Iki and Draconian alike.

The message came through to the current foreseer and Commander Arelix. He was stationed in orbit around Fareen upon his ship when the word of rebellion was announced. He had been monitoring Fareen, waiting for the tides of revolution to rise so that he could quell it personally. A dark and curling anger took grip in his gut, and set his coordinates to the city Ural. His reason was not only to squash the rebellion, but rumors of the Third Eye Order within Fareen were too reliable to dismiss as hearsay. If he could capture one of them, then perhaps he could infiltrate their mind and find the location of the Trichomes.

Arelix landed upon the city with a barrage of nuclear missiles, killing not only innocents and rebels alike but also his own people. Green toxic fire raged amongst the spatter of blood, and Arelix left his spaceship behind, wielding a plasma sword and taking to the battlefield on his own. Many tried to challenge the Draconian leader, but he cut through them all as if they were nothing more than flies in his way. He could taste the scent of magic in the air with the forked flick of his tongue and he followed the trail deep into the heart of Ural.

It was there that he saw a pile of Draconian corpses and a group of elite rebels fighting with relics he thought were lost to time. Ancient weapons from an era of old, imbued with powers that surpassed anything Arelix had seen before, and at the forefront of the battle was the golden Princess of Fareen. She wore the mark of royalty with a jewel-encrusted in the very skin of her forehead, battling as if she were made of wind.

Her robes billowed as she fought, with well-trained and honed movements, fluid and without hesitation. She plunged an ancient spear into the neck of a Draconian foot soldier, yanking it out a moment later and twirling her spear with a flourish. She was breathing heavily, and as she looked up from the falling corpse, she locked eyes with Arelix.

Everything stood still. The kicked-up dust of the desert city swirled between them in slow motion, and a foreboding sense of familiarity washed over the Princess, quelling her battle haze. The empathy of her heart rolled across the battlefield and touched Arelix in a way he had never felt before. It disarmed his mind in strange and magical ways. It stopped him in his tracks to the point that he felt as if he were frozen in time. It was Love. As simple and as plain as anything. The most powerful magic known to be.

Her eyes were the pure, unfiltered light of compassion, and they seized Arelix in their spell. No one had ever looked at him that way before. He was either feared or hated. Even the respect he gained was out of fear, not out of admiration. She looked at him with neither. Princess Cherena heard the sound of bamboo flutes on the wind as if the desert was singing to her, and the soul of the Draconian in front of her answered the wind's call. Like two stars colliding, their energies and worlds swirled around one another.

Their hearts met in a place where time and space did not exist, a place where all was Zero. This feeling sparked something in the universe. An impossibility wave. A meeting of two enemies locked in a field of time and space of their own. This feeling kindled something deep and ancient within the fabric of the cosmos. A new hope it spoke. A bond of beings bound to be enemies, and yet amidst the heat of battle, found something impossible.

Both of them were teleported to a different place entirely, a place within their minds that they both shared. A field of life and death. A realm of their own creation. But on the battlefield, with both leaders disarmed, some of the surrounding soldiers took their opportunity. A sword cut through the air. Cherena came to her instincts in just enough time to move slightly out of the way as a Draconian soldier slashed at her. She managed to dodge the brunt of the blow, but the poisoned edge tip of the Draconian sword cut down the center of her chest.

Arelix's eyes widened, and his voice tore rips in the fabric of space between them. He pulled out a knife an instant later, not thinking as he tossed it through the air. It found its mark directly between the Draconian soldier's eyebrows in the center of his forehead. He crumpled to the ground in a lifeless heap.

Arelix ran, his body moving as if it were running through thick molasses. Seeing the fall of the Princess, the people of Fareen grew enraged and attacked Arelix from all angles. Screaming all the way, Arelix parried and returned blows, slashing down all who stood in his way. The people of Fareen and the Iki fell to his blade as he closed the distance between him and the Princess. Meanwhile, he could hear another wave of Draconian soldiers approaching, their battle drums and cries unmistakable.

Even with their approach, Arelix only had one thing on his mind. He had to get the Princess to safety. He could not say why. She was meant to be his enemy, and yet all he could think to do was protect her. He picked her up in his arms as Fareen rebels charged at him with ancient weapons. But now that he had her, nothing would stop him. He used his shapeshifting powers and cloaked himself along with Cherena and they were no longer visible to the eyes of men.

Running through the shadows of a falling world, Arelix maneuvered through the blood stained whitestone with the Princess barely conscious in his arms. Cherena gazed up at him, her eyes never leaving his. She reached out a hand and touched his scaly, battle-scarred face. Her palm was warm despite the amount of blood she was losing. The warmth of her empathy ran through the commander's cold blood like a virus, taking root within ever cell of his body.

The Draconians were not bred to feel empathy. They were not bred for love. And yet he could not escape what powers held Arelix in their grip. He bashed down the door to a home, dropping his cloaking field and was met by scared and screaming citizens shouting in the language of Fareen. A small young boy grabbed a pan and stood in front of his mother and sister, wielding it like a sword.

Arelix placed the Princess down gently and witnessed the show of bravery and defiance from this small child. It disarmed Arelix even more. He found that even under threat, he could not take the boy's life. Arelix stumbled out of the house. He had done what his heart demanded. He had taken the princess somewhere safe. Fishing out a vial from around a belt, he handed it to the young boy, who looked at him with confusion.

It was an antidote. An antidote to the poisoned blade to which the princess had been struck.

Taking one last look into the deep eternal pool of the Princess's eyes, Arelix turned and ran. But he didn't get far before he encountered an Iki at the end of the alley. But it was not just any Iki. This being wielded an ancient sword and shield, and upon his brow was a symbol. A symbol of a vertical eye.

Arelix stopped in his tracks. He knew that symbol. It was what he had been tracking for the past hundred years. It was the symbol of the Third Eye Order. Being away from the Princess, already Arelix could feel her spell diminishing. He stared down Griek in the alley of Ural and drew his sword.

"Where is the manuscript?" Arelix growled, standing tall, about six feet larger than the short Iki.

Griek revealed the book from behind his robes, and

Arelix's eyes lit up with a wildfire. But Griek quickly veiled it again.

"It is bound to me. It burns should I die."

Arelix snarled a sharp-toothed grin. "Then I shall take you alive."

The competition held no challenge. Arelix burst into action, his powerful muscles propelling him forward at an alarming rate. Griek raised his sword and charged, but at the last second before impact, Arelix jumped onto the wall, his claws digging into the stone, as he ran on all four legs across it.

He leaped, and just as he was about to strike, the Iki smiled, vanishing into thin air a moment later. Arelix slammed to the ground, head snapping and tongue flickering, trying to catch the scent of the Iki. But Griek was gone. Gone in an instant, and before Arelix even had the chance to curse, swarms of Fareen and Iki were charging towards him. Arelix growled in frustration and cloaked himself, becoming invisible and climbing up the walls to the roof of the building. At the top, he saw his soldiers losing. The numbers of the Fareen and Iki were too many, and the weapons they carried too dangerous.

Arelix stood up tall on the ground once more and bared his teeth. He would need to call for backup. The commander pressed a button that summoned his personal space craft to him. It was floating in the air above the alley within seconds. Arelix entered his vessel, leaving the planet Fareen behind as he throttled back up into space. Arelix called back all his troops from the planet, ordering a temporary retreat. The planet was too valuable. It was the reason he told his men, but it was not the true reason in his heart. On another day, he would have had no issue slaughtering every being on the planet without hesitation. But even though he was no longer in the Princess's presence, he could still feel the warmth of her palm on his face.

He left the planet behind, and as the Draconian fleet retreated, the people of Fareen and the Iki slaves cheered and roared the applause of their victory that day. A victory won against all odds. And this victory was all because of Princess Cherena, although no one knew this. No one except for the small boy who had administered the antidote and cleaned Cherena's wounds. While his mother and sister had screamed and cowered, he had witnessed what no other being could claim.

He had witnessed the compassion of a Draconian. He had seen Arelix save the Princess. And unbeknownst to Arelix, this knowledge would serve to be a greater weapon than any blade or bomb. It was the subtle, soft, curved blade of hope. And hope, as all dictatorships know, is the flame that will set all Empires to fall.

Meanwhile, on the planet of Fareen, the rebels had succeeded in freeing themselves from Draconian rule.

Fireworks and celebrations broke out in the capital city of Ural, but they did not last long. They died almost as soon as they arose, for many of those who had picked up arms had become plagued with sickness. Not a sickness of flesh but of the mind. The weapons they held, the ancient metaphysical weapons, had begun to corrupt the hearts of many who bore them.

Almost as soon as the fighting was done with the Draconian, these corrupted Fareen and Iki began turning on their own people. The power of the ancient relics was based on the frequency of the emotions of those who used them. The ancient Fareen were masters of their emotions. The weapons that were used now, had been tools in the past, never once used for war. Over time, after hundreds of years of Draconian rule, the Fareen had lost their connection to their empathetic abilities. Now, as the curdle of vengeance and grief wrote their emotions out of control, the weapons began to corrupt them, drawing from the power of a dark and formidable place. Soon, chaos and pandemonium spread through the streets.

In The Dystopic Realm

Illuminatus X had lived for thousands of years within the Dystopian anti-matter realm and extrapolated many of this world's secrets, time not working the same as it did in the typical universe. Unlike the world he had come from, the majority of the beings here sought the destruction of light, not it's preservation and creation. Stars were black with dim rays of ultraviolet, and great creatures fed on the light, consuming black suns and plummeting solar systems into frigid darkness.

There were few in this realm who fought to protect the light, and those beings were seen as evil. This universe was slowly becoming submerged in total darkness, and by studying and impersonating the dark beings of the dystopic world, Illuminatus X had unlocked some of the esoteric secrets of this world.

There was a prime race of beings known as the Dystopians, and they thrived in destruction. It was their kind and their armies of multiple races that sought to plunge their universe into the beautiful chaos that had once existed at the start of all things. Order was a prison, a chain that bound and irritated them to no end.

The Dystopians were soul-less creatures, bent by destruction, almost formless in their makeup, existing more like wraiths of shadow. They guarded a black sun that emitted negative radiation, no longer seeping light but re-leasing a radioactive chemical substance that seeped into the universe and destroyed any light it touched.

Illuminatus X found that the Dystopian had engi-neered this sun themselves, using advanced sciences, but what was most interesting of all was the planet they lived on. It was a black and blazing inferno of void light. A light that had no shine but instead seemed to sap photons from existence. It hurtled in a chaotic orbit in close proximity to the black sun, and as Illuminatus X impersonated the Dystopian, he found that the planet itself was a massive anti-matter reaction waiting to go off at any moment.

If a single spec of matter fell upon it, surely entire uni-verses would crumble. Illuminatus X found that he took great pleasure in living like the Dystopian. He found their ideals of chaos and darkness to suit him, and a grand plan began to form inside his mind.

Kuma, the dog, stared wide-eyed as the child enjoyed his ice-cream. He was young, legs kicking playfully, back and forth on the large park bench. The sun was blaring on the hot summer day, and drips of rainbow hues fell from the cone and into the child's hand, slipping from skin to ground. Kuma ran over as he noticed and began to lap away at the puddle beneath the child's legs, wagging his tail back and forth in feverish excitement.

The child, who was directly above him, had to move his ice-cream back lest Kuma knocks it with his tail. Kuma's fur tickled the boy's skin, and he laughed, reaching down with a sticky hand to give Kuma a pet. Kuma looked up and noted the boy in passing before quickly turning his attention to the cone that was to be the source of the tasty puddle he had just lapped up.

Before the boy even had a chance to react, Kuma began to lick wildly at the ice-cream in the boy's hand, gobbling and trying to get a good position to grab it up in his jaws. The boy burst into a fit of high-pitched giggles as he watched, even pushing the ice-cream closer for Kuma to get more.

But before Kuma could take a nice bite, he felt hands pushing at his side. He retreated, letting out a soft whine as the ice-cream cone vendor waved Kuma off, angry and bitter in his approach and shouting curses as he did so.

Kuma felt the emotions hit him like a truck, and his tail ceased it's wagging, tucking in low between his legs. One more shoo and Kuma was off, leaving the tasty treat behind and racing to get away from the source of anger.

THE SEVENTH CHRONICLE

A Glimmer of Hope

In a cave nestled at the very peak of reality itself, touching the sky of Never, which so paradoxically acted as the ground of the physical plane, an ancient relic floated atop a pedestal. It shimmered in infinite variations of light, an inverted pyramid, rotating ever so slowly above a square keyhole, cut of rare alloys to fit the pyramids dimensions precisely. It was so known as the Trichome Diamond.

It hummed a gentle frequency, floating in stasis, waiting to be activated. The ancient relic was a conduit transistor designed to regulate the sonic frequencies of the universe. Symbols of light swirled on its surface, enchanted and cast in an infinity loop, constantly unravelling into zero as it rotated and back and forth into infinity.

The space between the pyramid and pedestal held the seed syllable frequency that bound the entire multiverse. Ohm. Master Zero's frequency.

Ohm bound the order of atoms, it defined the limits of space, it was the very current of time, and the fabric of materiality. Every pitch and vibration to ever exist stemmed from this frequency, and all is contained within it. The Trichome Diamond held the intention of Master Zero, polarizing the energies of the universe to maintain a constant balance.

Zero existed beyond materiality in a realm inconceivable. A place of nothing, a place of no relative time. All the material universe is contained within the space within zero, from which the seed syllable Ohm resonates. It is Zero's very existence, his infinite trance, that binds the universe together. Zero itself is the entity to which our universe maintains itself. Without Zero, the frequencies of reality would have collapsed as soon as the universe birthed itself.

Zero, being of non-physical origin, allowed itself to incarnate within itself as a Master of the universal dreamtime. Time in its relativity has undergone countless iterations and as prophecy comes to be, the time has finally arrived for the Trichomian Star frequency to be activated through the kinetic transmission of the ancient relic.

Within Zero's world, in a pocket of eternity created

just for him, the Beast King Ashka has lived beyond what any conscious being should live. Trapped in his immortality, Ashka degraded in the self-exile of his guilt and shame for betraying his people and losing the only planet he had ever lived on.

In his eternal shame, Ashka committed himself to penance, punishing himself with a vow of non-movement. For eons, Ashka sat planted in one spot, and eventually, his body grew hard and solidified into stone. Never allowing himself to let go, Ashka perpetually relived the destruction of his planet. His emotions formed ever-falling tears of sand that cascaded down the stone of his cheeks and onto the bedrock of zero. The once great and immortal king now entomb as a sandy statue of guilt and shame.

But even in eternal purgatory was the chance for redemption. Unbeknownst to him, in the distant realm of physicality, on the golden planet of Fareen. A spark had been struck. A frequency that had not been felt in eons. A frequency that vibrated with the exact resonance as the Trichome Diamond.

This ripple of frequency permeated every realm across the universes, including the one to which Ashka now sat. It vibrated through his stone body and carried along with it a glimmer of hope. Ashka had assumed the worst, had assumed that he had failed in his mission to protect the sacred knowledge of the Trichome. But as the ripple reverberated through the atoms of his stone body, he was granted a window into the mind of the sacred codes. Through a flash of vision, he not only felt the calling, but saw the Golden Trichome plant that he had sent out into the universe those many lifetimes ago, saw Raha continuing the legacy that Ashka himself had failed to protect.

He saw how it thrived in secret, growing in strange plots of lands, being taken care of by beings he did not recognize, and abundantly in the wild. He saw it untouched and uncorrupted. He saw the new race of being that had emerged because of its knowledge. A human. He saw how they acted as the unconscious caretakers of the sacred plant's wisdom.

At that moment, Ashka knew that it had been written in fate all along for the planet Trichomia to fall. Ashka took in a breath of hope. It was the largest breath he had taken in eons, and it cracked at the stone spot around his sternum. He found another deep breath filling his lungs and waves of emotions other than guilt and shame filling his being.

They rose from his gut in a great surge of power, rising to fill his heart. His emotions began to pulse in accordance with a heartbeat he thought he had lost. They continued to build up and up until an empathy shockwave burst from his chest, radiating in a giant ripple itself. It was the emotion of calmness and resolve. Of understanding. The shockwave broke out of the pocket of eternity to which he was trapped and intermingled with the resonant Ohm that emitted from the planet of zero.

It was a subtle shift, one that was hard to even notice, but in this pulse, marked the transition into a new era.

Ashka's heart pulse resonated through the walls of his prison statue, starting to crack and crumble the layers of stone that had solidified his state of mind and being. In a realm beyond where no stars reached and orbiting around the Trichome star were three Entity Moons, sentient luminary bodies, nodes acting as amplifiers to the sonic frequency of the Ohm chant resonating from the zero-point field of existence.

The shockwave emitting from Ashka's heart permeated the realms and began to harmonize with the ohm seed syllable of Zero. Even in nothing, there was always something to be found. The harmonics generated created a living aura, triggering the Three Entity Moons to align with one another and eclipse the glow of the Trichome Star.

From this frequency, a symphonic bliss was produced, echoing and reverberating back to where the Beast King Ashka sat in stone. Vibrating at such a high resonance, the tones of the Harmonic Aura began to liberate and accelerate his molecular movement.

Ashka felt a rich frequency permeate his cells, the divine golden thread unbinding him from the shackles of stone. Waves of sonic pulses began to generate and coalesce in his chest, and the outer stone of his form began to shatter. Ashka felt for the first time in eons, a fluid movement in his breath, the rock crumbling away first at the area of his sternum. With his heart pumping charged, sonic blood through his body, he began to grow feeling in his limbs.

Ashka clenched and opened his fists, and the stone fell away. He ripped one arm free, then another, and soon he was pushing himself up to stand. The Beast King rose, breaking away from the darkness of shame that had entombed him. The sand around his feet began to rise in response to the amplitude of his organic being. He was generating a bio-magnetic aura so strong that he created a field of sonic levitation.

He had shed the layer of his shame and guilt like a snake sheds its skin, and now the parts of himself he had let go floated in orbital swirls around him. Ashka raised his arms to the sky and roared a lion's roar, shattering the remaining stone that still clung to him.

Ashka breathed life into his body and sent pulsar waves out in all directions. In perfect alignment, the harmonic aura reached the Ancient Relic, sitting atop the endless sky and the polarized pyramid pieces connected. The inverted diamond pyramid was drawn inevitably into the keyhole like a magnet sucked back into place.

The seed of Ohm pulsed within the center of the ancient relic, reaching out through quantum beams and activating the Trichome Star Frequency. Ashka felt this alignment as it took place and understood that he had come to this place of purgatory for a reason. In this harmonic alignment, an infinity loop was created on the quantum plane.

Entangled to one another, the activation of the Trichome Star began to trigger subsequent activations to all other crystalline trichomes scattered throughout every universe. They began to vibrate and pulse a frequency of pure love, the highest frequency known to be.

The trichome crystals embedded within the sacred plant on earth lit up with this energy and were supercharged to their maximum threshold. This was the activation that the Lumarian Oracle had foreseen eons ago, and now that prophecy had arrived in full circle. This was the spark to kickstart the rise of all sentient beings back towards the golden age of consciousness. Of course, no evolution could occur in a single instant, but unconsciously, to most, sentient beings everywhere began to harmonize and align with the frequency of the sonic ohms.

The balance had been tipping in one direction for much too long. Suffering was rampant, and separation from the true divine code had left many disconnected from their true nature and, thus, the nature of the universe itself. So, the Trichome Star frequency in alignment with the subsonic frequency of the fabric of reality and the eclipse of the three Entity Moons began the tipping of the scale back towards balance.

The era of the Trichome Star had begun.

All Kuma, the dog, wanted to do was hide. He felt the reprimand still, felt the guilt of doing something he should not have done, and so Kuma ran. He people all around who had once seemed happy to him were now a threat. As his fear grew, the weather above began to change. Carried in on the wind from the other side of the city came the roll of dark rain clouds. People stopped what they were doing to look up to the sky, thunder cracking towards them. Then, the rain began to fall.

Slowly, at first. Just a couple droplets tricking here and there. In the next moment, it broke into a downpour. Sheets of water began to fall from the sky, and Kuma, even as he ran for shelter, became drenched to the bone. Shivering, he found his way to a bridge, slipping under it as lightning crackled down the center of the field. He turned around trembling, the sound of the sudden storm hurting his ears, and watched under shelter as the people all began to run for a shelter of their own.

THE EIGHTH CHRONICLE

Ancient Revelation

There was a message transmitted through the Lumarian Book of Prophecies that spoke of an auspicious time. When enemies become lovers, and the sleeping King awakens, so too will the world of Zero and One align, resonating a ripple in the fabric of time-space, and the sacred plant of Trichomia shall flicker for a moment from green unto gold. Love, pure and true, will rise in the moment of alignment, and those who resonate will feel the silent harmonics of Trichome's song. Those who fall into dissonance will miss the sweet beauty and be forced into the darkness in hopes that they may let go once and for all of the aggression and chaos that resides within.

The beginning of a new era is on its rise. The song for

love and the call to empathy. In the wake of a birthing star, so too must the tower fall, and in the destruction of the old, new life will rise. As the story goes.

As the story goes.

Arelix was an immortal. But even as an immortal, he found sleep still took him. His mind stretched through the bridge of space, his chaotic heart, hunting, feeding, killing. This was how all his dreams were, sword and tooth, knife and blade. Rage and hunger. Nightmares of his own demise. But on this night, as his mind dreamt, it conjured something impossible from the darkest depths. A light. It blinded him at first. He saw himself dissolve and felt it tear away his skin and bones, leaving him nothing but exposed. Exposed to the core, his ego ruined, and only the sensation of his tarnished soul.

He had dreamt of his death a thousand times, but this time was different. He did not wake, reaching immediately for the weapon by his bed. The dream continued to linger. He watched as the folds of light wove between one another and, in their center, a gem. A beautiful sparkling diamond of a gem, radiating shimmers of rainbow light. As the vision drew closer to the gem, he realized that at its heart was a person. His own heart yearned for this person and even with their form nothing more than a silhouette of light, Arelix knew to whom he gazed upon.

She was even more miraculous than when he had seen her fighting on Fareen. She had been wielding the metaphysical weapon of old like a dancer. Weaving between some of his best-trained soldiers like she was the wind itself. It had been a beauty. Something Arelix had never known. And now, as his dream continued, he stared upon beauty for the second time.

Princess Cherena. Her form stayed ephemeral, except the gem had shrunk while she had grown. It now sat atop her head like a crown, and her eyes came into focus through the veil of light. They were a bright emerald, shimmering like stars from another world. Arelix felt for the first time in his life, powerless. Totally and utterly powerless. No one in the history of time had been able to disarm him as she did with a simple look. He was at her mercy, a neophyte, no, a beggar at her feet.

What was he compared to her? What was he... She reached out in rays of light towards him. They grazed the battle-worn and brutal scars of his soul. He felt himself relax, felt the wounds heal and his soul let out a breath of relief that he never knew he had been holding. He knew at that moment that nothing in all the world would be able to match her beauty.

Arelix felt something strange inside him. It was soft and gentle. It was tranquil and calm. It was the touch of a gentle breeze and the gentle roll of a sleepy ocean against the shores of his heart. It was love. It was peace. And it was altogether foreign. Nothing like he had ever experienced.

There was no love in the ranks of the Draconian fighters. There was not even love in the families of royalty. Marriage was made only for political and power reasons. Love was a fool's concept, an emotion of weaker beings.

And yet here he was. Totally and completely submerged within an ocean of it. An infinite ocean of energy. Her hand grazed the hard set of his jaw, and Arelix found himself leaning into it. Soft and tender, like a puppy. He had left her on the planet wounded. He wondered if she was okay, and even as he asked it, he knew she was.

It was because of him that she had been wounded, but also because of him that she had been saved. He couldn't even begin to think what the other Draconian Imperials would say if they knew that he had spared the life of the Fareen Princess who had started the rebellion. But despite that, he could not take his eyes off her.

She smiled, and four words poured from her mouth.

I will find you.

It was all she said before the dream dissolved, and Arelix awoke in his chambers aboard his spacecraft. The glow of his heart was still soft from her love, and in that moment, he finally found his weakness. She was the single greatest threat to him achieving all his goals. He knew she would be the only one who could stand in his way. And he also knew that he would never be able to kill her.

Almost as soon as he realized it, a direct message came to him through the communication device on his wrist. It was a message relaying the status of Fareen. Arelix had to fight within himself to keep the memory of the princess away. He could not appear before his kin with a soft heart. The Draconians could sense emotions and taste them with their forked tongues. If any of his brothers sensed this strange feeling coming from within him, he knew there would be talk of mutiny. It was an inferior feeling, one a Commander could not be sensed to possess.

He growled and pressed another button on his wrist module. A novice soldier appeared in his quarters a moment later. The soldier stood at attention, and immediately, Arelix knew this soldier could sense the conflict within him. But he had known he would. In one quick movement, Arelix drew his sword and was before the soldier before the blink of a second, his sword plunged into the novice's heart.

Arelix growled and watched the life drain from the novice's eyes. Blood. Power. War. This was the creed of Draconia. He embodied it, quenched the fire of the love inside him and replaced it with savage brutality. He ripped out his blade and sliced the neophyte's head off, ending his life in a split second. This was who he was meant to be.

This is what he had been born to become. He cleaned his blade of the blue Draconian blood and stepped over the lifeless body as it crumpled to the ground.

He strode through the giant warship and entered a room of Draconian diplomats who stood around a sharp, obsidian-black table. He snarled, making it well known what he thought of them. They bowed their heads in submission, as was the custom for someone of a higher rank, but their emotions, like most, stunk of subterfuge and corruption. No one was to be trusted, even amongst those closest to his command.

They began to reveal why it was they had required his

presence. It was about Fareen. A dangerous topic, but Arelix made sure he hadn't wiped all the blood off his clothes, and he focused on the stench of fear the novice had exuded when Arelix had stabbed him. Focused on the stench of his death. Apparently, many of the Fareen who had taken up arms with those ancient weapons could not hold its power. They, like many before them, had been corrupted. The ancient metaphysical weapons were relics not to be handled lightly.

A flicker of vision darted past his eyelids. The Princess holding one, dancing across the battlefield effortlessly. He growled and turned the memory into hatred. Hatred towards inferior beings. The Draconian sense for emotions was high, but he knew none, but the best would have been able to taste his small slip. And on this ship, only Arelix was the best. He ordered them to stand away from Fareen. The people were too volatile, and the weapons they held to legendary. Blowing them up was, of course, not an option, as the resources they held were far too valuable. Arelix commanded that they let the Fareen fight amongst themselves. Let them slaughter one another, and only to return once the conflict had finished.

But of course, the sniveling rats that the diplomats were, they made sure he was aware of the fact that the King and Queen were unguarded. It was a good play, because they would be able to question his right as Commander should he pass on such an ample opportunity to seize them. The King and Queen would hold a high ransom, which could be used to negotiate with the rebels. It was well known that the royalty of Fareen were considered more like Gods than they were rulers.

They were a preserved blood lineage of old magicians. Arelix snapped the order to prepare his ship. He would go alone with a small group of mercenaries and retrieve the King and Queen himself. He left before he let himself think of the Princess once more. Only once he was secure in his quarters did he let the wall on his mind fall.

Return to Fareen? He had hoped he would never have to, and at the same time, he wished he could. But his task… To take the Princess's parents for ransom. He snarled. It was good. That way, she would have no choice but to hate him. Hate was an emotion he could reason with. Hatred was something he had dealt with every day of his life. He thought about what the diplomats had said, that the royalty was of an ancient magical line.

He assumed his feelings now were the effects of that old magic, making him weak and soft. The Princess was an enchantress, and she had gotten into his mind. He let himself believe this lie. Let it stir and fester and push him to the point of anger. The indication came that his ship was ready, and Commander Arelix strode to it with a new-found fire. He had retreated once, but now he would get what he needed.

Even as he started up the volatile ionic thrusters of his own ship, he couldn't escape the desire to see Cherena again. Just the enchantment. He thought. He refused to believe now that it was anything else other than that.

She had cast some powerful ancient magic on him,

and it would soon wear off. He set his JUMP coordinates for Fareen and was in their atmosphere a moment later.

In her wounded state, Cherena had caught a terrible fever. The young boy, looking after her, applied a medicinal herbal poultice to her wound as his mother had taught him, not trusting the vial that the Draconian Commander had given him. Yet he could see that the poultice was not working. With no other option, he ran into the streets. Blades were still clashing, and he did not know why people were still fighting. They had won, hadn't they? He was almost impaled with a blade, and he looked up to see one of his own people. The man who wielded the strange-looking weapon had milky eyes and dark veins pulsing from his body. Something had happened to him, some dark corruption overtaken his mind. The boy recognized this man as one of his neighbors and was stunned into fear. He couldn't move, even as the blade rushed towards him. The boy squeezed his eyes shut, but there was a clang and then a crash, and the boy found that he was still breathing. He opened an eye to see one of the Iki had saved him. The boy stared at the lifeless corpse on the ground of his neighbor, who had just been cut down, the milky fog disappearing from his eyes and the dark veins receding.

The Iki offered the boy a hand, and the boy took it. The Iki turned to leave, presumably heading back into battle, but the boy had a mission, he grabbed the Iki's hand and dared himself to speak. Griek allowed himself to be led by the boy to his house in a narrow alley, with a loose fabric as the only door or barrier between the home and the outside street.

Griek couldn't believe his eyes. He had seen the High Commander Arelix run off with the Princess. How was it that she had ended up in a peasant boy's house, of all places? It didn't make sense, but Griek didn't have time to reason. The wound on the Princess's chest would not have been serious, but with the poison-laced into the Draconian blades, it would be lucky if she kept her life.

Griek managed to gather as many of his compatriots as he could, those that had not been corrupted, of course, and they transported the Princess to a subterranean cavern beneath the city, a secret one mined out by Griek himself. It was here in the safety of rock walls that they began to try and mend the Princess's wounds and recover her from her fever that had been set on by the poison.

Meanwhile, Arelix re-entered the atmosphere of Fareen. He snarled at the destruction that had ensued. The chaos of Fareen would surely take a big hit to their resources. Of all the planets they had conquered, none had been so rich in gold and precious gemstones. Laser blasts from ancient weapons zipped past Arelix's ship, but he ignored them and went directly to the palace at the top of the city's natural marble mound.

The elite soldiers he had taken, however, were not so merciful. They sent blasts down to the streets where the lasers shot from. Explosions erupted, and Arelix could hear their childish growl of satisfaction over the communication devices. He chastised them for the insolence, commanding them to hold their fire, saying that they needed the city intact for operations to continue once the fighting amongst themselves had ended. They did as they were told, albeit with more than a hint of resentment. It was never good to restrict a Draconian's natural urge to destroy.

Upon seeing the destruction of the city, Arelix knew that he had to remain and restore operations, or else the losses would be devastating. Their void-energy, ionic thrusters that powered and propelled their spacecraft were built using the precious minerals that were so abundant on the planet of Fareen. To keep them in turmoil would put a halt on all his plans. Not only that, but the Iki, Griek, a member of the Third Eye Order, had slipped through his fingers before he could capture him and retrieve the knowledge he held.

Without the knowledge contained within the Living Manuscript that each member held, then finding the lost relic and knowledge of the Trichome star would be futile. In a moment of awareness, he realized the intricacies this mission would require. The first part was simple, capture the King and Queen, but the rest would require stealth and intelligence.

Arelix knew what had to be done. He barked orders over the comms and designed a party split. He sent his four elite soldiers to retrieve the King and Queen whilst he would search for the Iki. He cloaked his ship and split away from the rest of the team. His elite soldiers raided the palace, killing most of the guards and capturing the King and Queen. They had not known that the rebellion was going to occur and were shocked to hear that their daughter had been the mastermind behind it all. The Elite guards stormed through the palace, searching every room until they found Princess Cherena's. At first, they found nothing, but when they were about to leave, one of the Elite guards sensed something out of place. He pulled back a stone in the wall and found a secret compartment. Within the compartment, almost shining with energy, was a single book. The symbols on the cover seemed to almost breathe with light, and at once, they knew that this was what their Commander Arelix had been looking for. The Ancient Manuscript of Lumaria .

They also knew, however, that their Emperor Decepti Mortar was searching for it as well. With a twist of betrayal, they left the Queen and King behind, seized the living manuscript and returned to their crafts, zipping out of their atmosphere and heading directly towards the mothership. They knew that the emperor would be able to grant them with more rewards than Arelix ever could.

Arelix, unknowing of this betrayal, shapeshifted into a Fareen being and emerged from his ship in complete disguise. The streets were chaos, but no one paid him any mind as he walked amongst them. Some people bowed to him as they passed, which Arelix found strange until he spotted a reflection of himself. There were slight differences amongst those of Fareen. The upper Echelon Elite had different features, a lighter gold of skin with weaving swirls and patterns on their forehead. He was the perfect stature of an Elite Fareen. He looked entirely alien and all the more royal for it.

People didn't bow to him out of fear but out of respect, and he felt a strange sensation at receiving this misdirected praise. What would life have been like had he been born in another race? It was a dangerous thought, one he had never had before. Then, an even more dangerous one entered his mind. Would Cherena find this form pleasing?

As Arelix thought it, he forced it out of his mind. He had a mission, and there was no point in wasting his time wishing about things that he knew would never happen in a million years. A Draconian and a Fareen woman. It was unheard of, sacrilege, an abomination.

He tasted the air with his tongue and smelt it behind the guise of his shapeshifted form. There was a familiar scent in the air. There were many, in fact. Fear, uncertainty, death, and blood. But amongst all of them was another. Arelix had a sudden realization of the holder of that scent. It was the boy that he had handed the princess over to. He followed it through the streets, winding and weaving through alleys. The corrupted fighters tried to attack him, but he disarmed them and killed them instantly, not breaking a step.

These fighters were nothing compared to him. They were annoying fleas and pests. He turned a corner, and his eyes fell upon the boy. He was lying back against the wall, a blood-soaked hand pressed to his gut. Arelix's eyes widened.

Another foreign feeling ran through him. What was it? Arelix realized it was sympathy. And fear. Not only did he care, for some reason, that this boy was dying, but he also feared that if he was harmed, then what had happened to the Princess that Arelix had left with the boy.

Arelix tasted the air and sensed into the wound. He let out a puff of air as the diagnosis reached him. The boys' organs had been punctured. Such fragile things the Fareen were. Soft-skinned and easily pierced by a blade, with no exo-armour of their own. Even if Arelix was able to stop the bleeding, it would do nothing to the festering of his organs within. The kindest thing would be to put the boy out of his misery. But first...

"The Princess." He asked in the boy's language. "Where is she?"

The boy looked at him with distantly glazed eyes. He coughed, and blood splattered his clothes. Arelix could see that he was on the edge of death. It would be a slow teeter into his unmaking, but it was no use trying to communicate with him. Arelix sighed and drew a small blade. He stabbed the boy right in his heart and twisted. The boy gasped, and for a moment, they locked eyes. Then, the life was gone, and his head lolled limply to one side.

The boy would find his way to whatever afterlife the Fareen envisioned. Children always did. Their souls were still untarnished, and innocence lit the way greater than all others. Arelix stood and surveyed the scene around him. It would not be such an easy mission. The streets were much too volatile to find a Princess amidst it all. He would have to find the rebels, those that were uncorrupted of course, and blend in amongst them. They would take him to the source, to the Iki known as Griek, and per-haps to the Princess, as long as both weren't dead already.

Princess Cherena awoke in darkness, save for the flicker of blue fire that rested on the burls of ever-burning wood. She winced as the pain seared in her chest and could hear the murmur of voices coming from somewhere in the shadows beyond. She rose slowly, parched in ways she had never experienced before and was grateful to find a glass of mana liquid by her bedside. She downed the azure water thirstily and sat back with a pained sigh.

The Draconian had retreated. They had won. And yet, she couldn't shake the feeling of unrest within her. As if sensing her wakefulness, someone stepped in through the carved rock dome of the small chamber she lay in. It was Griek. Something tingled in the middle of her forehead. Something she was only beginning to understand. The power of her bloodline. The secrets of which had been re-pressed for generations. Griek had been the one to remind her.

He was a member of a secret society, one that spanned eons, unbroken. The Iki were a strange sort, taken from their destroyed planet, lightyears away and brought for the sole purpose of working as slaves for the Draconian Empire. There were many Iki scattered throughout differ-ent planets however most of their numbers were here. She greeted him with a slight nod, and a telepathic tingle sparked in the center of her forehead as he did the same.

He carried a golden liquid in his hands, and she frowned as he neared her. She could sense something within it. Vision streaked across her open eyes. She saw a diamond star twinkling in crystalline brilliance. She saw a sleeping lion and a planet filled with water. Surely not. Surely, the Iki did not carry part of the Trichomian elixir.

He nodded as if to confirm her suspicion. He set it on the rock table by her side and removed the bandages around her chest. The smell emitting from her wounds was foul. She spared a glance at the rotting edges of the wound, tarnishing her golden skin into a black blue. Griek applied the liquid to her wounds gently. It smelt of plants and sunlight. A warm and simultaneously cool sensation washed over the wound, numbing the pain.

Cherena watched in awe as the rotting flesh dissolved into sparkles of light, and the skin and muscles around the center of her chest reformed themselves almost instantaneously, weaving together like the fabric of a web before healing completely. Half of the bottle had been used. Griek met her eyes with a knowing gaze, and she returned one of gratitude, love, and empathy. Griek felt the waves rolling from her as if they were physical. She was an extremely powerful empath, the greatest he had met in generations.

The Iki were small and short, with disproportionately large eyes and hands. They lived long lives, longer than the people of Fareen. Unfortunately, most did not grow to be old. There was, after all, no use for an Iki who could not work any longer. But Griek had lived for thousands of years, only just reaching his half-life. Being a member of the Third Eye Order, he had access to powers and knowledge his brothers and sisters hadn't. He had planned for many decades before coming to Fareen and starting to plant the seeds of rebellion.

It had been heartbreaking at first. His kin and people had their spirits broken. None of them would listen, for they feared the wrath of the Draconians far more than they did life in eternal slavery. Griek had been getting nowhere until he heard of the birth of Princess Cherena. Her life had come on an auspicious day, and being well versed in the knowledge of the Living Manuscript, Griek had read the signs. She was the key. Griek had waited patiently, waiting for her to come of a certain age. He thought he would have to convince her to join his cause, but the stars did not lie. She had surprised Griek by finding him first.

With her powers she had been able to stoke the fire of the Iki souls back to life. She had used her powers of empathy to give the Iki hope. Hope, the greatest kindling of all. Together, they raised the rebellion, and with her intuitive senses, they tracked down the ancient burial site for the metaphysical weapons of another time. When he first saw her pick up a weapon, the very air around her had glowed with light. It was like a prophecy unveiling before his very eyes. But he had not foreseen that the power of the weapons would have such a corrupting effect on those not ready to wield them.

He revealed to Cherena what had happened after the Draconian had retreated with much dismay. It was a horror and shock to hear that her people were fighting amongst themselves. She had done this. Her people had been a peaceful race, their minds had not thought of weapons for generations until the Draconian had invaded. She had forced them to fight, and even when it should have stopped, it didn't.

"I only tell you this because you can stop it," Griek said solemnly.

Cherena stared at him. It was true. It could be done. But Cherena had only influenced small amounts of people. Griek had started by bringing small groups of Iki to her, and she had sparked their souls to life. With their torches alight, they had sparked hope in others. She was the bearer of the flame and she had only lit a couple. The others had done the rest.

To conceive of quelling the minds and hearts of so many. It was a task that seemed impossible, like lifting an entire desert in a single glass. Not only that, but these people would not be the same as the Iki. They had been willing to listen and had come of their own accord. The corruption Griek spoke about was a wild and devastating thing. Who knew how much of the soul was even left to convince?

But Cherena had done the impossible before. She suddenly remembered the Draconian Alpha. The High Commander Arelix. His name had been spoken amongst her people for so long. Spoken with disdain and hatred. She had never seen him herself. She had been young when he rose to power. Fareen had already been colonized, and he had taken over as the planet overseer in some Draconian political power play that existed beyond their atmosphere in some distant world.

But she remembered the moment with clarity. That had been impossible. Now that she thought about him, she could have sworn he had been in her dreams. A fragment of a tattered soul. It was all she could remember. She frowned as she recalled it, and Griek simply watched her. She was puzzled by the feelings she felt in her heart. Puzzled by the empathy, by the intimate way he had carried her to safety, cutting down his own people to do so.

She rose from the bed. Her body had healed. She had seen it happen, but it was as if her mind was still catching up with that fact. She winced even though there was no pain, the phantom scar of her wound leaving an invisible trace.

"Your wound will never truly be gone," Griek whispered. "I have healed it physically, but it cut deeper than your flesh."

She understood what that meant. Or at least she thought she did. But wounded or not, the battle was not finished. And Cherena was not the type of Princess to leave her people when they needed her most.

"I have to do something." She said, pushing closer towards the door.

"My Queen." Griek humbly bowed his head, but there was a debate on his lips. "Four Draconian stealth ships were reported entering the atmosphere. It is not safe. Without you, the rebellion will crumble. You must remain hidden."

"With all due respect, honorable messenger, without my people, there would be no rebellion. Without my people, I am nothing." She met the Iki's eyes with a stern and unshakeable affirmation. "I must do what I can. And if I should die, it will only serve to stoke the rebellion's flames further."

Griek went to retort, but Princess Cherena was already pushing past him. She strode out of view, and Griek let his humble mask fall away. He had known all along that she would not accept his words. But he said them anyway because sometimes opposition did the job of further affirming what must be done.

He could not see into the future. That was not the task of the members of The Third Eye. His task was simply to carry on the legacy of the twelve Lumarian Oracles, to continue the groundwork that Raha had set into motion. The ancient manuscript held windows into the future, but they were purposefully vague and wrapped in metaphor. Griek knew that Princess Cherena would have a large part to play in the upcoming chronicles of the time, but he did not know what would come of her fate.

He followed along behind her, watching her with an immense curiosity. She was living proof of the great Oracle's prophecy. She was an incarnation of Fate itself, and she played a role larger than any of the others he had met. He not only watched her, but the people that she passed in the hidden catacombs. They all stopped what they were doing to bow or tap three fingers to their forehead in recognition of her royalty.

Wherever Fate led her, she would become a God. She was a walking legend in the making. Already, her name was spoken on every lip in hushed whispers. Griek was not the only one watching, all of Fareen was.

He quickly jogged to catch up with her. The Fareen were much taller than the Iki and one step for them was roughly three for an Iki. "What will you do, Princess?" He said with a bowed head, resuming his mask of humility.

"If what you say is true, that my people fight amongst themselves, then I must unite them once again." "But it is the weapons that corrupt them, your highness."

"Yes." She replied. "Weapons, your order and I provided." She said coldly. "We must assume responsibility for the harm we have caused. Only then will there be balance again."

"What about the Draconian Empire?"

Her brows furrowed. "If they should seek to control Fareen again, then they must go through me. I have handled more than five before."

"But your health, Princess. You have not yet fully recovered."

"I thought you a being of faith, Griek." She replied. "Do you not feel the potential in the air?"

Griek was a being of faith, but he was an archivist, a keeper of records and tradition. Whatever she felt was beyond the scope of his senses. He remained silent.

"When the potential is this great." She continued. "It would be a crime not to step into its power."

As soon as she said it, they emerged into the light of day. Griek was caught by the brilliance of her. Her golden skin shimmered like a newborn star in the sun, refracting rays of ultraviolet in its hue. Almost immediately, one of the corrupts turned his head to her and charged. Griek shriveled back almost instantly, an instinct of the Iki race that was at the peaceful core of their genetics. But the Princess didn't even blink an eye.

Suddenly, Griek felt an incredible burst of empathy radiate from her chest. His feelings were blinded by it as if it were the cleansing wash of pure white light. The corrupted Fareen rebel suddenly froze in his tracks. The weapon fell out of his hands, and he dropped to his knees. Griek looked at Cherena, and she seemed to be glowing. Slowly, she approached the man and lowered herself to his level. She smiled at him with glowing eyes and kissed his forehead gently.

The dark corruption faded from his veins, and the light of his true features resumed their place in his body. He dropped the weapon, and it clanked to the ground. Griek hadn't known when it started, but he found that he was crying. The hot tears dripped down his hybrid amphibian face. Love. That was all he felt. Immense and totally obliterating love. The light began to retreat, and suddenly, the world felt all the darker for it. So, this was the power that the Princess held.

She was speaking with the newly uncorrupted man, holding him in her arms as he released his tears of guilt.

"It is not your fault." He heard her say. "The fault is mine. The sin is mine to bear." Princess Cherena stood and turned to Griek. "I must get high enough to where all can hear my words."

Griek nodded wordlessly, and already he found his legs were moving of their own accord, as if her word was a command that he had no choice but to oblige. So, this was the Princess that the Oracles foretold? A wave of gratitude washed through him. Gratitude for the fact that he should be lucky enough to serve such a noble being. That he should be on this side of the great story that was unfolding. That he had not incarnated through the role of the darker opposition.

He guided her with ease through the city. All whom they passed ceased their fighting and dropped their weapons. Princess Cherena walked slowly and with purpose, extending her aura of empathy so that all who were encapsulated in it were reminded of their heart's true nature.

Through the civilian streets, he led her and up to the great onlook of the Fareen tower. It had once been an outpost for Draconian surveillance, but there was no sign of them now. Cherena walked out to the edge of the balcony that overlooked the streets and gazed out upon her beloved city.

The white stone of the city was laced with gold veins. But both colors were stained with blood. There were people running and people chasing. Warriors fought, and warriors fell. Most of the people still on the streets were corrupted. Those who had fought and kept their minds were no longer there, most likely having retreated into the many hidden chambers that Griek and his followers had carved.

This was her fault, and her heart churned with grief every time she watched one of her people fall to a blade. It was made all the worse that the fighting should be over; this should have been a time of celebration, and yet all she felt was fear and terror amongst those below. Cherena closed her eyes and dug deep into the chambers of her heart.

She had not known she had a power until it had been triggered in battle. It had awoken inside her suddenly, like the plug on a dam being yanked free. She could still feel the walls blocking much of her inner power, but there were cracks in the wall, cracks teeming with golden light that was yearning to break through.

She dug deeper, and unbeknownst to her, she began to radiate that light. It was so bright that Griek had to shield his eyes from it. From below, any onlooker who gazed upwards would not have seen the form of their Princess Cherena in the tower but a star.

A Rise from Exile

Back in the World of Zero, Ashka burst free of the rock that had kept him in exile, having undergone a great metamorphosis of soul within. The guilt, pride, and shame had imprisoned him like it had many a great man, but now he was free of the shackles of the lowest frequency emotions. He rose like a phoenix from the ashes or rather a lion beneath the warm rising of the dawn-light sun. His main billowed in a phantom wind, and he radiated a state of pure bliss, which manifested as a pure and undifferentiated diamond light. Redemption.

Once known as the Beast King, Ashka was born anew as the King of Diamonds, fulfilling the ancient prophecies of the Lumarian Oracle and standing once again in his eternal reign as the gatekeeper and protector of the knowledge that lay within the Trichome diamond crystals.

Through his newly attained state, he vibrated at a harmonic frequency of the trichome star, the single highest frequency known to any being, the frequencies of which permeated every molecule and atom of his being. Ashka had become tuned to his ultimate purpose and, in so doing, evoked the Master of Zero himself to draw forth from the permutation of space and time.

Ashka saw the world he was in. Saw the world of Zero through flashes in the fabric of his mind. He saw the Trichome star shining true, and in apparition, the Master appeared before him as a translucent fold of light before revealing the Star in its wholeness. The King Ashka no longer slept in his dark and twisted hibernation, and as the time-space warped, a vortex formed before the awakened Lion Eternal.

Ashka's eyes burned in the face of the Trichome Star before him. They peeled away every shred of darkness in the void and exposed Ashka to his very core and bone. Brave as he was, Ashka could not help but bow down to one knee. The force to which the Trichome star radiated was no match for him, even in his newly enlightened state. All he could do was radiate and keep his eyes fixed as the Trichome Star Knowledge was transmitted unto him.

Through the folds of light, Ashka knew what he had to do. It was a quest tasked upon him by the very heart that now beat in his body. Attuned to the Star Frequency, he was a living emissary of its divine right and the passage through destiny that it offered. Ashka was granted the vision, and the very knowledge of the Trichome lived in his heart. He did not need to carry around a tome manuscript or ancient message. He was now the living embodiment of the light which he had been tasked to guard.

He could see in this vision how every moment since his birthing had been twined in this fate. He saw now how far the Oracle of Lumaria peered, that everything from the fall of Trichomia to the torment of his self-induced exile was written in the strings of fate and the dance of the three moons around the World of Zero and the star to which all life orbited.

The vortex realigned in twists of fabric, space, and time and from his will, Ashka manifested a vessel of that same diamond that was to carry him through the portal, just as how the Lumarians had countless lifetimes ago. He slowly glided forward on the tides of the Celestium, disappearing from the world of Zero as the portal closed behind him.

Through trillions of lightyears and none, the end of the vortex opened in the sky above the planet Fareen. He was the only being to have ever bridged the gap between the worlds of mortals and the realm at the center of the universe to which the Trichome star existed. And it is here that Fate is most obvious. For the planet was caught in the tides of war amongst itself. Despite that the Draconian forces had been pushed back.

Had the Princess of Arul, the leader of the rebels Cherena, not engaged the Draconian forces, they would still be present on the sparkling planet. The Draconians would have seen the portal that tore open the sky, and they would have found King Ashka in his diamond light craft. But as the story goes, they did not.

The passage through the portal of immortality from one realm of existence to another barely left Ashka conscious as he descended upon a remote part of the planet covered in shimmering blue and gold sand. Whilst the Draconian were not around to see his arrival, a local indigenous tribe had. They beheld the great King of Diamond's descent from the vortex.

But even in Ashka's strength and might, the journey left him feeling disoriented and sick to the stomach.

Having spent so much time in the womb of Zero, the return to materiality was a crushing shock on his system, and especially having maneuvered the single greatest rift in the cosmos, he could barely hold his space vessel enough to land.

When he did, he was overcome with nausea and inter-dimensional sickness. Ashka's ships dissolved before the eyes of the indigenous people of Fareen. At first, they were timid, retreating and watching from the mouth of their cave homes. But over time, their fear of the unknown turned into curiosity. They eventually drew near enough to inspect the fallen star that had appeared before them, and even in his coma, Ashka radiated a beautiful and blinding light, one that soaked his protectors in frag-mented knowledge of the Trichome's secret codes. Seeing that he was no threat, the indigenous tribes of Fareen took him under their wing and carried him on an ornate palan-quin to a cave system beneath the rock formations in the desert sand.

One of the indigenes, a young tribal princess who went by the name of Zaya, fell in love with Ashka almost as soon as she saw him. She was small and barely a child, but she demanded that she care for him whilst he slept. Zaya was special amongst her people. She was born with the eye of a dreamer. Whilst she inhabited the body of a child, she was recognized as an old soul, a soul who had been through many lives, incarnated in many realities and who held a frequency of the Lumarian star system. Though she was only six on the planet of Fareen, she had dream memories of another time, and she recognized Ashka.

She asked that Ashka be taken to the most sacred place of their tribe. Deep within the rock and caves was a sacred underground spring. It had never been seen by anyone outside of their tribe and was a closely guarded secret. Within the waters were the codes of the liquid diamond crystals of ancient Lumaria and the healing aspect of the Trichome Star.

At only six years old, she carried the beast King's massive body upon her back through the caves of bio-luminescent fungi, which many of their tribe consumed in ritual to commune with the stars. It was an enchanted mushroom forest aglow with life and encapsulated by crystals, all cohabitating with the sacred holy water. She lay him down in the sacred pools so that his mind, body, and spirit could recover. Her touch revealed the memories of a being's life, and she could see all the trials and perils Ashka had undergone.

She used the healing waters to tend to the wounds of his inner heart, and as her hands flowed, the water moved and glowed, reacting to the waves of empathy he was still emitting from deep within his being. Zaya had been there at the time of his coronation. She had been there eons ago when they were forced to leave their beloved planet of Lumaria . In fact, she still existed there, for time does not run in line with the mind of an awakened being. Part of the work of the Lumarians was to incarnate at various times, their hearts and souls anchored in the singing crystal forest, and branches of themselves spread into different realms and dimensions. Whilst the Lumarian civilization itself was no more, the souls of Lumaria continued to incarnate in various physical forms through various beings throughout the universe. This was what had become of them.

Zaya could see that the ancient prophecy was in effect and that it had been her task all along to help the King of Trichomia to rise once more, to recover him from his self-exile in the world of Zero, and activate him once more, so that he could become the instrument for the prophecy of the universes.

*

Shining like a star above her people, Princess Cherena felt veins of empathy running to each of her people like the roots of a tree, connecting her to all of them. She felt those channels that were corrupted and began to direct her power there. A surge of loving energy poured from the core of her heart, tapping into a well of energy that seemed infinite.

But even in Cherena's naivety to her own power, she knew that its infinitude was finite. At least, it was until she was able to crack the final walls in her heart. Walls raised by a lifetime living in the shadow of oppressive rulers. She lashed at the wall with an inner force, and the cracks deepened but did not give way.

Already, she could feel the vast amounts of energy the

corrupted took from her to renew their hearts and minds. She was siphoning so much energy that, at her current rate, she would be empty in a matter of minutes. Her eyes shot open, and she desperately willed her mind to channel inspiration. Inspiration from the wounded, from the injustice. But it was not enough. Her glow was beginning to dim already.

And that is when she saw him. Atop one of the distant rooftops, hundreds of meters away. It was a distance that made the man look small, yet somehow, their eyes still locked, like two polar magnets. He wore a different face.

Wore a different body altogether. But those eyes were still the same. She knew the man at once. It was the Draconian commander, Arelix.

Their bond was unspoken, their distance pulled into a place where there was no space or time. Their souls were entwined, and it was the final force that broke the walls down entirely. The chambers of her heart burst open, and an infinite magnitude of love created a shockwave that threw Griek off his feet and cured all of the corruption in an instant shockwave.

Princess Cherena felt her arms splay to the side and upwards, and the force of the energy lifted her up into the sky. She was unmade in her name and plunged into the infinite ocean of the light inside her. It was a peace and stillness like no other. A total and all-consuming everything.

Light poured from her eyes and mouth and shot out in

rays from her fingers and palms. It pulsed from her chest and stole her breath away. She heard distant music, the music of the stars playing in her mind, and even though she could no longer see him, she knew that Arelix felt it as well. It was not just her that felt this freedom. Arelix's soul was entwined around hers in the rising of energy, like two snakes wrapped around one another in a helix of DNA. Their hearts and genetics entwined, bridging the space between them in a quantum leap of entanglement.

The shockwave rippled throughout the entire city, and everyone felt it. The people of Fareen were drawn from their homes and hiding places like a moth drawn to a flame, and when they beheld the star of their Princess floating in the sky, they dropped to their knees and lowered their heads to the ground in prostration.

It was the thing of legends.

Interlude Six

The storm came and passed. Kuma, the dog, sat and watched the entire time, staring at the trillion drops of rain that cascaded to the ground. And as he sat in quiet presence, his fear began to dissipate. It was a quick flash, and before he knew it, the sun was peeking back through the cracks in the sky, and the wind tossed the clouds aside, clearing way once more for the blue above. Tentatively, he laid a paw out. The sun crystallized in small, tiny starbursts against the wet dew of his fur, and Kuma felt the first touch of warmth again.

Kuma stepped from beneath the bridge just as people were beginning to return from under the cover of buildings or thick-leaved trees. And where once was nothing but the grey and fall of rain was laughter once again and people blooming all around.

THE NINTH CHRONICLE

Unconditional Love

The High Commander Arelix's disguise was stripped from him as the shockwave hit. But he was not conscious of his body. He was in another world entirely. Dropped to his knees, he felt the divinity of love devour him. He felt the light fill every vessel of his cold blood and warm it until he thought he was going to catch on fire. In a matter of speaking, he was on fire. Except it was not one of flesh and blood. It was a spirit fire, burning wild and pure.

In the fire he saw the actions of his life and saw how all of it was impure compared to this light. His murders and his fight for power had been deemed honorable in his society and were, in fact, disgusting in the light of this fire.

Everything he knew, everything he was, burned in the sanctity of his holy retribution. It was all engulfed in love, wrapped in the warmth he had often witnessed from other mammalian beings, parents hugging their children, lovers entwined. He had always witnessed it but never understood why it was done. Now, it was all that he was. His intellect drowned in this awareness, and as all his life burnt, he was brought to a single moment of memory.

When he himself had been a child. There, the fire did not burn. There in the heart of him as a child, was a spirit worthy of this love. He was confused and perplexed. Arelix had always assumed that it was the Draconian nature to be the way they were. But there in that memory, he relived a feeling, a pure and honest feeling, one that had very much existed but had been buried and destroyed under years of upbringing in the Draconian Legion.

The color of the fire burned the color of his white skin pigment. He had been born different. That difference had almost crushed him under the weight of the judgement from his peers and those around him. Then, through the veil of his younger self, he saw her.

She burned like a pure white phoenix, like the core of a burning star. She reached out a hand, and Arelix was scared as much as he was drawn to it. Her hand promised his death. Not the death of his body. But the death of Arelix. Of the being, he had grown to be. It would be the death of his ego, and whatever came after was a complete unknown.

His goals and aspirations were nothing to this. They

were false shadows in the truth of what the Princess radiated. His fight for control and power was not his own. He had been dreaming a dream not his own. It was the dream accumulated from millennia' worth of Draconian ideals, ideals born from a hostile planet in a chaotic three-star system.

None of it was his. And yet, it was his legacy. Could he so easily forgo it? The pulse of love vibrated again, and Arelix could not fight as his struggle melted away, turning into grief for all the suffering that had occurred because of his hands. He did not deserve this, and yet Princess Cherena stood before him. She smiled, and Arelix could no longer hold himself back. He went to reach for her hand, but before they even made contact, there was a great flash, and both vanished through the folds of space and time.

*

The shockwave from Cherena and Arelix's entangled hearts continued outwards, rippling across the entire planet, out towards the desert tribes where Zaya and the Beast King lay in the sacred waters deep below. The waters began to ripple first, resonating at the frequency and rising in waves of cymatics resonance. Zaya felt the first wave run through her, and the pools began to glow even brighter than they already were.

She knew this light. She knew this love. Even though she was just a child, the frequency of it reminded her of another life, of another time, and all the memories of Lumaria came streaming through all at once. She remembered a time of prophecies and creation, of crystal singing forests and peaceful love that could be drank like water all around.

She began to splash playfully in the water, like the child she was, and as she did, in one swift moment, the Beast King's eyes shot open.

The massive second shockwave burst through the caverns of the desert people of Fareen, and in that moment, it sparked King Ashka's heart to life. He awoke with a gasp in the sacred waters beneath the desert of Fareen. A child splashed in the water before him, and in the air was the frequency of Love that Ashka had not felt since his first contact with the Lumarians eons ago. His heart was attuned to the frequency, and a triangle of resonance began to bounce between the King and two unknown points of contact. He could feel these other hearts in the place beyond space, could feel the love that vibrated between them.

Somewhere in the far reaches of the astral planes, someone was watching. Zaya could feel the presence of them, staring through the veils of density upon them. Barradow floated in the realms of ether, his heart having attuned to the awaking of King Ashka, a person he had thought to be dead, more than dead, erased from existence.

Barradow could traverse many realms and planes of existence, but the World of Zero was a place untouched by him or any other sorcerer within his ranks. But as soon as the King had returned to the mortal world, something inside Barradow had awoken, triggered by Ashka's presence.

He had gone and taken the astral winds, following the calling within his heart. So, it was here that Barradow stared down upon the missing King. How long had it been? It felt like millennia had gone by. And despite the fact that the King had awoken, Barradow could tell something was wrong.

The King was not rising like he should. A great cosmic energy surged around him, but a part of him was still damaged. Barradow trilled and convened with the ancient records, knowing that he had little time. Though time was relative within his realm of the astral, in which he spent most of his time now.

He was less a physical being now and more one of light. The mortal world had been lost to him for so long, and now, like a magnet, he was pulled back. A part of him already knew what was to be done. This was not just about Ashka anymore. This was about the Fate that intertwined them all. This was for the good of life and the good of the universe.

Barradow had lived eons of time. Now, it was his moment to let go. Harnessing all the power at his disposal, Barradow began to unwind the very constituent ether that bound him to form. It was love in the form of sacrifice. The High Priest began to pour his life energy into Ashka, willing every ounce of it to go.

Ashka closed his eyes and smiled, and the softness of

his mane began to glow against the backdrop of the sacred pool. Whilst this was a sacrifice of form, Ashka could once again feel the merging of minds between him and Barradow. Oh, how long it had been separated from the one true love he had ever had.

He rose slowly, lifting from the ground, and as he did, the child stopped her playing. She stared up at him with wide, curious eyes. Ashka and Barradow were joined again, the last of his material ether merging into the body of Ashka, and suddenly, from the spark of the love they shared, great owl wings burst from the space between Ashka's shoulder blades. Giant wings. His eyes burst open again, and the ritual was complete.

His wings beat, and, in their beat, he felt Barradow within him. They were twined eternally in each other's minds. They would never have to separate again, and Ashka was no longer himself, nor was Barradow. Together, they became something else. They transcended what they had both had been, merging for eternity into the King of Diamonds.

"Thank you for guarding over me, little one," Ashka spoke gently to the child with a deep and powerful voice. "It has been many lifetimes since we last met."

The child returned his smile and stood as well. "Will you help me?" He asked her.

She nodded and walked towards him as Ashka extended his hand. She took it on her own. The King's hand was massive compared to hers and soft with fur. She looked up to him as he stared through the fabric of time and space. Seeking out the two hearts that had triggered this cosmic event. He could feel them twined in one another, and Ashka began to hum, opening a gateway of sound that tunneled through the realm of space.

He called to the source of the shockwave. In his heart, he felt the beat of two more, and he felt the source heed his invitation. In the next moment, they were there with him in the sacred pools, embraced in one another's bodies. Even the King was shocked by what he saw. A golden Fareen Princess was caught in the loving embrace of a silver-skinned Draconian male.

Ashka had never thought it possible for the Draconians to love. He himself had witnessed firsthand what destruction came in their wake. He had lost his entire planet to them. And yet, here was the impossible right before his very eyes. Two natural-born enemies caught in the embrace of a frequency so profound it had activated him and sent a shockwave throughout the entire planet.

The little girl by his side stared up in awe at the two lovers. They slowly descended from the opening in the sound portal at the top of the cavern and gently lowered into the waters, where their feet touched down on the surface as if they weighed nothing more than feathers. Ashka closed the portal and watched in equal awe. The two lovers turned away from one another and faced Ashka. Both of their hearts radiated the pure vibration of the trichome star, undifferentiated and harmonically resonant with one another, the same frequency that ran through Ashka's blood at this very moment.

The woman was the first to talk. "What is this place?" She looked around at the subterranean cavern, her hand joined with the Draconian's.

"This is the sacred heart of my people," Zaya replied. "We are the Yakuta of Fareen."

The Princess looked at the child with unyielding love. "Of course," Cherena replied. "It is my honor to be welcomed into this divine sanctum."

Arelix remained silent.

Ashka looked at both of them. "You may or may not be aware, but the union of your hearts has triggered an ancient prophecy. One that was foretold eons ago."

None of them responded. They only looked at one another with great love in their eyes.

"Together, your souls are resonating a melodic vibration that has awakened me from my deep sleep and triggered a shockwave that will no doubt be felt throughout the entire universe. Even as we speak, the heart of this calling lives within a realm at the core of the universe. At its heart is the Trichome star and the world of Zero, which I have been in for many lifetimes. As both of you know, a great spiritual war rages throughout the universe." He turned to Arelix. "Your former people have gotten hold of the map to the sacred invisible star and desire the ancient relic within the world of Zero. If they should reach it and bend the power of the Trichome to their will, the entire universe will be plunged into chaos. Your union could put an end to this. Your love could stop the dark prophecy from being fulfilled and instead unfold an era of infinite peace."

This time, Arelix stepped forward towards Ashka and bowed on one knee.

"I know of you, great King. My people were responsible for the destruction of your planet, and I bear their sin on my shoulders. Let me be an ambassador of this era for peace. Let me aid you in any way that I can. My people have good in them. I am a living example. They are prisoners to lifetimes of generational trauma and horrors.

They do not know the nightmare they are caught in. It is my wish to unbind them from their shackles as the Princess has done for me. He looked to Cherena. "I have been granted a divine gift. Greater than any I deserve. It would be our honor to aid you in spreading the frequency of love throughout the universe."

Princess Cherena nodded. "I once thought that the Draconians were evil to their core, that they were born simply to oppose. But I have fallen for the enemy and in this love, we together have discovered the ancient secret that has been buried for countless eons. Arelix and I will be of service for as long as we shall live."

Ashka smiled and raised his arms. "Then so shall it be. Together, we will form an alliance of beings with a mission to spread a New Unity throughout the many universes. But before we do, I sense that there are stories still yet to be told. It was not chance that brought the two of you together. A great story has been unfolding for many millennia, and it seems you two have always been a part of it, whether you knew it or not. I am sure there are many questions that need answering."

"We sense it, too." Princess Cherena smiled as she looked at Arelix. "There is a member of the society here on Fareen. He goes by the name of Griek. He is a keeper of records and a keeper of the sacred knowledge of the Trichome."

Ashka was in awe. He still couldn't quite believe that the Third Eye Order started by Raha had spread so far. He had seen the vision of Raha and the former Trichomians so many millions of years ago. The fact that the society was still around was a great testament to the will and mission of his people.

Princess Cherena smiled again. "Very much so. It was under their guidance that I began to gather forces for the rebellion. If it were not for Griek, the uprising may never have come. And Arelix and I may never have met."

"It seems all the threads have been leading to a single road," Ashka replied. "We must locate Griek, and he may accompany us on our mission."

"What about me?" Zaya asked. Her voice is as soft as a crystal flute. Ashka laughed. "Well, of course, you can join us, ancient one." Zaya giggled at the name he called her.

Arelix stood, and he sniffed at the air with his tongue. "I sense our friend Griek is already on his way here."

"Then we shall wait," Ashka confirmed. "Little Zaya, will you not spread the word that a celebration is underway?"

Zaya nodded eagerly and ran from the sacred pools. She began to sing and twirl as she headed through the cavern tunnels, back towards where her family and the rest of the Yakuta people. King Ashka gestured forward with an arm.

"I worry that it may be a shock for these people to see a Draconian in their home. It is my understanding that they have remained hidden for quite some time."

Cherena squeezed Arelix's scaly hand. "It may be a shock initially, but the frequency we carry will quell their worries quickly."

As they strode through the chamber and into the main cavern, there were already people looking out from their homes carved into the rock, whispering and muttering things to their neighbors. But as soon as the halo of Cherena and Arelix's love passed over them, they all went silent. The bioluminescent fungi lit up the walkway, and Zaya soon returned, pulling her mother's arm. Her mother, Eneela, was the tribe's chieftess medicine woman and was often counselled in matters pertaining to greater outside influences.

Her mouth dropped as she saw the couple walking through the main cavern with the Beast King Ashka at their side. She did not bow, but Cherena offered a submission of her head, bringing three fingers to her forehead in greeting.

"My name is Princess Cherena." She said softly.

"We know of you," Eneela replied, offering a gesture of peace. "Even in the far deserts of Fareen, the wind carries your name." Her attention was already shifting towards the tall Draconian male, with slight worry.

"Do not fear," Cherena said calmly. "He has been cleansed in the same spirit that runs through your waters. That runs through the fabric of the universe, through the sacred plants of knowledge and wisdom, and through the light of the eternal star." She looked at him lovingly as Arelix bowed his head. "Our hearts have merged in the light of the Trichome."

Arelix bowed to Eneela. "I deeply regret the struggles and harm me and my people have put your through, but I hope that the peace on Fareen may be the start of reconciliation."

"We have lost many brothers and sisters to the brutality of the Draconian ways," Eneela responded.

She could feel the waves of love emanating from him and the Princess, but that did not erase the memories of the past.

"Come now." Ashka interrupted. "There can never be peace until all who have been wronged let go of their grief and allow change to move forward. I can personally vouch on behalf of the former commander."

Eneela turned to him. "And who are you to vouch for

this being?" She paused. "We found you on the fringes of our desert, but we do not know anything of your deeds. Although Zaya has seemed to have taken a liking to you, and she does not take to many, even amongst our own."

Zaya pulled on her mother's arm and indicated for her mother to bend down so that she could whisper in her ear. Eneela's eyebrows raised as Zaya whispered softly, and then once Zaya was done, she stood tall again.

"Zaya here tells me you were once a great King." Zaya pulled her mother's arm again, frowning.

"Sorry, my mistake..." Eneela corrected herself. "Are a great King."

She narrowed her eyes and looked Ashka up and down. "May I?" She asked. Reaching out a hand.

Ashka nodded and let her take his. Eneela's eyes rolled up into her head, and she saw through every memory that Ashka had lived. They flashed before her vision at a timeless rate, but the exchange only lasted a couple seconds before she withdrew her hand again. This time, there was a look of understanding in her eyes.

"You have experienced much, King Ashka. More than any mortal might. If your judgement of these two is pure, then I shall confer."

At last, Eneela bowed to both Princess Cherena and Arelix. "The home of the Yakuta is yours to share. May you find refuge in our walls."

King Ashka, Princess Cherena, and the High Com-

mander Arelix all bowed to the matron of the Yakuta people and the daughter Zaya by her side. Eneela beckoned
some of her still hesitant Yakuta people to retrieve some
drinks and food. And together, they all sat, awaiting the
Iki, known as Griek, to arrive.

Interlude Seven

Kuma, the dog, felt alive once more. Not only alive, but invigorated, renewed with a sense of life that felt as if it were something long forgotten and simultaneously been there all along. Inside him was a feeling, a source of warmth from beyond the sun that hung above him. He bound across the field and back, stretching limbs and spreading that feeling around, spreading it like dust falling pollen off a flower petal. Running to meet the new chords of life.

THE TENTH CHRONICLE

A Joint Mission

Griek had seen two stars rise in the sky at that auspicious moment. The Princess herself and an unknown body on the far side of the city. The shockwave that emanated from them had been so strong that Griek had been utterly consumed by it. When he awoke back into his body, the princess had vanished, and so had that second light. But the traces of their energy had not.

Back in the Yakuta caves of Fareen, there was some movement from up above, and Griek appeared in the entranceway to the great cavern.

"Oh, it seems we have another visitor. Griek, member of the Third Eye, welcome back. It seems you are just in time, although I am sure it is no coincidence."

Griek smiled and bowed, acknowledging the matron of the Yakuta people. She nodded an acknowledgement back before turning to address the caverns of waiting for tribespeople. She raised her arms and voice so that all could hear.

"Fareen is free for the first time in millennia! Let us celebrate!"

A loud burst of cheers and howls erupted from the cavern, and already drums were being played, people rushed out to start preparing for a grand feast. Griek humbled himself before the Princess, not even noticing that Ashka stood beside her. His forehead touched her bare feet, and she shook her head.

"Please, Griek, you do not need to lower yourself on my account. We are all equals in this." He nodded and stood, and that was when he noticed Arelix for the first time.

"It is I who should bow, noble Iki," Arelix said and went down to one knee. "The Draconians have disgraced themselves amongst countless races, and I believe we have done the most harm to your people."

"It has come to be," Griek said, in awe and not in fear or hatred. "The Prophecy has come true." He began to recite it. "When enemies become lovers, and the sleeping King awakens, so too will the world of Zero and One align, resonating a ripple in the fabric of time-space, and the sacred plant of Trichomia shall flicker for a moment from green unto gold. Love pure and true will rise in this moment, and those who resonate will feel the silent harmonics of the Trichome's song. Unto those who fall into dissonance, will miss the sweet beauty, and be forced into the darkness, in hopes that they may let go once and for all, the aggression and chaos that resides within."

That was when Griek turned to King Ashka. "My King, we have been waiting for your return for eons. The first members of our order were founded by Raha himself under your divine instruction. I cannot believe that it is you I see before my eyes. What stars guided the fate that allowed me to be alive in this blessed occurrence? It seems all too much like a dream."

Ashka smiled, and Cherena spoke. "What is the difference between a dream and the heart of the universe, noble Iki? All of this may vanish in a single moment, and neither you nor me would know the difference. What is reality but not the incarnation of one's dream into an infinitesimal multitude of refracting experiences." She smiled. "Our grandest notion may be an insignificant spec on the bottom of a furry creature's foot for all we know. Our entire history, a single day in the life of a dog. But that is neither here nor there." Her eyes twinkled and she exchanged a look with Arelix. "Noble Griek, I fear I must ask of your service once more before the celebrations truly commence. There is a thread that bonds Arelix's and my fate. Do you not keep records of such things? Would you help us trace our link? For it may uncover a secret that we have yet to learn."

Griek nodded eagerly. "It would be my pleasure Princess. I have a ship that has access to a living part of the Trichome. The singing crystals will answer any questions you seek."

The four of them emerged into the desert, and Ashka smiled deeply as he recognized the familiar design of the spaceship. It was designed like a grasshopper with wings for atmospheric propulsion. He could see that there were slight modifications to some of the technology, but the shape had remained intact.

"I cannot believe my ships still live." He said, grazing an affectionate hand over the legs of the grasshopper. "Raha was very persistent in keeping the ships identical to the originals," Griek replied with a smile.

The four beings, each of completely different origin, walked onto the spaceship as the long metal boarding bridge unfolded from the base of the craft. The inside was full of Lumarian symbols, the ancient language of a civilization that was thought lost to time. The rare metals of Trichomia curved seamlessly throughout, and in the center was a capsule radiating golden light. Inside was a part of the sacred plant of Trichomia.

King Ashka's eyes widened as he saw it. "I never thought I would see the light of the Trichome crystals ever again." He whispered breathlessly. "I never thought I would hear the singing within."

Princess Cherena was also enamored by the sacred plant. It pulsed and sang and called to her in ways that were altogether familiar as if it was reaching out to her and speaking directly into her mind in the way of dreams. A memory as a child wandered through her vision, and she realized in that moment that the Trichome had been calling out to her even then. That this light, this song, was the source of her power.

Griek turned his gaze on her and Arelix. "Within the Trichome are the records of the universe, past, present, and future." He said, bowing to Cherena and Arelix and then to the sacred plant.

Around the capsule were four chairs and Griek indicated for each of them to sit. Cherena and Arelix sat opposite one another, their energy still tightly entwined with one another. And the Trichome crystals within the plant reacted to their presence. Images began to appear in the space within its golden light. Then, almost instantly, their minds were ushered away from the present and carried to a far distant past, in a realm and world unknown.

*

It was a dark planet. The land was barren and scorched. Black rocks jutted from the ground in sharp spires, and strange factories made of dark metal churned smoke and chemical fumes. Through some omniscient view, three Draconian Emissaries walked amidst a giant temple made of the same stone that was native to the planet's dark matter.

It was gothic in appearance, with sharp angles and spires that extended to cathedral heights. It was an ancient temple of Necromancy. An ancient Draconian practice that had once been the closest thing to religion that the Draconian Galactic Empire ever had. The energy was foul and decrepit, and the stench of death was thick in the air.

Cages hung from the tall spires, and within were the slowly dying bodies of mortal beings. Giant batlike creatures fed on the flesh of these mortals and tore at their eyes. Their moans and screams filled the air for as far as the ears could hear.

Eshu strode behind her parents as they led the way through the Necrotic temple. Her jaw was clenched and tongue tucked away so that it could not taste the foul stench in the air. She had been raised in the brutal and cruel manor of the Draconian Elite, but even still, the existence of this place was a shock to her.

Even though she was of age, she had not outgrown her innocence, and the brutality of what surrounded her was a horror to behold. She forced her emotions to calm, forced herself not to look at the grotesque sacrifice all around her. Her parents had told her it was an extreme privilege to be invited into the temple. It was the closest thing to a sacred place that the Draconians had. Mortal beings were sacrificed to the Dark Deities of the Draconian Empire, and those of true power within the Empire's ranks fed on the life force of these beings to extend their own lives in unnatural ways.

Veins of metal ran through the structure of the temple, and various colored blood ran through these veins, feeding the energy source that sat in the center of the main alter hall. A dark crystal with what looked to be a black sun radiating in its center, ultraviolet rays leaking in a halo of deep violet around it. Eshu had been told it was a portal to another realm. A dimension where the dark Gods existed. The remnants of the first one. The one who had once been named Lekiam or known to the Draconians as the Dystopic Ones. The origin of the one who questioned.

The Gods were what fueled the Draconian power and allowed them to call on these necromantic powers themselves.

"Eshu." Her father, Menshuk, called her name. But she didn't hear him over the sound of screaming. He called her name, this time louder, growling in frustration.

Her eyes snapped towards him. They were standing in front of giant black-stone doors. She didn't know when they had arrived there or how long they had been standing outside them.

"We are to speak with the Temple Necromancers." He said sternly. "You must await us here as we discuss the terms of your initiation." He said with a slithering tongue. "Stay put where you are, and should you be accepted, I expect you will finally be of some worth. This role will bring honor to our family."

Eshu's mother hissed. "Do not disappoint us again. This is your final chance to make something of yourself."

Eshu swallowed something like revulsion and nodded obediently. Her father turned with a snarl, and the giant black doors opened. Eshu caught a glimpse of the Draconian High Council within the cathedral-like room, seated around a long slate table. She had to hide her shivers of disgust as she saw that almost a dozen mortal beings hovered above the table by means of dark magic, their life force slowly being sapped towards the High Council members through dark tubes that fed directly into their veins.

The being's eyes had been sucked within their skulls, and their mouths were agape, releasing soundless screams as blood drained from their bodies. It was all she saw before the doors closed behind her parents, and she was left alone in the Citadel's central hall.

Time seemed to stand still. There was the whisper of haunted spirits in every rogue wind that managed to find its way through the tight cracks in the fortress. Eshu could not help but feel on edge as phantom limbs seemed to reach out and touch her scaly skin. There were pleads from those dead or alive. Eshu could not tell the difference. But it all surrounded her in a chaotic maelstrom of emotions.

Then she felt it. The pulse of the dark star. Her back was turned to it, still facing the large double doors as she had been instructed to by her parents. But the black sun within the crystal seemed to creep under the folds of her scales and pull her attention towards it. Reluctantly, she turned as if against her own will. At first, she didn't even notice the body that had been ritualistically nailed below it. At first, she had been too entranced by the dark pulsars and lashes of energy that flowed like tendrils from the heart of the Draconic crystal.

The ultraviolet light was altogether wrong. An inverse

of light, the opposite of life-giving as most stars were symbols of. It was a void, life-draining, and if it were not for the practices her parents had instructed her on, practices of willpower and shield obfuscations, she may have been drawn into the star's power and left a husk of her former self before her parents returned.

It so happened, however, that she could pull her eyes away from the dark center, and when she did, they fell upon what looked to be the corpse of a body. Her muscles tensed as she withheld the withered form. It had two legs and arms just like her but had the hollowed, almost corpselike face of what she could just recognize as a Fareen male.

She was shocked, for this male showed no sign of the race's typical vibrant and golden skin. Instead, it was dry and black as if it had been singed or rubbed with charcoal. It was shriveled in places like a grape left to dry in the sun. Then she heard it. The pathetic rag of a breath. A breath so thin it should not have been a breath at all. This being was alive, albeit on the brink of death, but a sliver of his spirit still clung to the possibility of life. To some, an existence of suffering was better than no existence at all. The threat of death can leave even the most fate-filled man clinging to life.

Eshu could feel that willpower as if it were a texture in the room. In this horrible place of darkness, where all those trapped here shared the common wish of death, this being will be akin to the rising of a lotus in the heat of draught. Eshu found herself before him, not remembering having made the decision to move, and dropped to her knees. One of his eyes was half closed, the other staring somewhere past her as if he stared into another world.

She touched him, and a cold shiver passed through her nervous system. What sorts of torture had this being been subject to? And for what reason? Her eyes instinctively drew upwards to the black crystalline star. She could feel the channel of energy that flowed between this male from Fareen and the sun. She felt the man's life force being syphoned towards it.

Then, a strange thought occurred to her. How could she be so close and not feel the star's heat? The cold shiver ran through her again, and Eshu reached a curious hand towards the pulse of darkness. There was no heat, but a bitter cold threatened to freeze the blood in her veins and still her on the spot. Even still, Eshu reached forward.

She touched the strange crystal and was surprised to find that it was hard, like stone. Her touch rippled through the surface of the star, and under her palm, Eshu felt something crack. Shocked, she quickly withdrew her hand and found that it was sung in a similar fashion to the Fareen male beneath her, blackened and shriveled. But Eshu was Draconian, and the once withered flesh reformed into bright emerald scales as her regenerative healing took effect.

Something moved within the star, and she felt a presence appear in more strength. In a moment of clarity, Eshu realized that it was not the star that had a presence, but something within it. There was a smoky movement beneath the surface of the dark exterior, and Eshu felt a dark grief well up inside her.

"Are you trapped as well?" She whispered compassionately to the spirit.

There was a pulse within the sun, and the emotions that streamed towards her were undeniably a 'Yes.' "You poor thing." She replied, stroking the surface of the star again.

There was a sound of movement, like dust falling, and Eshu could see that the being below her had opened his eyes a crack more. They stared up at her in confusion as if he were seeing an apparition. She gave him a look of empathy.

"I am sorry you have both been confined to this fate. Maybe I can..." Eshu's voice suddenly trailed off, and she turned to look at the large doors that were still closed. "No, I mustn't..."

She pulled away from the star with reluctance, and the spirit within pulsed its emotions of sadness. A sadness so deep it stopped Eshu in her tracks. What was this strange entity at the center of the entire citadel? She had assumed that whatever deities resided here would be as evil as the Necromancers who worshipped them. But perhaps this entire star was yet another ritual of blood sorcery.

At that moment, Eshu knew that she would never be able to follow through with her parent's plans for her. She would never be able to become what they wanted her to be. That would inevitably lead to her death, whether at the hands of her parents or the hands of the Necromancers. The forms of punishment that followed dishonor within the upper echelon of Draconian society were not kind. She realized that it may soon be her lashed up, or caged in the citadel's towers, slowly dying and pleading for a quick delivery into the afterlife.

What a life that would be. To go against her nature, to resist until her fight finally paved the road to her own death. She turned back to face the strange formless spirit that lay imprisoned within the black sun. But where would this road lead her? The thrill of the unknown rushed to greet her. Since Eshu was born, her entire life had been planned out for her, and she had followed obediently at much cost to her own values.

But here in the heart of a black star was the promise of an alternative future. One that was completely her own. This would be her decision. Even if this choice ended in death for her, she was okay with that. Death was never far away anyway, and she had come to terms with it a long time ago. Eshu stepped back towards the star, and she felt a swell in her heart. The rays of ultraviolet light seemed to beam brighter in that strange anti-matter way. It wasn't so much that they shone, but rather they removed most of the light spectrum that was already there, leaving only the hue of ultraviolet.

The Fareen being croaked beneath her and extended his arm up towards her. Eshu quirked her head and kneeled at his side. She met his distant eyes and took his hand.

"Whatever happens next, we will be in it together." Eshu smiled.

She touched her hand to the star, and the cracks grew larger. The love and compassion in her heart acted like a spell, breaking down the barrier of the prison. At that moment, the large stone doors opened, and her parents stepped out. They were being accompanied by a few members of the council, all of them seeming like they had come to an agreement.

It was Eshu's mother, Ighriru, who noticed her first. She stopped dead in her tracks and froze, making the heads of Menshuk and the council members turn to see what was wrong. They followed her gaze to Eshu, knelt by the crystalline void in the center of the citadel. Before they even had the chance to scream, the starburst.

Dark violet filled the entire room in an inverted polar field of light, making everything appear in strange shades of black and violet. From the center of the star emerged a chaotic maelstrom of smoke.

"What have you done?!" One of the council members shouted.

Eshu's head turned, and she could just make out the dark features of her parents. She felt the mind of the spirit she had just freed. She felt its rage seething, and at that moment, she knew it would kill them.

"No!" Eshu spoke to the spirit in an authoritative command. And surprisingly, it listened to her.

Already, she could feel the spirit slipping from the mortal world, sifting back into the realm from which it came. But surprisingly the Fareen male reached out an arm towards it. There was no hesitation. The spirit drove itself into the remains of the body. Eshu watched as the body writhed and convulsed, eyes turning pitch black, the same color as the spirit's energy. Then everything went still.

The light was starting to return to normal, and Eshu could see that the Citadel necromancers were already coming towards her. Time went in slow motion as she realized this was the end of the road. They would capture her, and she would be subject to the cruel punishments reserved for traitors. Her family would be dishonored, lose their rank, and be shunned from the Draconian Empire, forced to live in exile on one of the colonized planets.

She saw the Necromancers cast spells of binding and felt the shadows of their magic reaching towards her. But before the tendrils of darkness could reach her, the Fareen male suddenly rose from the ground. He did not stand but began to float in the air, eyes hellbent and vicious. Eshu's heart reached out to him, and she felt a wave of emotions return. They were bonded.

The spirit within the body crossed his arms over one another, and in an instant, a void-shield surrounded them, cutting off the magic reach of the Draconian Necromancers. Then the spirit released a wave of dark energy, sending them and Eshu's parents flying back. Her head darted to him, and he grabbed her in his arms, holding her close to his body. She clung to him like a damsel in distress as he made for the exit of the citadel.

Eshu clung so close to him she could feel the dark seethe of his power; it was chaos incarnate, and she could feel that even in this fragile state of his, he was extremely powerful. The dark void bubble that surrounded them shrouded her in that strange absence of light as it had before. She could only make out the outlines of shapes and people as they flew through the grounds of the planet.

Spells hit the bubble, but it was impenetrable, and they bounced off, the force of them being redirected right back to the Draconians who cast them. Eshu hugged the spirit with all of her heart and whispered into his ear to get them away from this planet. He assured her she would be safe with a flow of emotions. They had opened a telepathic link from the moment she set her hand to the now exploded crystal that had been the bridge between two realms and the dark dystopic God's prison.

Their hearts were bonded in ways Eshu had not thought possible for two beings from such separate walks of life. Even amongst her own race she had not ever conceived that someone would be able to return the vast amounts of love and compassion she carried in her own heart. Alarms were blaring, and the gruesome bats that had been feeding on the prisoner sacrifices shifted their attention and headed straight for Eshu.

Get us out! Eshu thought desperately.

But as she thought of her escape, her heart went to those who were still trapped. She doubted she would be able to save them, but she could at least put them out of their misery. The spirit felt her wills and desires and saw to them like a lover sees to his partner. Shards of shadow shot out of the void bubble and found their mark on the prisoners pleading for death.

They were silenced instantly. She felt a wave of relief at having freed those souls of their torment. They would no longer be slaves of energy to the dark forces of the Draconian Necromancers. With that task done, she felt the spirit shift his will. There was a great rumbling as he stretched out his hands and ripped a hole in the fabric of space and time. It tore like a claw ripping through the firmament of reality, and in the next instant, they were inside it.

Eshu felt the form of her body twist and writhe as they were transported through the wormhole. She felt stretched and elongated, then squished to painful densities. All the while she felt the tether of the spirit twined around her own soul, keeping her safe, holding her from completely being torn apart.

They passed through the other side, and Eshu breathed in desperately. The edges of her vision blurred, and the boundary of where her body began and ended was still wavering back and forth in uncertainty. She felt the arms of the Fareen male wrap around her and pick her up, and in the distance, she could see the light of a shimmering city before her mind gave in, and she was swallowed into unconsciousness.

Back on the ship on Fareen, Griek held the space as

Cherena and Arelix viewed this ancient memory through the lens of the great Trichome plant. He, too watched this ancient scene take place for the first time. Within the infinite facets of the Trichomes, all knowledge of past, present, and future existed. Like an all-seeing eye, the entirety of the universe's moments lay within the power of the singing crystal forest. It seemed the story they witnessed was a love story very similar to their own. A story founded on two beings that loved one another against all odds.

Eshu awoke inside a small cavern that the spirit had carved into the desert rock. The spirit, which now shared the body of the Fareen male, sat in meditation, waiting for her to arise, and the second her eyelids flickered, he was at her side. She stared at him with a distant gaze before raising her hand to touch the dark withers of his cheek. And she smiled.

"You did it." She managed to say. "You freed us both."

"No." He replied. "It was you who set us free. It was your spell that broke the bonds of my prison. I am in your debt."

Eshu laughed lightly. "Well, if that is the case, noble spirit. Then you can start by telling me your name."

He frowned. "I am afraid I do not remember. I have been a prisoner so long; it seems I have lost my name in the process."

Eshu felt the pain in his voice. "Maybe together, we can find a new name for you." He smiled. "I would like that."

Eshu frowned and stared into the eyes of the man. Within, she saw two spirits. She saw the Fareen man, who had endured endless torture, and she saw the strange being whose soul had been imprisoned within the dark star obelisk within the Draconian Citadel. She addressed the latter.

"What world do you come from?" She asked. The spirit had to take the time to think about it.

"I come from a world much like this except all his in opposition. Where things attract here, they repel in my dimension. Where light shines, all his dark. Where nature here is good, it is corrupt in my world. Very few break away from the darkness. I fear that if it were not for my imprisonment by the Necromancers of your world, I too might have fallen subject to the darkness and corruption that is everywhere. But forced to observe how your Necromancers took the lives of others, I grew something in my heart that was not there before."

"And what was that?" Eshu replied.

"Empathy. I could not stop my nature, however. The Necromancers continued to use my powers to sap the lives of others, but as they forced my powers, I communicated with the spirits of those who they tortured and killed. I learnt of the good that they had within them, and I helped to numb their pain. The Necromancers were unaware of this, of course, and I had resigned myself to this fate. That was until you came along."

Eshu smiled and reached out a hand to touch the body that the two spirits inhabited. She could feel them become less separate, learning to merge with one another. The two lived in the wild of the cavern for a long while, and Eshu began to call the spirit Terya, which meant bringer of hope in her language. They eventually gave birth to two opposite twins. One had strong Fareen genetics, a golden sparkling baby, and the other had dominant Draconian genes, with scales and teeth and all.

At this point in time, Eshu had shapeshifted into a Fareen woman, and they were living in the heart of the capital city. Fareen had been colonized by the Draconians for the better part of ten generations. It was once a shining and sparkling example of life within the cosmos. Planet Fareen was a beautifully abundant planet, with a rich diversity of life, tucked in gentle orbit around its mother sun.

They were a highly spiritual and scientific race, merging both together to create incredible feats of technology. Many believe that the two disciplines were inherently separate in nature, but when the spirit lies at the heart of the universe, it must also inhabit the essence of technology. Without it, then beings may fall victim to their own creations. It has occurred on many planets and in many civilizations.

When a society or group of beings moves away from spirit and instead invests all their energy in the faulty pursuit of materiality, their souls will wither, and soon, their technology will outpace their own evolution, giving rise to the potential of darkness to take root.

The people of Fareen were wise and noble. They had pentagrammic, humanoid bodies with shimmering golden skin. Their skin adapted in such a way to better absorb the rays of their sun. Through their skin, they could store heat and energy, conserving it within the largest organ of their body.

Most of their technology was powered by this accommodation. Not only could the people of Fareen absorb energy from the sun and harness it for themselves, but they could also transfer that energy. This could be used to heal those who had developed sickness or to share energy in battle.

When it came to technology, however, the Fareen could pour this storage of energy into their devices, essentially powering their technology with the potential energy of the sun converted through their own bodies. Their technology was magnificent, carved from the light porous stone that lay at their bedrock. It most closely resembled a mixture of chalk and marble, laced with veins of gold throughout.

The veins of gold were perfect conductors for the energy they held, and the porous quality of the stone around it could hold that energy within its structure. They made their cities out of this stone, their architecture, their orreries and their technology. In a way, the people of Fareen and the cities they lived in were not separate from one another. Therefore, a desecration of this stone, or vandalism of any sort, was considered a great sin to their people. It was from this ancient art form and spiritual science that the Fareen people fashioned the first mystic weapons and fought the initial Draconic invasion.

But the people of Fareen were not a war-faring race. They were highly advanced and extremely intelligent, and for a long while, they managed to hold back the forces of the Draconian empire. But again, war and battle was estranged from them. Swordplay and artistry in weaponry were not anything new. Many Fareen nobles partook in dueling and sparring matches with one another, but it was seen as an art form closer to dance. They never struck to kill, and whilst they developed intricate and beautiful fighting forms, these were not effective or reliable in actual battle.

Their advanced technology was the only thing that managed to delay the initial invasion. Upon learning of the Draconian's advance, the technicians of Fareen fashioned powerful solar ray cannons that acted as high radiation and incredibly high-powered heat beams. These beams could obliterate a Draconian warship in a single fire. The Draconians had not anticipated how quickly the people of Fareen could adapt.

But truth be told, the people of Fareen never stood a chance. Their planet was rich in resources, and to the Draconians, it was an investment that they simply could not pass up. They increased their forces and rained down upon the planet in a scourge of ships that was too great to number.

The people of Fareen were outmanned and outclassed. The Draconians had been born into war. Trained from practically the moment of spawn. They were not only efficient and brutal but smart and deceptive as well.

Many capital cities were lost. Many Fareen perished. And like many other civilizations before them, the people of Fareen were put under the martial law of the Draconian Empire.

Their advancement of technology was halted, and many were forced to work for the Draconian government. The Fareen forgot many things about their true nature and lost a lot of the knowledge their ancestors once held. That being said, many still sold wares, and life was allowed to continue as a fragment of what it once was.

Fareen people hated the Draconians who continued to patrol their city, desecrating their lives with their mere presence. Eshu and her partner Terya fled to Fareen, knowing that little place was safe for them. She could not walk the streets as herself, for she was now an outlaw amongst the Draconians. So, she shapeshifted into a Fareen female, and they hid away for a while in the far reaches of the planet.

Terya had once been a Fareen, and Eshu had hoped that returning to his planet might restore some of the damage that had been done to his body. But no such thing happened. It had been sapped and aged to a point that was no longer renewable. He still resembled the race, except his face was hollow and sunken, and his skin no longer a shimmering gold but the dark of slate. Whatever soul had inhabited his body before capture was no longer what it once was. It had merged with the spirit from the crystal, and together, they had become something else.

Eshu did not care for the form, for as a Draconian, she knew how malleable and insubstantial a body truly was. It was what was inside that mattered. She and Terya shared a similar past. They were both born in a world that wanted them to be dark, a world that taught only cruelty and corruption. And both of them had resisted. Both of them had tried to seek another way. It was ultimately that seeking that had led them to one another.

In their darkness, they shared a solidarity in the guilt of their ancestors' sins. In the darkness, they strove to fight each day. Just because they were removed from any immediate influence, that did not undo the years of conditioning and horrors they had both witnessed and committed.

However, then, they had not known any better. Now they did, and slowly, they began to build a life for themselves. It was not easy, for whilst Eshu looked and appeared to be Fareen, she had none of the mannerisms and collective mindset of a true Fareen. She did not know their customs or their stories, language, or songs.

And Terya was something else entirely. He was of Fareen and recalled a life before he was captured. But his appearance was disconcerting, to say the least. His skin was so withered it could barely touch the sunlight without causing him pain. He had to wear thick robes and covered his arms in bandages, and any who lay eyes on him muttered prayers beneath their breath.

They hid away for many years, but Eshu would often

frequent herself to the larger cities and study in the ways of the Fareen people. After several years, she was recognized by many, even liked. She made friends, knew the merchants, and avoided the Draconian patrols like any other. Together, Terya and Eshu moved to the capital city and found a life for themselves there. Eshu soon forgot what it meant to be Draconian and fully embodied her new Fareen way. She became like them, was them. And yet she was not.

To the surprise of them both Eshu and Terya conceived children. They saw it as a great miracle, a miracle from the cosmos itself, and an acknowledgement of their fortune and the path they carved for themselves amidst all the darkness surrounding them.

And on the day when they came, Eshu gave birth to twins. One Fareen, the other Draconian. A female and a male, respectively. To Eshu, her children were the most beautiful things she had ever seen. They were not only perfect to her as a mother, but they represented something impossible, something inconceivable. A Fareen and Draconian born from the same womb. Mortal enemies joined through blood and love.

Eshu loved them more than anything, and Terya soon learned what it meant to have his soul fully invested in that of another, to love something and to care about a being above himself. But their joy was not long-lasting. There was no way Eshu could raise a Draconian child within the walls of Fareen. His mere presence would be a hostility to the Fareen and an alarm of her whereabouts to the Draconian empire.

Either way, it would most likely end with the death of her son. He would not grow the organ that allowed Draconian the ability to shapeshift for many years. It was different for every Draconian, and some never learned how to shapeshift at all. It was all genetic. But considering Eshu's lineage it would be very rare if she did not pass on the gene to her son.

Still, twenty-four years was a small amount of time to that of a Draconian. Barely even a spec in their lifespan. Regardless of that, the days would be long spent in hiding. She could not simply let her son grow in hiding. Hiding from the world only to shapeshift and hide himself some more.

She had to find another way. But there was not a single hospitable planet in the galaxy that did not hate the Draconian. Even those few allied races of beings who aided the Draconian in their conquest only did so out of their own desperate greed. Eshu could not return to Draconia, and she could not raise her son here. So, once again, she had come to a crossroads.

It was Terya who suggested they send him to Draconia. At first, Eshu was outraged. She could not even think of sending her son there to grow amongst the monsters that had raised her. But Terya made her see reason. Not all Draconians were monsters. That much was fair to say. It was a large number, burdened by brutal tradition and forged from the desperate need to survive as they evolved. But Eshu knew of kind beings within the Draconian Empire.

Draconians who removed themselves from the politics and war efforts and foul vampiric practices.

"We are the breakers of laws, the breakers of tradition," Terya spoke softly to her. "Since the dawn of our kind, no match in history has occurred like this. We will not pass down the trauma of our forefathers. The forge of this bond is what lives in our son's DNA. It will be carried on for eternity to come."

Of course, Terya was right. But just the mere thought of separating from her son almost tore her to pieces. "We have no other choice."

So, in secret, Eshu reached out to her aunt, who lived on the far reaches of a fully colonized Draconian planet. An aunt who had spoken her own disquiet about the Draconian regime to Eshu herself. Her aunt Derini had been cast out of the family for being upfront about her contrary beliefs, speaking about peace in a world that she wanted only to conquer.

It was in the dead of night under the veil of a stolen craft that Eshu handed her only son to Derini, baring the truth of his conception. Even as a radical amongst her own race, it was a hard pill to swallow for Derini, but she took the child regardless.

"I will raise him as my own." She vowed.

Never having had a child of her own, Eshu had given

her a gift despite what grief it caused her. "Take care of him. Try to guide him in the ways we have come to know."

Eshu wished she herself could have stayed. That all of them could have hidden out there. But her husband and daughter were also to be considered. If she remained in the colony then it would be her daughter who had to hide.

She would have to separate them. They would grow on separate planets with their own kind. At least they could live normal lives in the hope that one day they would meet one another later in life. She left her son behind, not able to bear the sight of turning back. Hoping and praying in her heart that he would come to find the good in himself, as she had done.

But the day would never come for Eshu to see her children grow. She would never get to see what came of them. For upon return to Fareen, upon return to her partner and daughter, she was intercepted. The Draconian militia had detected the stealth of her craft and seized her before she could even enter the atmosphere.

The capture was quick despite Eshu's efforts to evade them. They locked her out of her control and seized her in a gravitational beam, rendering her craft useless. She did not even have the chance to look back to the planet before she was injected with the Draconian fluid, which forced her to return to her original form.

Her head was covered with a bag, and the soldiers that captured her jumped directly to the Draconian home planet, where she was thrown on the ground in front of the Imperial Judicator. He found her guilty of the crimes of high treason and was sentenced to death after torture. They tortured her for days, trying to squeeze information out of her. Information about where she had been hiding, and who with... But even as her scales were peeled one by one from the flesh, Eshu never gave in.

Weeks went by in starvation, hooking her up to torture rigs designed to extrapolate the most pain imaginable. Still, Eshu never cracked. She died soon after and, in the moments before her death, caught a glimpse of the realm beyond. In that single moment as the light faded from her eyes, she was allowed a single perception of the future. Of a shimmering Fareen princess and a Draconian General meeting eyes across the battlefield, locked in the shock of love.

Then, all at once, her soul was gone. Untethered from the mortal realm, undone and never to be born again.

A chord struck in the heart of Cherena and Arelix as they witnessed this. The time within the vision of the Trichome sped up, and they watched the children grow, give birth, and die. The cycle of life repeated for ten generations until it was their own faces that they saw being birthed. The vision suddenly ceased, and the truth of their blood bond had been revealed.

Cherena and Arelix had been bound to one another through an ancient ancestral lineage. Inside both was the blood of Draconia and Fareen, and in their souls were the traces of the dark spirit that had been freed because of their great ancestor Eshu's compassion.

"It is true then," Ashka confirmed. "Prophecy has written your fates together."

Cherena and Arelix both stood and embraced one another, both seeing and feeling their bonds tracing back thousands of years.

"It was our ancestral parents that first joined our races together," Cherena said softly, looking into Arelix's eyes.

"It was because of Eshu's bravery. It was because she went against the rules of the Empire that we stand in front of one another today." Arelix added.

"We must continue her legacy," Cherena said grazing her fingers over Arelix's cheek, mirroring the action Eshu had done with Terya thousands of years ago. "Our heart connection holds the key to restoring peace and spreading the light of the Trichome throughout the universe. We must set out and align the universe."

Arelix nodded. "We are two halves of the same moon. With the light of your compassion, destruction must come in the face of the old ways. Our connection to the Trichome Star will light the way as you build the new world. I will destroy what no longer serves the path of prophecy. In this way, we may seek to reinvent our universe and those within it."

They both turned to Ashka and Griek.

"Will you help us?" Cherena asked, biting gently on

her lower lip with the anticipation of hope.

Griek bowed in service. "I am here to serve the Trichome and the prophecy of the ancient Oracle." He paused. "Excuse my blindness, for I am only a servant of the way, but I cannot see what you all do. I must ask. Will our actions truly make a difference? You speak of a new world, grown from the sacred Trichome frequency, but it was the Lumarians who once held that knowledge in their singing forest. At their time it was said no darkness existed. And yet, it was a Lumarian who eventually strayed from the divine law of the Trichome Star and manifested all the destruction and chaos we know today. If we do manage to stop the Draconian forces from seizing the ancient relic in the world of zero, then who is to say that the events of the past will not just repeat themselves over and over again in an endless loop. Does any of it even mean anything?" Arelix nodded thoughtfully.

"It is true what you say, honorable Griek," Cherena responded. "It can be easy to get lost in a nihilistic tendency when observing the greater cycles of the cosmos. But since the Lumarian epoch, have we not learned anything? The Lumarians were so set in their ways that they could not stop Lekiam from falling. The Oracle did nothing to ease his questions, did nothing to guide him. As wise and noble as the Lumarians were, they did not hold the agency of will as we do today. They were bound to fate, like a leaf to a river current. They were so insubstantial in their physicality that they were more ether than matter. We have grown, not as individuals, but in the soul archetype to which the Lumarians set into motion. Do you not see that the external manifestation of our circumstances is a physical representation of what is occurring in realms beyond our observable mind? We may not have the eyes to stretch across infinities horizon, but we are a part of a larger story."

"The cycle may repeat again and again, as you said, not by ourselves, but by other people in worlds and times so distant from now that we cannot even fathom what they should be. The battle itself may be eternal, but that does not mean we should not fight. It is not the lack of chaos that we seek but harmony with the resounding melodies of the universe. There will always be those who seek to strum a dissonant chord, and who are we to say that the dissonance is not part of all? How else can we understand what we are if not in the face of such an opposite mirror? We do not fight for some great cosmic notion of morality or truth. I fight to save my people and my family. I fight for a world where my people may grow and prosper and feel love until their last breaths."

Arelix nodded. "We all have our reasons for why we do anything. Were it not for the destructive ways of my people, this meeting would never have happened. Perhaps we should not be focusing on future moments or what lasting effect this will have in our timeline, but instead, be cherishing each moment that we are experiencing right now."

Ashka smiled. "And our answer lies somewhere in the

middle of it all. At the heart of us all are three primary instincts. Regardless of how evolved we like to think we are, at the core, only three tones resonate. Destruction. Creation. Preservation."

"Is there not a fourth?" Griek asked.

Ashka frowned. "What would that be, Noble Iki?"

"Non-action," Griek replied. "To simply exist without motive."

Ashka smiled, and his eyes lit up, turning his smile into a hearty chuckle. "I guess you are right, Griek. A state that supersedes even the primal forces themselves."

"How could that be?" Cherena asked. "Surely it is impossible to exist without motive."

"It may be hard to conceive, and yet it is possible to achieve," Ashka said knowingly. "Very few ever come to know the state of non-action, for even to strive for it is to miss the point." Ashka chuckled again. "But that is neither here nor there in our matters. Each of us has chosen what role we shall play in the coming events. Though those roles may differ in nature."

Cherena looked to Arelix and knew that he understood. "I have to use my powers. They are amplified by the alignment of the entity moons and the Trichome star. The Ancient Relic has been activated by the shockwave Arelix and I created, but it is meaningless unless we use it to our advantage."

"What is it you have in mind?" Griek asked.

"I must go to the front lines of battle. I can use the Trichome's energy to aid our forces in the battle against the dissonant. I can inspire and uplift our forces, raise them into the frequency of the Trichome and grant them an advantage over our enemy." Ashka nodded.

Arelix growled, and heads turned to him. "I wish I could come with you to the frontlines. But there is unfinished business that I must attend to. Decepti Mortar still seeks the Trichome Star. There is no doubt that with the activation of the Ancient Relic, his forces have locked onto the quantum signal. I need to stop him. I need to destroy them before they destroy themselves and the universe along with them."

Cherena met his eyes and held them with an overpowering sense of trust. "I believe in you." Ashka nodded. "It seems you both know what you must do." He turned to Griek. "As for me, I must return to the place I fear most. I believe there is still something I must do there. Will you join me?"

Griek hesitated. For a moment, he almost considered joining the King. But something stopped him. It was not a thought with reason but a knowing. Something he could not explain. "I do not know what role I must play from here on out. It was my task to guard the knowledge till the day of the prophecy came to be. I have fulfilled my function. There is no purpose required for me any longer."

Ashka went to retort, but Griek shook his head.

"I can see it now." He said softly, and a small smile

grew on his face. "It lies there, just on the other side of where nothing and all join to one."

Arelix frowned, and so did Princess Cherena. "I must go now," Griek said with finality.

"Where?" Princess Cherena asked, emotions welling in her heart.

He smiled at her. "I do not know."

Cherena blinked, disarmed by his answer. "You can't! We need your help!"

They had been working together to save the planet of Fareen for so long, and the Princess had found a great friend in the noble Iki. Tears started to flow at the thought of him leaving them. King Ashka put a hand on her shoulder. She looked up to meet the beast King's eyes.

"Griek must go his own way, and that is his choice to make. Just like each of us." He said softly. Cherena began to cry, and she rushed over, kneeling down and pulling Griek in for a hug.

"I will never forget your kindness in helping my people." She whispered.

Griek only smiled and returned the hug before pulling away. "I am sure I will meet each of you again. When all is said and done. Whether it be in this form or another."

Ashka met Griek's eyes knowingly. "Farewell, noble Iki."

And with that, Griek bowed and walked off the ship,

disappearing into the shifting sands beyond.

Princess Cherena stood at the opening of the spacecraft and watched the horizon for a long while after Griek had vanished from sight. After almost an hour had passed, Arelix came and stood by her side. She felt the presence of his emotions, his love for her thick in the air. She turned away and buried her head in his chest.

"I may be very new to this," Arelix said. "To the connection of hearts across the folds of time and space. But now I can see that even though we are separated in form, we are never truly alone."

Cherena nodded and allowed Arelix to guide her back into the craft, where King Ashka was waiting for them at the console. When he faced them, both Arelix and Cherena saw something else in his eyes. A second spirit was living within him.

"What Arelix says is true." The King said, through a voice that was both his own and another.

The Owlinian Sorcerer, who had merged with the soul of the King, also spoke. The King had something in front of him. He was mixing several compounds together in a flask and even took a golden drop from the sacred Trichome plant, mixing it into the rest of the alchemical liquid.

"We have the tendency to be limited by our senses." Ashka continued. "If we want to continue our communication across the vast distances that we will traverse, then we should partake in an ancient ritual I once learned about from a dear friend of mine."

The liquid the King had made swirled in the container, and Ashka handed it first to Arelix, beckoning him to drink the cup.

"This will ensure that our minds are connected, no matter how far apart we are from one another."

Arelix looked to Cherena, and she nodded her encouragement, and together all three partook in the sacred alchemical elixir that King Ashka and Barradow once shared.

"We must make haste now," Ashka said. "I will leave you with the craft that once carried my people through the cosmos."

"What of the sacred Trichome plant?" Cherena asked.

King Ashka smiled. "I think I know a people to whom we may entrust it with."

Moments later and, the King re-entered the cavernous homes of the native Fareen and knelt down as Zaya stared up at him with bright eyes.

"I have a very important task for you." King Ashka said. "I need you to look after the sacred knowledge contained here. Plant them if you like. I trust you to do what you know to be right."

Little Zaya accepted the capsule that contained the sacred golden plant and hugged it close to her chest.

"I bid farewell to you now." King Ashka extended his powerful Owlinian wings that extended from his shoulder blades.

They were massive, reaching an eleven-foot wingspan, and he took off into the air. Smiling one last time at the small girl whose soul he recognized from lifetimes ago, before taking to the stars and heading towards the unknown, following the calling in his heart.

Meanwhile, Princess Cherena used the grasshopper spacecraft that King Ashka had gifted her and took off toward the capital city of Fareen. She could sense in the fabric of spacetime that the shockwave she and Arelix had created had sparked great unrest amongst the universes. With the elevated state of awareness also came the fall of those who were not ready to step into the power and light that it offered.

The Draconian empire and their subsidiary races were launching a full-on assault, having picked up on the frequency. Arelix guided Princess Cherena on where to land and together they rushed into his Draconian space craft. It was there that they found that Decepti Mortor had pinpointed a quantum coordinate for the Ancient Relic.

Arelix had known of its existence only through myth, but Princess Cherena knew it to be real from the stories she had heard from Griek. Whilst they were gathering every one of their fleets, the shockwave sparked rebellion from all the colonies they inhabited. Races and beings of all kinds were fighting to bring down the Draconian Empire, and they needed Cherena's help.

"I have to go to the frontlines," Cherena said with urgency.

Arelix understood, even though it killed him to know she would be putting herself in danger. "Don't worry. The Trichome will protect me." Cherena said, sensing his emotions.

"It seems like we have only just returned to one another again after so many lifetimes, and now we must separate."

But the effects of the elixir were already taking place, and though she said it, she knew it was not true. She could see herself through Arelix's eyes. She could feel every ounce of the love they shared, not only from her side but radiating from him.

He smiled a genuine smile. A gesture she had never seen in a Draconian before.

"I must go too." He spoke. "I must bring down Decepti Mortor. If he falls, the Empire will be without a leader, and I must take his place."

She nodded. "I will see you in the end."

They embraced and the infinite feedback of their emotions echoed back and forth, the shockwave strengthening in power, and continue to send ripples of inspiration throughout the cosmos.

Taking all the will he had, Arelix separated himself, and Cherena retreated back into her spacecraft. They both took off and jumped to different parts of the universe, knowing that even though their bodies were separated, their minds were one, not only in the magical elixir of the plant medicine but in the unbreakable connection of their heart.

THE ELEVENTH CHRONICLE:

Universes Align

The entirety of the Draconian star fleet under the command of Emperor Decepti Mortor was in vicious search of the location of the Trichome star to which the ancient relic was said to exist. After receiving the intel from Arelix's stray dogs, he had set his sights on it. Decepti's life was coming to an end. He had relied on the ancient practices of vampiric necromancy to prolong his life far beyond any Draconian before him. Even though he lived, his life force was a meagre thread of what it once was, his spirit frail and his body weak. He lived on the teetering edge of death.

The cost of such rituals had eventually taken its toll, and he needed more and more life force each day to barely sustain himself enough to carry out his basic requirements of rank. The only reason he had not been usurped by the younger Draconian generals was because he held the knowledge they all sought.

He had been searching for the Trichome Star since his first rise to power all those eons ago when Lumaria had first been destroyed and the knowledge of the singing crystal forest transferred to the planet of Trichomia.

The universe had been split into two factions since the resonant shockwave that emitted from the origin of Cherena and Arelix, fracturing the timeline into a perfect balance of polarity. Those who aligned with the empathy shockwave became harmonic in alignment with the highest frequency of the universe, but those whose hearts had failed became aligned in perfect dissonance with the shockwave's vibrations. Most of the Draconian Empire had become disharmonic and were now ravaging the planets they controlled.

War had broken out in every inch of the universe. A war of the opposites beings in alignment with the Trichome and those against it. And so, the Trichome wars had begun. Desolation and Armageddon were in every solar system. The Draconian and their disharmonic allies expended all their resources, but Decepti reigned them in an all-in attempt to reach the mythical World of Zero.

Their destructive ionic thrusters tore through the fabric of space, and they shot, commandeered, and destroyed any spacecraft that got in their way. Already, the three active members of the New Unity, Princess Cherena, Arelix, Ashka and Griek, could feel the mass destruction that was going on in the universe. Within the grasshopper ship that Cherena flew in, a great map of the entire universe lit up with the light of war.

Ashka could feel and see through the eyes of both Arelix and Cherena and trusted them in the task of stopping the Draconians, not only from winning the battle against the rebels but from reaching the Ancient Relic that lay in the World of Zero. Despite that, Ashka could not shake the feeling that there was another threat. A threat perhaps even greater than all the others that they were facing.

With his astral mind granted to him by the merging of Barradow, he surfed the cosmos and tried to locate the source of the threat, following the sense of impending doom in his chest. But no matter where he looked, there was nothing visible to him in the known universes. Barradow's part of him came back time and time again with no results.

Even though no threat could be found, Ashka knew where his task would lead him. He could feel the familiar pull of a hidden part of the universe. The pull back to the world of Zero.

Meanwhile, Princess Cherena hyper-jumped to the closest warzone, appearing right in the center of the battlefield. Chaos ripped through the material plane. Warships from all races were in a full-out assault on one another. There were the recognizable Draconian locusts, among many. Some were in the shape of long cigars that fired seismic pulses of destructive energy. Others were giant whales of crafts, swallowing smaller ships in their hangars and crushing them in an inferno of fire and metal.

Small zip fighters shot around the battlefield in squads at extreme speeds. They were easily the most agile and nimble ships, firing lasers and moving like a hive of wasps. Princess Cherena was in shock at what she saw. The waves of emotions she felt through her empathic abilities were pure chaos.

"This is madness!" She muttered to herself.

She could see that the tides were not in favor of the rebel forces. The Draconian army was simply too large and mighty for the rebels of this star system to fight off. She knew from the scanner on the ship that many more of these battles were occurring in different parts of the universe. There was no way she alone could turn the tides. She and Arelix would have to work together. She needed him to take down Decepti. All Cherena could do was help to alter and raise the consciousness of the rebels fighting for peace. But even then, her power was limited.

Cherena closed her eyes and dug deep into herself, finding that endless well of light within her. This was her connection to the Trichome star, the power she had been blessed with as a part of a long ancestry of Fareen royalty.

Channeling the power of the Trichome through her body, she emanated another pulsar wave of strength.

Everyone on the battlefield felt it, even though she hung back on the fringes of the battle. Those who fought on the side of peace suddenly tuned into the frequency of the Trichome. Their eyes lit up with celestial fire, and their minds became enhanced. They could see deeper into the fabric of time, and the Draconians felt the opposite. The Trichome's energy dragged them down, making them sluggish as they resisted its pull.

The rebels could see moments entire seconds before they happened, allowing them to dodge missiles and projectiles that otherwise would have killed them. The tides of battle quickly began to shift. Despite this great advantage, Cherena knew it was only a small change. She still had many more systems to aid, and even though the rebels here had an advantage, the Draconian fleet still outnumbered them greatly.

She feared that as soon as the effects of her empathic vibrations wore off, the rebels would fall once more. If it were not for her connection to Arelix, she may have fallen victim to the tides of hopelessness. But his drive pushed her onwards, and sending out one more pulsar wave of inspiration, Cherena jumped to the next system.

Arelix wove through the tunnel in the fabric in space, locking his coordinates onto Decepti Mortar's mothership. He had stolen one of the vessels left behind by the troops on Fareen. No one had heard of his sudden turn of sides, but he was notably an advisory towards Decepti Mortar. Arelix would have to shapeshift into one of his troops in order to get close enough.

The only issue with that was the closer he got to Decepti, the deeper he went into the mothership, the more defenses he would have to go through. Being Draconian, they were all highly suspicious of their own kind. They were well aware of how easy it was to shapeshift past security protocols, so they had technology that revealed if one was showing their true selves.

Once Arelix got to that point, there would be no choice but to reveal himself. It didn't matter, though, because the light of the Trichome was on his side, enhancing his senses and clearing his mind. The wormhole through space opened up and he burst forth into the airspace around Decepti's mothership.

Before he shapeshifted, Arelix consciously connected with Cherena. Their souls joined, and she reached into the womb of her power, seated in the infinite ocean of potential, and as it pulsed through her veins, she let the power flow through Arelix. He felt the strength she radiated, and it gave him everything he needed. Their souls were with one another.

Arelix proceeded to the main docking bay. Approaching the ship, he could already see the hyperjump thrusters powering up. It would not be long before they ripped open a massive wormhole and leaped towards the World of Zero, towards the quantum location of the ancient relic, which continued to emanate the frequency of the tri-chome star like a cosmic antenna.

Arelix shapeshifted into a high ranking officer within Decepti's command and was greeted with salutes within the hangar bay from several of the lower soldiers. He growled and strode past them, embodying different characteristics and mannerisms, presenting a domination that he had honed through thousands of years of practice.

But before he made it very far, he was stopped at one of the adjoining doors to the main part of the mothership.

"Officer Igrax, we were not expecting you back so soon. We thought you were fighting the rebels in the Serenian system."

Arelix stared the Draconian down. "You think I would have returned if I didn't have reason?!" Arelix had to think quick. "There is something the High Commander Emperor needs to hear. It pertains to the treasure he has been seeking. If you do not step aside, then I will make you. And your head will no longer be attached for you to process the fact that I have done so."

The draconian hissed, but he stood aside, opening the door. Threat of beheading was often a good way to get what you wanted amongst the Draconians. Arelix thrashed his head and strode through into the main body of the mothership. All sorts of preparations were being made for the JUMP, which was good for Arelix because almost everyone was occupied.

It took a lot of power and resources to tear a hole in

time and space big enough for the mothership to fit through. Not only that, but they had to keep it stable during the entire journey, or there was a risk that the wormhole would collapse and crush everything within it.

Arelix knew that the ancient relic was in the World of Zero, and it would not be easy to get to. He strode through the ship and made his way to a maintenance tunnel. A mechanic looked up and was about to question Arelix's presence there, but Arelix killed him before the draconian even had the chance to draw a breath. Arelix destroyed his body with an incinerator gun and assumed the draconian mechanic's identity.

The maintenance shafts and tunnels wove like a network of veins throughout the entire ship. The gates and doors would raise too many questions, and the technology would unveil him, so instead, Arelix decided to creep unseen through the part of the ship that only lowly mechanics would normally have access to, bypassing the security protocols on the main parts of the ship.

Arelix had lived on this mothership as a youth. He had been forged in the brutal training regiments here. And he knew every inch of the ship. Arelix ripped free a hatch and clambered inside, moving stealthily through the inner arteries of the mothership towards the High Commander Decepti Mortar.

Meanwhile, Ashka was flying on the wings that had been born of his merging with Barradow, heading directly towards a natural stargate at the edge of the Fareen sun.

The stargate was a natural ripple in the fabric of spacetime that would allow him to take the organic avenues back to the place where he had exiled himself.

It was a harrowing mission. Ashka never thought he would return to the world of Zero. He had spent eons wasting away there, turning to stone, and the memories of that guilt and shame were still fresh despite all that he had witnessed in the last days. If it were not for the bond he felt with the two others who fought to uphold the universe and also with Barradow, who now was one with his soul, Ashka would not have been able to take the leap.

But as the natural stargate pulled him in, Ashka allowed himself to let go, to let his heart bring him back to where the universe needed him. In his next blink, Ashka was no longer surrounded by the familiar texture of the void around him. He stood on the planet of zero as liquid metals swirled beneath his feet.

In the sky, hues of purple flowed like the rivers of the etherium, and as Ashka gazed up to the heavens, he noted for the first time that the three entity moons were in the perfect eclipse of one another, with the crystalline, diamond, Trichome Star eclipsed behind them all. The edges of the Trichome star still leaked out, like light bleeding through from the edge of a curtain. It cast the planet of Zero in a diffraction of light that stretched the shadows.

Ashka knew this place to be the purgatory where he had spent countless eons in his own exile. Though he had been locked in a chamber deep within. The surface of the planet was alive with living metals, though there was not another soul in sight. For some reason, this place was calling to him. Ashka turned and took a step forward. The metal beneath his feet fragmented and crunched before turning back into a solid-liquid that he could walk upon.

In the distance was a massive mountain that shot up from the ground like a jagged spire. At the very tip, an archway in the stone revealed a glimmering object that shone a ray of rotating light. He could feel Barradow in his thoughts, and he knew that Arelix and Princess Cherena also saw what he saw.

All three of them stopped to stare through King Ashka's eyes.

"The ancient relic." Their voices said in unison through one another's minds.

It stared back at them. This was what Griek had been speaking about. The relic that controlled and modulated the Trichome frequency throughout the universe. It was this ancient relic that had picked up on the frequency shockwave that Arelix and Cherena had produced and transmitted its energy throughout the universe, radiating the alignment of the three entity moons and the Trichome star itself.

Other than the relic there was no other movement on the planet Zero. It was eerie and haunting to be walking on the ground of such desolation. Yet, in the very back of his mind, King Ashka could hear a sonic vibration emanating from the planet. Perhaps the very vibration that caused the metals to flow as forms of liquid.

Ashka blinked. "Why have the tides of the cosmos carried me here?"

It was Barradow's mind that replied within the King. "Perhaps the task you have been brought here for is still yet to be."

Meanwhile, back at the mothership, Arelix had returned to his stealth mission through the engineering tunnels and air ducts of the spacecraft. It was hard to keep focused with his awareness being split into three different minds. He could see and feel his lover, Princess Cherena, continuing to inspire and invigorate the rebel battle troops throughout the various parts of the universe. And the King had reached some part of the universe that did not even seem real.

But Arelix had to keep his mind focused. He snuck through the tunnel systems of the ship, and soon enough, he could sense power in the air. Flicking his tongue out, he tasted the familiar scent of his former mentor. Decepti was nearby. Peering through the gap in the air grate, he could see into the large cathedral-like room that was Decepti's throne chamber.

He was a shadow of his former glory. Around him was the fresh scent of rotting corpses, and he had wires and tubes hooked up to him. Decepti was drinking from the blood of one of his soul-leeches, a warm-blooded being who was kept captive solely for the purpose of keeping Decepti alive through ancient vampiric practices.

Arelix had once participated in those practices. He remembered the power that would flow through his veins when he sapped the life force of another being. But Decepti had far extended his life span. He had been alive for eons of time. His body was thin, and Arelix assumed that it would take more and more life force just to keep him alive.

He sat at his throne above a long table of black obsidian, and around the table sat his member of the council. If Arelix burst in right now, the council members would be upon him before he could end the Draconian Emperor's life.

Arelix snarled under his breath and retreated back into the shadows of the maintenance tunnels. He needed to find another access point to Decepti, and Arelix had been in the emperor's throne room enough times to know where.

Princess Cherena jumped to the fourth battle star system. The scene here was just the same as many others. An all-out celestial war. The Draconian forces were a horde of destruction. There were dozens of star systems still to visit and already Princess Cherena was feeling the fatigue of using her powers in such rapid succession. The power of the Trichome star was endless and eternal, but her body was still mortal. Channeling the immense power of the Trichome diamonds was taking its toll on her body.

It was like running millions of volts of currents through her nervous system all at once. Being of Fareen she had been born to channel the power of her sun and use it to activate the various technological stations throughout the planet. But she had only been channeling the distant rays of her system sun, and only ever in small amounts. This was something else entirely. It was like trying to tame the force of a lightning bolt. Rather, thousands of lightning bolts. Her nervous system already felt on the fringes of being fried.

She needed to find a way to channel the energy of the Trichome without killing herself in the process. There were still many star systems to visit, and if she didn't stop the Draconian forces, then it wouldn't matter if Arelix succeeded in killing Decepti. Another Draconian General would just usurp him. She needed to ensure that their forces were not in the condition to take over once Arelix sized the emperor's throne.

Cherena turned to the console within the ship. The King had thought it best to ensure that the sacred living plants of the Trichome frequency had been left behind on Fareen just in case Cherena was killed in the frontlines. But Cherena had requested that one be left behind. She pressed a button, and in the center of the vessel, a capsule rose, revealing a golden, glowing plant.

There had to be a way to use the plant. Perhaps she could use it like a transformer, stepping down the frequency of the Trichome light so that she could bear it within her body, then amplify it once more as it left. Reaching out within the network of minds, the princess reached past the King and straight to Barradow, asking him directly. They were all connected. They knew each other's memories and deepest selves. She knew of his past and knew that of all of them, he would be the one who could help the most. It was his elixir after all that had connected them.

Princess Cherena felt the deeper fusing of Barradow's mind. She could see him understanding her problem and felt his mind as it began to find a solution. Cherena let go of her control and let the Owlinian sorcerer step into her body, let him move her limbs like a puppet. His mind was like a supercomputer. She had never truly felt an intelligence as incredible as his. He was not limited by the function of neurons and a brain. Barradow was an astral entity capable of accessing the *akasha*, which offered endless knowledge of the past, present, and future.

As he accessed her, she could feel him tracing the veins of her power deep into her connection with the Trichome star. Vast amounts of knowledge passed through Cherena, and a seemingly infinite number of connections seemed to circulate in her mind's eye. Then, together, they began to work. Cherena snipped a piece of the golden trichome flower off of the plant and began to use an advanced crucible to heat the golden trichome nugget.

Through the vast amount of knowledge, she was processing, she knew that if she heated the sacred plant, she could extract a vital component from it. She could already see what Barradow was planning, even though he did not communicate with her verbally. Extracting the vital component, together they began to synthesize it into a liquid.

In haste, she assembled a rig with tubes and vials and steam pumps. The golden liquid passed through many stages, diluting itself into a potent extract that dripped slowly into a beaker.

She could smell the fumes of the plant, and just inhaling the runoff, her mind was already beginning to expand even more than it had before. Geometric swirls of patterns began to appear in the spaces between objects like there were invisible threads connecting everything together in some divine tapestry.

She could see that the plant was alive, radiating an aura of golden symmetry. Once invisible, biochemical signals were now visible to her, and she could see how her nervous system interacted with the plant. She reached for the beaker that was now full and hesitated as she raised the golden liquid to her lips. Then, closing her eyes, she slowly sipped the sacred liquid.

Her entire body filled with warmth. The warmth of an infinite sun is synthesized into a living plant and transmuted into golden nectar. It was sweet and, at the same time tasted of the ground and soil. She could trace the warmth as it descended into her stomach, and as soon as the liquid began to digest, she felt something activate. Her veins began to glow with the golden light as the spirit of the plant integrated with her body.

It filled her nervous system with a profound strength and vitality. It regenerated the fried nerves and healed her system. She could feel an endless power surging through her, and when she reached once more for her power, for the well of infinite energy that was directly connected to the trichome star, she knew that this time it would not do her any harm. The golden nectar she and Barradow had created acted like a shield, like a conduit for the energy to surge through her without overloading her nervous system.

Cherena opened her eyes, and her golden skin was glowing, an aura that extended far beyond her physical body. In fact, she could see the aura, shimmering in brilliant glory, extending even past the walls of the spacecraft. She not only felt her connection to Arelix and Ashka, but she felt a profound connection to the universe. Her entire life, she had felt separate. Integrating the sacred medicine of the living plant of Trichomia had undone that. She saw herself in everything as if the cosmos was one great mirror reflecting her greater self-back to her. She was not alone. She had never been alone. Everything was connected. Everything was part of the same universal heartbeat. She saw the invisible etheric threads that connected everyone, enemies and allies alike. This was all one great symphony, and she was part of it.

Smiling, Cherena dug back into the well of power and let loose another empathy shockwave onto the battlefield. This time, the Trichome liquid plant was there to help, and the energy passed through her without harm, blasting forth in a shockwave greater than she had ever produced before.

Arelix felt the shockwave and was stunned in his place

deep within the guts of the maintenance tunnels. Love poured through him, and he felt what Cherena did. He felt the profound connection to everything, every bolt and screw, every cell and spec of air. He even felt a connection to all the Draconians upon the mothership. He knew that he and them were one and the same. And from a strange part of his mind, he knew that his final act would be an act of murder on himself, and this act would be one of kindness. He would not kill Decepti in hatred. He would finally free the emperor from the chains that had been holding him back his entire life. The very chains that had once ensnared Arelix himself.

Arelix forced himself to stand. He was now directly above the emperor's throne, looking down upon him from a grate in the ceiling. He could hear Decepti's ragged breaths. The Draconian emperor was mere moments away from death. If it was not for the fact that he continuously sustained himself using dark magic, then he would have died a long time ago. Arelix broke the vent and dropped.

The emperor did not even sense Arelix falling. Arelix pulled out a knife in mid-air. Some heads from the council turned in shock. But in the next moment Arelix hand his knife deeply embedded in the emperor's chest. All of a sudden, the rest of the world melted away, seized by shadows that encased Arelix and the emperor in a cocoon.

The emperor now lay on the floor, gasping for breath. Arelix knelt by his side.

"N-No. I was so close!" Decepti Mortar growled, reaching towards the shadows with a grey-clawed hand.

He had lost all color and pigment in his draconian scales, and his regenerative abilities declined after so many years of extending his life. The tubes that continuously fed him blood had been disconnected, and he now lay bare before Arelix.

"Don't you see?" Arelix said softly. "The knowledge of Trichomia. It was never something physical. It was never something you could take by force."

"You lie!" Decepti retorted, coughing up blue blood. "I saw it for myself. I heard the crystal singing forest with my own ears." He turned to Arelix with rage and betrayal in his eyes. "You are a disgrace to Draconia. With that knowledge, we would finally be able to settle. All the war and conquest would have come to an end."

"That is where you are wrong," Arelix replied. "The knowledge of the Trichome star was always available to you. The singing forest was merely it's physical manifestation, a window upon which to gaze into. It's true knowledge lives within the very fabric of the universe itself. A wise Iki once told me that its knowledge was always ready for those who sought it with pure heart."

Decepti went to speak, but he only coughed up more blood.

"I am afraid that all you would have found at the end of the road was your own destruction," Arelix replied and bowed his head. "May you find peace in death; I offer you forgiveness for all you have done. You will see that you and the Trichome Star have never been separate but connected all along."

Arelix dug the knife in deeper and dragged it up, raking through organs. At first, Decepti's expression furrowed into confusion. But as death began to take its hold on him, Arelix watched as the emperors' eyes shifted from confusion to understanding. They widened as if to express he were peering in on something great. An invisible light, but a light all the same, filled his vertical pupils, and Arelix knew that Decepti could now see past the chains of his mortal life.

Instead of reaching for the shadows, Decepti now reached for the light. A small smile appeared on his face, and as the final breath escaped his lips, they formed into two words.

Thank you.

Then, in one quick motion with his other long sword, he cut off the emperors head holding it with his hand as the light left his eyes, and Decepti's body went limp and fell to the ground. Arelix closed his own and took one breath in the presence of death. The unexplainable shadows that had encircled them fell away, and all of a sudden, reality came back into focus. All the council members were on their feet, weapons drawn. Arelix stood calmly and faced them all.

"I am your Emperor now. If any wish to challenge me, then you may step forward now."

Decepti Mortar had been killed. An emperor and war general who had been leading the majority of the Draconians for countless millennia. The council members all exchanged glances with one another, and then, one by one, they knelt down on one knee and lowered their heads in submission to Arelix's takeover. As was the Draconian way.

Arelix pointed to Decepti Mortor's body. "See to it that he has a proper Draconian burial fit for an emperor."

Draconian attendants rushed into the room and removed the body. Arelix watched as Decepti Mortor was taken out on a hovering golden stretcher. Once the body was removed, Arelix sat down on the throne and looked down upon the council members.

"As my first act as Emperor, I order the nulling of the JUMP. Power down the mother ship."

A council member went to object, and Arelix threw his knife into the Draconian's throat before the words could escape his mouth.

"Does anyone else have anything to say?"

They watched as the council member's bodies crumpled to the ground, shaking their heads and rushing off to cancel the JUMP. Arelix did not like what he had to do, but he knew the Draconian way. They only responded to violence and power. It would take many generations of reprogramming to revolutionize the Draconian ways.

It was done. Arelix had taken over the largest Draconian Empire in the universe. He ordered the immediate retreat of his armies, and for those draconians that were not under his control, he sent troops to pacify.

Princess Cherena had just made it to the final star system when all the troops retreated. She had not even used her powers and knew through her connection with Arelix that the fighting was finally over. She slumped down in exhaustion. Even with the aid of the golden Trichome liquid, it had been an exhausting task for herself. She had seen so much death in the last relative days, and the weight of that death was finally taking its toll on her.

Meanwhile King Ashka had made it to the top of the mountain, watching as the ancient relic sent cosmic gong-like reverberations outwards, radiating the Trichome signal and literally altering the vibrational fabric of the universe. It was obliviating. Completely all-consuming. It took all of Ashka's will not to melt into the frequency. There were wavelike cymatics patterns flowing through the air, geometric codes of energy diffusing outwards into open space. Ashka was filled with awe as he beheld the Trichome frequency resonating in such purity through the relic. Even within the facets of the singing crystal forest, the sound waves of the Trichome Star were distant, ephemeral, and long travelled echoes of what he felt here.

For a sharp moment, he stared into the eye of creation, stared into the blueprint of the many universes this frequency bled through. But beneath that awe, beneath the glory of witnessing creation, was something else. At first, he could barely sense it at all, consumed by the radiating sounds emanating from the relic. However, bit by bit, it began to creep up on him. It started with a small knot in the King's gut, barely large enough to fit on the head of a pin, and as he tuned into that sensation, it grew louder, dissonating in a frequency of dread that rose up from the pit of his stomach and into his chest.

Something was coming. It felt wrong. Wrong in the most perverted of ways. It was everything the Trichome Star wasn't. As the feeling began to grow, Ashka realized it was the exact inverse of the frequency rippling outwards from the relic. Suddenly, feeling fear, King Ashka turned his head to the heavens, gazing up into space. But there was nothing. It was empty, save for the entity moons in eclipse with the Trichome. All was well... And yet it was not.

He reached out to Princess Cherena and Arelix with his mind, but they had already picked up on what he was feeling. He needed them. He didn't know why, but he needed them. Whatever was coming, Ashka would not be able to face it alone. He thought he was strong enough. But the power that he was tapping into that wrong and dissonant frequency was just as consuming as the Trichome Star, but in all the worst ways. If the Trichome frequency held love and creation, order, and harmony in its vibration, then this opposition was... It was hatred. It was malice. It was the vicious tear of chaos and destruction.

"We are with you." Came the voices of both Cherena and Arelix. At that moment, Ashka drew in a sharp breath, breathing in the currents of the Trichome Star. His eyes filled with a fierce solar light, and he extended his arms outwards, clapping them together a moment later, creating a powerful shockwave force that split a crack in the fabric of spacetime. In the next second, Arelix and Cherena appeared before him in veiled silhouettes of light. Barradow helped to hold the portal open, and as Ashka released his hands, both lovers materialized in the space before him.

Ashka stared at them with the ferocity of a sun in his gaze. "The fight is not yet over. There is still one last thing we must face. And we must face it together."

Princess Cherena could feel exactly what the King was feeling. It lay under the tides of the Trichome. An ominous force, larger than she had ever felt before, growing closer and closer. She grabbed Arelix's hand and set her soul to the moment. They would either stop what was coming or die trying.

Meanwhile, in the dark and empty reaches of space, at the farthest corner of the universe, lay a black hole. This black hole was the portal into an inverse universe, a realm of antimatter, the exact opposition of the knowable universe. At the center of this inverted universe was a Black Diamond star, one which destroys all life, spreading tendrils of malice amidst the antimatter.

Amidst this universe, the ancient demonic spirit beings known as the Dystopian thrived. Their hearts had collapsed upon themselves, creating internal black holes.

Their bodies are wrath-like, chaotic maelstroms of energy and hateful intent, and they inhabit a dark comet that orbited the black diamond star.

No being from the known universe had ever found a way to travel to the inverted realm, for any matter that made contact within the antimatter universe was instantly annihilated. When matter and antimatter make contact, they cancel one another out, destroying each other in a burst of energy. If any being of matter were to find a way to traverse into this realm, they would be instantly destroyed as well as any spacecraft they had used to travel

there. Though one being did make it and was living amongst the Dystopians at this very moment.

The Dystopians had been harnessing the power of the Black Diamond star to create an extremely advanced weapon of mass destruction, purely out of the desire stemming from their own nature. Just as beings yearn to create, manifesting beautiful works of art and tools for creation, the Dystopian wished to destroy, and their weapon was their magnus opus.

If this weapon were to find its way into the known universe, it would cancel all atomic matter in a single moment and annihilate the whole of existence in every universe and dimension of matter. It was an invention of terrible greatness. It was a weapon to end all, returning all into the blank space of nothing.

The dark occult master Illuminatus X managed to survive the destruction of Trichomia when he was captured there. Using dark magic, he managed to save himself by inversing the field of his atomic structure. As a result, he was inverted into the opposite universe and found himself wandering in the realm of antimatter.

It was from these beings that the partner of Eshu came, the spirit who became one in the withered form of the Fareen male. Terya. He had originated from this realm, and the Draconians had been drawing from its power for countless generations. It had been harnessed but never ventured. The only way the two realms could interact was through the boundary crystals that acted as bleeding points between the veil of the two realms.

Terya had grown and was forged in the destructive impulse of the Dystopians. Where beings in the known universe contained souls of life, the Dystopian held the opposite within themselves. The nature of the soul was to create, to preserve and to blossom. To go against the nature of the soul was to destroy it, to invert it, much like what the Draconians did to their own souls. Like a star, the soul lived in a being, growing as its nature was fulfilled and diminishing when gone against.

The Dystopians were unmakers. They began with the tearing, maelstrom chaos of a black hole at the center of their being. Any soul, if corrupted and violated, had the potential to become something similar. That was the truth of a universe with free will. Likely, the potential for the black hole essence of the Dystopians, if fought, could eventually become a soul. Everything here was in inverse after all.

It was through this free will that Terya managed to free himself from the chaos of his destructive essence and grow within him the beginning of a soul. The Draconian's using dark magics had managed to infiltrate his realm and he was by chance captured amongst many of his kind, bound within the dark crystal that lay at the center of the Draconian Citadel. It was here that he was forced against his will to harm and sap the life out of other beings, granting power to those of the Draconian nobility. Until the day came that Eshu set him free.

If Illuminatus X had any semblance of a soul before entering, it was destroyed and wrought to nothing in the chaos of his transformation, in the inversion of his atomic structure and mind. The Inverse anti-verse was not unified in its structure like the known universe he had come from. It was fractured and chaotic. There were no rules that coincided with one another. It was complete freedom. Or so freedom was how he and the Dystopians saw it.

The rule of order was a prison to them. The order of the known universe, the unification and the single seed syllable that ran through it was to be locked into a law of nature. Illuminatus X had never known freedom like this before. Freedom to destroy and unmake however he so pleased. This was the answer he had been searching for his entire life. The beings in the known universe thought they had free will, but they were bound to the natural laws, they would never know what true freedom was.

This inverse realm was beautifully dark and chaotic and order-less. Free of boundaries, with laws crumbling and crashing against one another. Many different types of beings existed within this realm, but the Dystopians were dominant, just like the Lumarians had once dreamt in the opposite universe. However, with all their chaos, they still bound themselves to certain rules.

In the center of the realm was a black diamond star that did not radiate outwards but inversed inwards, consuming and ravishing life instead of creating. For some reason, the Dystopians venerated this star, honored and protected it. It seemed to be a very contradiction in the way they should live.

It seemed that even in chaos, some order existed. Just how in the universe of order, there was chaos. The polarities and balances were shifted, however. But Illuminatus had seen both sides, a privilege that few, if anyone, ever got to see. Was there something beyond it all? Was there something beyond the polarity? He learned over time that even in the chaos, the Dystopian beings were bound by their attachment to a lack of order, which was a prison in itself.

Illuminatus sought to find something greater.

There had to be something that superseded all of it. A true freedom in the lack of chaos and order, beyond destruction and creation. He yearned to find this state of existence. But first, he needed to know more about the Dystopians and this strange realm. Without the laws of the known universe on the inverse matrix of the anti-verse, beings were not bound to space as others were.

Illuminatus only had to will, and it was. He shapeshifted and found himself amongst the Dystopians. They were wraiths with erratic behaviors. Their forms are never pinned down, always shifting, always changing. Their time flowed from moment to moment, place to place.

There was no true pattern to their behaviors, no rhythm, no cadence. But at the same time, they were bound to that lack of rhythm, bound to their disharmony. They were not free; Illuminatus came to realize after long moments of imitating them and learning their ways. He found he could not imitate one as he could in the known universe, but all he had to do was not imitate them, un-bind himself. It was the opposite of how he learned to shapeshift in the other realm. Instead of learning from them, he had to unlearn himself.

They were beings untethered from the limiting scope of the ego. They were the quantum field before it col-lapsed, except there was no pattern of waves, no laws to create synchronicity. There was a great knowledge here in the unlearning of what one believed to be. In the unrav-elling of identity and the unleashing of pure, destructive, chaotic energy.

Except it was not mere destruction. Things were cre-ated as well. It was impossible to avoid the duality. How-ever, creation was the rare event of a supernova black hole in the known universe. Where stars destroyed to create there, here it was the opposite. Stars are created to destroy.

And even within the forges of endless destruction and constant unmaking, something managed to survive. Something managed to withstand that destruction. Just how the purest diamond could withstand the hardest drill, an ancient dark relic existed, immune to the destruction around it.

It grew a way to adapt. It unmade and made itself constantly, dissolving and reappearing. Where did the antimatter go when it was absorbed back into nothingness, and how did it return? The relic fascinated Illuminatus, as it did the Dystopians. It had been created as a by-product of the Dystopian's destruction. The aftermath and fallout had birthed its existence. An eternal anomaly in the chaos and constant desolation of antimatter.

Over the millennia, Illuminatus studied the ancient dark relic and learned how to harness its powers. Stretching his mind through the fabric of the inverted universe, using the Dark relic, he caught wind of the Dystopians and found the weapon they created. The weapon was, in fact, the comet that they lived on. Their world was a ticking time bomb of ultimate destruction, only held in balance, like a cosmic clock, because of its orbit around the Black Diamond star.

All it would take to set it off was to find a way to bring it into the regular universe. Illuminatus X reached out to these dystopic beings by casting an inverted form of his astral body, amplified by the strength of the Dark Relic. They were surprised to see a being other than themselves, and at first, they tried to destroy him.

But Illuminatus X was strong and well-versed in the dark arts. Using the power of the relic, he managed to create a bubble of antimatter around his astral form, which protected him from being consumed.

Illuminatus X knew of their passion for destruction, having observed them for some time, and proposed his plan. He told them of his universe, that there were beings of love and creation, and told them of King Ashka and the singing forest. He told them of the Trichome Star, and if left unchecked, it would eventually destroy the Dystopic way of life. Illuminatus X needed their weapon, and he would use every ounce of his power to get it.

So, Illuminatus X gave the Dystopians something they had never truly known before. He gave the order. Structured thoughts, series of events, time in linear motion. They revulsed and writhed against it, fighting the prison of what Illuminatus offered them through the channeled power of the dark relic.

He bound them to it, imprisoning them within the knowledge he had taken from the other side. They begged and pleaded to be set free. Illuminatus again revealed that this was what beings on the other side fought to protect.

Reveling his power over them, he dominated their

chaos. He beat rhythms into the fabric of their world, creating them, solidifying them. To the Dystopians, it was the ultimate form of torture.

Only when they were on their last limb did they finally give in. They said they would allow Illuminatus X to take the dark relic so long as he freed them from the prison of order. But being the Draconian he was, Illuminatus didn't free them, and took the relic regardless.

There would be nothing left of them to remember what they were once his plans came to fruition. With this relic, he could find the truth. If this dark relic existed, then on the other side of the realm was one of opposition. Only when these two relics, dark and bright, came together could Illuminatus know the freedom he had been seeking. The place beyond chaos and order, the knowledge that came at the end of all existence, when the great dream was sent to rest, and all returned back to what was before.

Illuminatus X harnessed the power of the dark relic and seized the weapon with his psycho-telekinetic force, transporting himself and the weapon to the inverted black hole that bridged the inverse universe with the universe of matter. All he had to do now was use the dark hole as a gateway, and the second the antimatter weapon made contact with the material universe, all that was known would be gone in a single instant. But little did he know that simultaneously, in the other universe, the trio of Ashka, Cherena and Arelix were waiting.

Ashka began to feel the crushing force in his soul as

that dark, inverted frequency drew closer and closer. It was unbearable, the opposite of everything good, threatening to unmake and destroy him in every moment. Arelix growled and bared his teeth as he sensed it as well. All three of them looked around, scanning every spec of space, yet they could see nothing. It was then that the ground before them began to shift and move. Liquid, purple metals crystalize into geometric fractals.

It startled the trio, but almost immediately, they knew that this was not what they should fear. From the ground rose a form, deep violet like the far voids of space, where new life was nothing more than gaseous clouds of cosmic color.

Greetings, protectors of the Trichome.

A voice sounded in all their heads, and the crystalline, metallic being focused his featureless face on them. Cherena felt overwhelmed by the amount of awareness this being held. Ashka, on the other hand recognized that awareness, recognized that voice.

"Who are you?" Arelix asked.

Though just as he asked it, he knew the answer through Ashka.

I am the ground you walk on. Replied Master Zero in their mind. *I am the resonance that emanates from the ancient relic. I am the zero-point field upon which all creation rests.*

King Ashka bowed his head in acknowledgment, as

did Cherena.

"Master of Zero," Ashka spoke. "Something terrible is coming. We can all feel it, and yet we do not know what it is."

The strange avatar of Master Zero's form turned away from them and looked out to the eclipsing moons. *You know not what it is, dear Ashka, because it is not.*

Master Zero took in a breath that sounded like crystals clinking together.

A being you once knew as Illuminatus X has found his way to the inverted universe. A thing no mortal should be able to do.

Ashka shook his head, frowning. "That is impossible. I thought Illuminatus X to be dead. On the day when Trichomia was destroyed by the Draconian fleet."

The day you should have died? Master Zero asked.

It was true. King Ashka should have died. But instead, he had ended up here.

When your heart brought you here to the base of creation where the Trichome lies, Illuminatus was simultaneously sent into a universe directly opposite to your own. It is the way of our world. A balance had to be struck.

"You mean it was because of me that Illuminatus X still lives?" Ashka replied.

Yes. As it was always meant to be. As was written in

the stars at the very beginning of creation, before the Lumarians lived, and before the first neutrons thought to join.

"I don't understand," Arelix said. "What does this imply?"

He has found the inverted relic. He seeks to return.

"And do what?" Cherena asked.

To unmake all that has been made. To revert the universe back into a place beyond even nothing. Beyond zero.

Cherena held a hand to her heart. "But why?"

It is not my way to understand the will of mortals.

"Balance must be struck..." Ashka mumbled to himself. "He is the counterweight..."

Cherena, at that moment, understood. "Whilst we seek to save our world, he acts as the second swing to the pendulum momentum."

"Exactly," Ashka whispered.

Then, without warning, he turned sharply towards the ancient relic. "If Illuminatus X holds a relic, then we must too."

Ashka reached for the relic, but before his hand even drew close, he hit an invisible force field of frequency, the reaction of which sent him flying backwards. Ashka slammed hard against a wall of rock.

You cannot seek to wield the power alone, Fallen King of Trichomia. Zero said in his mind.

Ashka winced as he moved to stand, his wings aching from the hard impact. Within him, Barradow could feel Ashka's struggle.

"We have to stop Illuminatus X!" Ashka roared. "He grows closer and closer. Why are you doing nothing, Master of Zero?! The state of the universe rests in what ensues here."

Master Zero glided across the ground. He did not form legs, but instead, the crystalline metal of the earth shifted and slid as his form moved across it. He reached up a hand towards the relic, and as it touched the energy field around it, a spark struck against his fingertips.

Even I do not wield the power to possess such an item. My form is merely an arrangement of molecules formed from my will, my power bound by the natural laws of the universe. It is not my place to wield such an object. It is a part of me, and yet I cannot access it.

Ashka struggled to stand. The intense shockwave from making contact with the ancient relic still coursed through his nervous system. At that moment, the planet Zero rumbled. Ashka felt an immense pain as he sensed something terrifyingly massive, trying to push through into their realm. "It's here. It's coming." Ashka's eyes went wide.

Princess Cherena gripped tighter to Arelix's hand, and as she did the old Draconian Commander felt her love. His heart understood at that moment. His eyes darted to the side, and he lunged for the King, stretching out his hand to grab Ashka's. The love that passed through Cherena passed through Ashka like an unbroken circuit.

"You may not be able to wield the relic alone," Arelix growled. "But together!"

Ashka felt a surge of power rushes through his veins. He looked over to see Cherena's eyes alight with gold. She was harnessing the potent power of the Trichome Star through her ancestral genetics. A halo began to radiate around her and encapsulate Arelix. There was the smell of burning flesh as the heat coming off of Cherena singed into Arelix's scales. But the Draconian did not let go.

"It *must* be you!" Arelix yelled. "Go on! We will hold the currents of the Trichome frequency!"

Ashka did not hesitate, for he could feel the impending doom that was mere inches away from breaking through into their universe. He ran, one hand linked to Arelix, the current of the trichome surging through his veins in a primal fire, the other hand reaching out towards the relic. In the next moment, a massive tear in the fabric of space warped open. Ashka grabbed the relic. It almost destroyed him to do so, as a pain beyond anything he had ever known. The pain of being burned alive threatened to break him. It was a terrible pain, and yet, in the heat of the fire was the purest of lights. Love emanated from that flame like a cooling balm. Ashka held on, and just as he pulled the relic from its place, Illuminatus X broke free from the Dystopic universe and unleashed the power of the dark relic upon their world.

In a single instant, the force of explosion and implosion collided with one another through all levels of time and space, throughout all the universes and dimensional planes.

All went into silence.

There was chaos and order. Destruction and malice meet creation and love like twin fires lost to time. Ashka was no longer himself, and yet he was. All he could feel was his heart. Glowing molten hot and connected to three others. These others were not who he knew them to be, for Arelix, Cherena, and Barradow were no more. Instead, they were bright suns themselves, each radiating the pure frequency of the Trichome.

They stood together, though they had no form. And if space still existed, Ashka could not feel it. A force pressed against them. A single force, that resonated at the exact opposite frequency to their own, matching them in power. A perfect inverse vibration.

Still, no sound arose.

It was all going. Ashka could feel it. The two forces were cancelling one another out. Creation and destruction meeting in a match that neither side could win. Then, from the silence came a single sound. A melody, a harmony, a rhythm. A single harmonically perfect tone resonated in its purest form. It emanated from the three stars around him. And Ashka realized that it came from himself as well. As their sound arose, so too did the sound of the inverted, black diamond star. It emitted a counter rhythm and a dissonant melody.

Opposites.

There was no way both could exist simultaneously. And yet... The wavelengths of sound met each other, like waves on either end of a lake travelling to meet in the middle. And when they met, something entirely unexpected happened. At first, they began to syncopate. The beats displacing one another. But in that displacement, the ripples that followed began to synchronize with the inverse waves, creating a state of superposition. They did not harmonize, but instead, they began to crystallize into a complex geometry.

It happened in an instant. And as the sounds truly met, they undid once more into silence. Then, from the silence came a flash of light.

*

Lives are neither born nor do they die. Through the expanse from universe to universe, from realm to dimension, a single life may seem small, but its reach surpasses the bounds of time and space. A soul arises from the very essence of creation, a single droplet of ether within the vast ocean of existence. When all things seemingly die, they only return to the great all. It is not oneness; do not mistake, for all does not exist as a singular, but simply is what everything is. You may think if a universe crumbles, the lives and souls within that tapestry of geometric matrixes are lost forever. But that is not true. Lives are neither born nor do they die, for they arise from something beyond life and death. They arise from that which supersedes even the highest of cosmic orders.

The notion of birth is only a misunderstanding of the true origin of our existence. The notion of death is to misunderstand the decay of a physical body. Souls transpose dimensions. They transpose the fabric of what we call reality itself. We may forget that we ever existed separate from the all, and yet some force, perhaps the grand play of it all, calls us back from time to time, across realities, across dreams and dimensions, across space and time. Where we once forgot we were ever separate from the all, the great play inverts its expectation, and as we dilute a single drop from the very essence, we, in turn, forget that we were ever a part of the all, instead becoming so absorbed in a singular perspective that we begin to believe we are the lives we live.

It is the great cosmic conundrum, the paradox of life, and for our heroes and those who fought to uphold the light of an eternal star, their lives will never truly be lost, nor those who fought against them.

As each fractal of time passes, from one dimension to another. Everything is, the one. Nothing is the zero, of everything.

In all the worlds, civilizations, and kingdoms, there is drama, and in those stories we hold so dear with such importance, we then realize it was just a dream, of another dream, of a Dog.

THE TWELFTH CHRONICLE

The End and the Beginning

The sun shone brightly as it began to set upon the fields of existence. Both primordial suns existed simultaneously, mirror images of one another on either side of the mirror plane. Zaya laughed as Kuma, the dog, licked her face. As they played together, she noticed a sparkle of golden dust upon the fur of his paw. She picked it from the hairs and held it up to the light of the two opposing suns.

It was nothing more than a spec of crystal dust, the remains of golden light. In it she felt a large sense of familiarity, like she had known it before, seen it in another life. It twinkled before her eye, reflecting the sun and sparkling bright. As she stared into it, she saw worlds being born, worlds ending, life unfolding and life unveiling. She saw a flash of light and felt a wave of love wash over her. She laughed, and as her breath exhaled, the crystal dust was blown from her fingers and cast once more into the open air. The light of the setting sun pierced through the trichome crystal, reflecting trillions of worlds in a single ray.

Kuma sneezed as the dust dispersed, and that made Zaya laugh even more. Kuma's tongue lolled out of his mouth as he panted cheerily. Zaya stood and began to twirl, riling up Kuma, who ran after her, jumping and barking playfully by her side. The flakes of crystal dust that still remained swirled and twirled around their dancing bodies, trailing currents in the wind. As Kuma jumped, a single spec landed on his coat, and the light of two suns was reflected once more in the crystal dust shimmer.

Kuma jumped on Zaya, and together, they fell into a roll on the ground. Zaya splayed out her limbs and lay on her back, and Kuma lay his happy head down on her chest. She petted him gently, staring off into the two suns through each eye.

"What is that sparkle in your paw?" She whispered.

He shifted his head to look up at her as she spoke, and a glint shimmered in his eye. "It looks like a little sun," Zaya added, squinting her eyes.

Rays of light stretched out from the spec as the sun reflected upon it, and she swore she could see people moving. There was a flash of gold and the image of a lion.

But before she could gather anything real, Kuma licked her cheek, causing her to lose her focus and break out into a series of giggles.

"Oh, maybe it was all just a trick of the light." Zaya smiled.

The glint sparkled in her eye this time, and Kuma let out a howl of joy. And together, they lay on the endless fields, joking and laughing as the sun set for its final bow. As the sun dipped below the horizon both Kuma and Zaya settled, their eyes growing heavy as the dream they had conjured began to diminish with the last rays of light.

Kuma's eyes slowly fluttered open as he awakened from a deep slumber. He stretched his legs and shook off the sleep, only to realize that something was different. Kuma looked around, slightly confused, and realized that he had awoken from another dream. This wasn't the first time that this had happened, but it still felt strange to his mammalian brain. In this new dream, Kuma found himself in a vast, empty field, surrounded by golden plants that swayed gently in the breeze. The sky above was a deep shade of purple, and the stars twinkled like diamonds. Kuma felt a sense of calm wash over him as if he had been transported to a different world entirely. He padded through the field, feeling the soft grass beneath his paws and the warm breeze ruffling his fur. It was a peaceful, serene dream unlike any other it had experienced before. As Kuma continued to explore, he knew that eventually, he would awaken once again. But for now, he was content to roam this dream world, to soak up its beauty and tranquility, and to savor the feeling of being alive, even if he was only in a dream.

To Kuma, the world was a place of infinite wonder and possibility. From the tiniest ant crawling on the ground to the vast expanse of the sky above, everything seemed to be connected in some way, a part of a grand and mysterious web that was both beautiful and bewildering. But Kuma was not alone in his curiosity about the world. Far above, in the depths of the cosmos, the macro verse also held secrets and mysteries beyond comprehension. In the vast and wondrous expanse, galaxies collided, and stars were born, each one a part of a cosmic dance that had been unfolding for billions of years.

And yet, despite the seemingly insurmountable differences in scale between the macro verse of Kuma and the micro verse of the cosmos, there was a certain harmony and balance that existed between them. At the micro level, every creature and organism played a role in the delicate balance of the ecosystem, while at the macro level, galaxies collided and merged, each one a piece of a larger cosmic puzzle. Kuma, in his own small way, was a part of this grand cosmic design, just as much as the stars and galaxies that glittered in the night sky. It was a humbling realization but one that filled Kuma with a sense of wonder and awe. For in the vastness of the universe, he was a part of something much greater than himself, a tiny but essential piece of the cosmic tapestry.

To all ends and all beginnings. For they are one and

the same through the stretch of time.

ZERO

A Day in the Life of a DOG

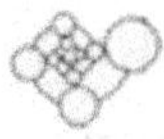

Kuma awoke at the exact same time that Zaya did. She blinked her eyes repeatedly, the traces of her dream fading away almost instantly. Though as she met Kuma's eyes, she seemed to remember a little flicker of something. Of laughing and playing in endless green fields and the light of a setting sun far in the distance. Kuma sat up suddenly, and Zaya smiled. He let out a small gruff then gestured to the window. Zaya leaned over and opened it a little more. Kuma stuck his head out of the back of the truck window as his family drove from the long stretch of empty countryside road towards the city. There was only bliss as the wind rustled his fur, and he watched as liquid butterflies fluttered and electric grasshoppers fly humming along the fields of sunflowers that whizzed them by.

In the life of a dog all is the present. And in this present, with his head out the window and the wind in the air, nothing could have been better. All was perfect as it was. His heart was full as the car began to slow, loud and strange sounds filling his ears. He tucked his head inside to make sure all was okay, and the little girl in the back seat giggled and ruffled his hair.

Knowing all was well, Kuma stuck his head back out the window, taking in the views of the sprawling city stretching up into the air all around him. There were lots of beings here, many just minding their own business, walking by, some other beings waved at him, and he barked happily back to them in response.

His tongue hung loose, and a large smile spread up his furry cheeks. The car went around a corner, and Kuma spotted something in the corner of his eye. At the mouth of an alley, a tabby cat sat calmly, grooming her paws.

Kuma's ears suddenly perked up, and he barked from the window.

The cat spared him a passing glance, seeing that he was far, and continued licking her paws. Some primal instinct in Kuma wanted to play. He grew excited, and his tail began to wag madly back and forth, batting the young girl in the back, tickling her chin, and making her giggle even more.

As the car pulled to a stop, Kuma took his chance. Without warning, he kicked off the back seats and jumped out of the car window. The parents in the front didn't even notice, but the young girl named Zaya did.

"Kuma!"

This got her parents' attention, and they spun to see Kuma running on the sidewalk, almost making unaware passers-by stumble over. Startled, they knew they needed to pull over, but the light went green, and honking behind them made them move onwards. Zaya turned around in her seat, watching as Kuma began to chase the tabby cat, turning left into a dark alley.

Kuma chased after the cat, but this was her terrain. She leaped onto a dumpster and was out of reach even as Kuma stood on his hind legs and tried to play with her using his paws. The tabby cat was not impressed, and she hissed rather scornfully at him before resuming her grooming session.

Kuma's barking woke a blind man who had been asleep in the alley. He rose from beneath a blanket of cardboard. As he sleepily gazed with blind eyes upon the world, he felt Kuma and stumbled to his feet. He turned over the box and fished around until he found the remains of an old sandwich. Slowly, he approached Kuma and set it at his feet.

This got Kuma's attention, turning him away from the cat and his tail wagged as he began to munch down on the half-finished meatball sub. The homeless blind man kneeled down to the ground and put his hands together in prayer.

"Hello God, my name is Raha. I hear you come from

the 3 star system, the invisible Trichome Star of Sirius, and you are the spirit being of canna, the Dog God. I know we haven't spoken in a while, but I hope this sandwich shows that I haven't forgotten you."

Kuma licked his chops happily and looked up at the man who had given him the sandwich. He gratefully licked the man's hands that were still clasped in prayer. The man chuckled and gave Kuma a pet back.

"Oh, thank you for forgiving me, God. I promise I will try to do better." Raha said, meeting Kuma's eyes with a blind mans stare. "If you follow me, I will show you my favorite dumpster to dive."

Kuma's ears perked up, which made Raha laugh. "I thought you would like the sound of that."

The man led Kuma away from the alley, and they turned the corner just as Zaya and her mom and dad entered the alley.

"I saw him go in here," Zaya said.

She looked up to see the cat on the dumpster and knew that it was Kuma who had chased her. "Well, he can't be far." Said her mother, Cherena. "Let's keep looking."

Meanwhile, as Kuma and the Raha enjoyed a gourmet meal from the number one dumpster in the city, the tabby cat jumped down from its perch. The only sound it made was a slight graze of its paw over a crinkled plastic bag.

Kuma's head snapped in the direction of the cat, and

his ears went high. A moment later, he was chasing her at a wild pace. The homeless blind man looked up from his food and waved with a dirty, toothless smile.

"Bye, God! Thanks for stopping by!"

Kuma bound after the orange tabby cat, barking playfully. The cat took a sharp turn, deeper into the maze of alleyways, with Kuma quick on her tail.

Two men stood deeper in the alley, hidden away from prying eyes. "I'm telling you, Ashka. This is the best flower I've ever tried."

Barradow pulled out a baggy of cannabis. The veins were laced with golden trichome crystals. "What's it called?" Ashka replied, eyeing the bag with an impressed look.

Barradow smiled. "My supplier told me it was called *Dog Star.*"

Ashka raised his eyebrows.

At that moment, the orange tabby cat zipped through their legs. "Woah!" Barradow exclaimed. "What the hell is that cat on?"

Before they even looked away from the cat, Kuma came bounding through. He barged through the two of them, and Barradow was knocked backwards, stumbling over a piece of trash, and the baggy of flowers flew up into the air, slipping free from his hands. He watched in slow motion as the keef crystals of the cannabis were tossed inside. A single crystal escaped a small gap in the zip of the mylar bag, and a small beam of sunlight reflected off one of the back alley windows, caught the golden shimmer of the crystal.

The tabby cat ran circles around the men's ankles, and Kuma chased the cat around as the crystal slowly drifted downwards. The tabby cat zipped off in another direction, and as Kuma got his bearings, the crystal landed on his foot, nestling deeply into the furrows of his fur.

"Quick, catch the baggy," Barradow yelled.

Ashka leaped and managed to catch the bag, and as he did, he felt the ripple of something far away tingle inside of him. He felt a glow, like the light of an ancient star, and he stared down at the baggy in awe.

"Shoo!" Barradow yelled.

But Kuma was already running off, the little trichome crystal seeded deeply in his paw, shimmering an old and distant light.

Through the folds of his fur, through the very atoms of the crystal, was a flash of light. A speck of dust burst into the infinite unfolding of a universe. In a single instant, a microcosm was born. And from this burst, rose.

Three Infinite Entities, giving birth to the World of Zero. From nothing an atom was born in the foundation of cosmic balance, growing into. Molecule and expanding to form the light of the Trichome Star.

The tabby cat managed to escape Kuma up a tree on the outskirts of a park. After several minutes of trying to climb up himself, Kuma gave up and turned his attention away from the victorious cat. As he turned he spotted a small boy happily enjoying a snow cone, kicking his legs happily whilst sitting on a park bench.

It was a hot summer day, and Kuma was panting. He eyed the snow cone with wishful eyes, and as the boy took his next lick, a big drip of ice plopped onto the ground beside him. Kuma's head perked up, and he quickly sauntered over, licking the drips off the floor. The little boy smiled and reached out to pet Kuma's head.

Kuma let him and pushed up off the ground to sit beside the boy on the park bench. The boy offered Kuma his snow cone, and Kuma took a very grateful and slobbery lick, making the boy laugh even more.

Meanwhile, from the light of the Trichome star, the planet of Lumaria was born, and crystal rain showers fell like sparkling comets onto the planet, forming a forest of song and mystical knowledge. Prisms reflected in the light of a million facets, shimmering in the energy of the Trichome star. From this place of light, beautiful beings were born, beings born of the light of the Trichome star.

Through seconds and infinite moments, the planet of Lumaria rose and fell, falling into destruction, and the beauty of the singing forest was transported from its original birthplace.

The snow cone vendor saw Kuma licking at the little boy's cone and pulled out a fabric cloth, waving it at Kuma.

"Shoo!" He yelled, dipping his fingers in a bucket of ice

water and flicking it at him.

Kuma felt the negativity of the snow cone vendor and jumped off the bench, hurt by the man's harshness. He whimpered and ran away, leaving the boy behind. He walked by the edge of the fence, letting his fur dry after being splashed by the cold water. He sat down and, for the first time, wondered where his family had gone.

He quirked his head, looking around, trying to find any sign of them. As he turned his head, he heard a growl. A large Pitbull stared at him through the gaps in the fence. He was chained up to a post with a metal collar, and when Kuma quirked his head, the Pitbull began to bark viciously. Kuma jumped to attention and backed away. The Pitbull stuck his head through the fence and started snapping with his jaws.

Kuma whimpered and scampered off, not wanting to get bitten.

As he ran, within the world on his paw, a planet amidst the pull of three suns was born. From the planet, a vicious race of reptilian beings was born. Born almost as a reaction to the snaps and bites of the Pitbull, a mirror of Kuma's fear and loneliness.

He wandered aimlessly in the city, tail and head drooping low. People barged into him without concern and Kuma continuously looked up, smelling at the different scents, trying to find one that felt familiar to him.

With no luck, he eventually found his way to a park. His head slightly perked up as he saw people having fun.

There were some young kids throwing a Frisbee and many others sitting beneath the warm sun on picnic blankets, talking and eating with one another. A child turned away from the food his mother was trying to feed him and locked eyes with Kuma.

Kuma quirked his head and raised a single ear, the other flopping down. The child waved him over, and at first, Kuma approached timidly. Now unsure of whether or not he would get in trouble as he had done before. All of the family turned when Kuma got close, and he was suddenly poured with attention and affection. Kuma rolled over happily onto his belly as the family gave him rubs and called him cute names.

"Can we feed him mom?" The boy asked. "Please." "Okay, but just a little." The mom said, smiling.

The boy took out some ham from his sandwich and held it in the air. Kuma's eyes went wide with excitement, and he began to lick and bite at the ham, pulling it from the boy's hand and munching it down in one go.

The boy continued to feed Kuma until his mother told him it was enough. "You don't want him to get a tummy ache, do you?"

The boy shook his head. Kuma continued to sniff around their picnic blanket when a single group of grey clouds rolled across the sky. A single droplet of water fell onto Kuma's nose, and his head jerked upwards. The boy also threw a ball for Kuma to catch at that exact moment. Kuma ran for it, leaping into the air and catching it in his mouth before it ever hit the ground.

"Oh no, it looks like it's going to rain." The boy's father said, and the family quickly packed up their stuff.

As they were walking off, the boy turned around and held out his hand to Kuma, but his mom pulled the boy away.

"He doesn't belong to us. You don't want his family to miss him, do you?"

Kuma sat in the grass with his head slightly tilted and ears drooping, watching as they left, ball still in his mouth. As he watched them go, he put the ball on the ground and placed his paw on top of it. He was alone again.

Upon the planet of Trichomia, a new King was born, and that same King fell. His planet was destroyed, and an infinite forest of knowledge transformed into the sacred cannabinoid living organism, dispersed throughout the universe and hidden away in the folds of time and space.

Kuma was drenched as he trudged through the muddy grass, still holding onto the ball that the boy had given him. At the edge of the park, beneath a bridge, Kuma stumbled across an empty large drainage pipe. He ducked his head and made his way inside, seeking shelter from the rain. Sad and alone, he lay down and rested his head on his front paws, watching the sheets of rain falling. Pools of mud formed on the ground and there was no one in sight. All was grey for a long, long time.

Kuma fell asleep and woke up hours later. Water still

dripped in the opening to the pipe he had hidden in, but as he yawned, grazing one paw over his head, he noticed that the rain had stopped outside. Sun was beginning to peak through the clouds, and he rose, poking his head out to sniff at the air.

A droplet of the water fell onto the tip of his nose, and he let out a heavy exhale, shaking his head and his whole body to rinse his fur clear of the water. He took a step out and a slant of sun reached down through the gaps in the clouds, surrounding him in a halo of warmth. Kuma looked up to the sky and closed his eyes.

There was a glint in his paw, and grasshopper space-ships landed on earth, just as the dinosaurs were oblite-rated in the cataclysm of great comets. Man evolved from their ashes, and the secrets of Trichomia were passed down.

Kuma had a bit more spring in his step as he left the park. Now that he was dry and the sun had melted away most of the clouds, he used his smell and began to follow a trail. Through all the smells of fresh rain on grass and the smell that comes after as the sun warms it all away, Kuma smelt a thread of scent that was familiar. He felt a tingle of joy and a rush of excitement. His nose locked on to the scent, and he began to chase hurriedly after it.

Meanwhile, his family had given up the search for him and decided to go home to make missing posters with a reward. Zaya drew pictures of Kuma and continuously looked out the window to see if he had come home yet.

Kuma followed the scent out of the city, walking on the edge of the road through the large fields of delicious-smelling wheat baking in the sun. He followed the trail, led by his nose, weaving in and out of highway roads. Cars honked, hurtling towards him, giving him barely enough time to run out of the way. He looks up and doesn't recognize any of his surroundings. Suddenly broken from the trail of scent.

The smell of car exhaust and asphalt fills his nose, and the loud noises scare him, but he continues onwards anyway. His body began to tremble as he carefully walked on the side of the large highway, constantly looking up as cars zipped past him.

After hours of walking in the baking sun, Kuma grew overheated and exhausted, coming to a slow stop under the shade of a small tree on the side of the road, panting heavily. He dropped onto his stomach and tried his best to stay awake, but his eyelids slowly fluttered closed, and Kuma was ushered into the dream world.

Within his dreams, he saw a world with a sky of liquid purple, saw the shadow of a figure amidst a world of Zero, and a King with a lion's head. Kuma wandered amongst this strange, dark world. The earth was made of metal and shimmering gemstones. He continued to walk forward, but the world seemed to loop upon itself, and quickly, Kuma grew disoriented, all the smells leading back to nothing, as the liquid purple sky seemed to grow closer to him.

Anxiously, he settled down and remained put, his eyes fluttering closed once again, and his dream blossomed once again into a dream within a dream. Master Zero dipped his head through the liquid purple sky, and in his eyes were the swirl of light and darkness. Kuma looked up at this great and godly being, whimpering slightly, but the Master coaxed him with a gentle hush.

"All will be well." Master Zero's voice echoed through the fabric of his world. "You will soon find your way."

Kuma understood and decided to trust this strange being in the sky. He allowed himself to settle down, and as he did, he saw a girl. Kuma recognized her. It was his owner. It was Zaya. His eyes shot open, and he was back beneath the tree in the light of day. Immediately, his tongue drooped out, and he began to pant because even in the shade, the heat was sweltering.

But now that he had some rest, and spoken with the master of Zero, Kuma felt confident to set out once more. As he sniffed the air, he caught the scent of the trail again and continued down the long country road. A car passes by and suddenly stops in front of Kuma. He paused, turning his head to the side, unsure of what was happening, when a man got out of the front seat.

Kuma doesn't recognize the man, but a second later, the window rolls down, and three children stick their heads out. They all smile and wave at him, and Kuma's ears perk up.

"What are you doing out here all alone?" The man

asked, kneeling down and patting Kuma's head. "Are you lost?"

Kuma stared up at the man with wide eyes.

"Why don't you come with us? My name's Griek. You look hungry and thirsty."

His eyes wandered to the children, and they opened the side door. Kuma smiled and ran to them, jumping into the backseat and making them laugh and giggle. The kids cuddled him up and made him feel welcome, but Kuma still had one eye out the window, glad to have found a safe place, but still worried about where his true family was. The father started the car, and together, they drove off down the long country road, leaving the city behind.

Amidst the world of Fareen, war broke out between the rebels and Draconian soldiers. The battle raged, and people fought for the freedom of their kind. Through their fighting, the words of an ancient Oracle whispered in the wind, and across the field of impossibility, two eyes met. A draconian commander and Fareen Princess fall into the weave of bond despite all the odds stacked against them. A shockwave of their opposing forces emerged as their hearts came into union beyond space and time.

In a sacred pool, deep within the recesses of a cavern, a King stirred from his slumber, greeted by a child from another world. Through her eyes, he saw the ancient promise of Lumaria and rose to the call of empathy, opening a portal in the fabric of space and summoning the Princess and Commander to join his side.

Kuma had lost his collar somewhere along his journey, and without it, the family that picked him up had no way of returning him to his rightful home. They allowed him into their own home, feeding him with a cut of steak and giving him a warm place to rest outside of the unpredictable elements.

Despite the cozy house, and loving attention, his ears still drooped, and his heart still called out to his own family. Seeing this, the kids began to pet him, taking his mind away and bringing him outside to play. They set the sprinklers on, running and laughing through the spray of water and calling for Kuma to join them.

Kuma let go of his woes for a little time, and bound through the water, chasing and parking with joy, playfully biting at the water and shaking it off when his coat got too wet, spraying the kids more and earning even more laughter. But as the playing started to come to an end, Kuma's ears perked up, and his nose caught onto the whiff of something familiar.

Suddenly, the urge to run went through his bones. On the wind, he caught the scent of home. His heart was torn. Torn by the love and affection he was receiving and the desire to find Zaya and his family once again.

The gate opened by the side of the house that led into the backyard and Kuma took this as his opportunity.

He sprinted out the gate, leaving the kids and family behind. They shouted for him to come back, but Kuma disappeared into the wood nearby, stopping one last time at the edge of the tree line to give a farewell bark to the kids who took such good care of him.

His nose was locked onto a trail of scent, and his nose turned up as he sniffed his way through the woods.

He wove through the trees until there came a clearing. The woods opened up into a beautiful meadow, where a young girl sat amidst a field of purple flowers. He stops just as she turns her head. His ears quirked upwards, and a big smile spread across the girl's features.

He could recognize her scent from a mile away. Kuma bound towards her, and at the same time, Zaya stood, running towards Kuma. They crashed together into a heap of cuddles, kisses, pets, and licks. She laughed as he licked her face.

"Kumaaa!" She giggled, trying to avoid the onslaught of licks, wiping her face and kneeling upright to give him a fond pet on the head and a tight hug.

Kuma sat in ecstasy, tongue handing out, eyes only half open as she petted him with one hand, picking a flower with another and placing it so that it sat just above his ear. Over the horizon of trees, the sun began to set, plunging the lower sky into a bright cast of orange and stretching to die the clouds a cotton candy pink amidst the light of blue above them.

Together, they sat in the light of the setting sun, and in another world, Zaya held the Sonic Cannabinoid Flower in a realm of both beginnings and ends. And the cycles of life started to turn from day into dusk. Together, a Goddess and God. A young girl and her dog. And the world was complete once again.

All universes begin with a dream and a dreamer, and what role we play within that dream is but a facet of the greater picture. There are oracles who can see the greater picture and children who understand but do not know. There are others who lose themselves in the wrapping of illusion and try with all their might, despite their ignorance, to pull the dream apart.

But for songs and for stories, all that was written was said. And in the beginning was the primordial sound, stretched from the mind of the young child who dreamt in her bed or the joy of a dog who barked and played. All starts where it ends, and all ends come before the start. But for Zaya, she was just happy that she was reunited once again with her one and only dog.

In a dream, of a dream within another dream.

Kuma wakes up! His family says to him, "Let's go bye-bye." Kuma is so excited that he runs and jumps into the car, immediately popping his head out of the window. The family laughs and giggles as they happily drive down the road.

The simple happiness of the dog's love for his family, the car ride, and the wind blowing in Kuma's face is a monumental peak of his life.

Each precious moment of time in all the infinite multi-dimensions, significant or insignificant, occurs in this single point of time, the now. The trichome crystal shards are of the time-space continuum. These are the glimmering reflections that manifest "Fractals of Time."

Trichome Star

Copyright © ® 2024 by Teodoro Castro III

www.ingramcontent.com/pod-product-compliance
Lightning Source LLC
Chambersburg PA
CBHW061504120726
48001CB00004B/1200